W9-CIJ-935

Summer's
Fortune

Summer's Fortune

Joan Reeves

Five Star • Waterville, Maine

Five Star Romance Series.

Published in 2002 in conjunction with Joan L. A. Reeves.

The text of this edition is unabridged.

Cover design by Thorndike Press Staff.

Set in 11 pt. Plantin.

Printed in the United States on permanent paper.

Library of Congress Cataloging-in-Publication Data

Reeves, Joan.
    Summer's fortune / Joan Reeves.
        p. cm.
    ISBN 0-7862-4450-X (hc : alk. paper)
    1. Houston (Tex.) — Fiction. 2. Rich people — Fiction.
3. Hitchhiking — Fiction. I. Title.
    PS3568.E4714 S86 2002
    813′.54—dc21   2002069306

This is for Adina, who believes in Cinderella stories
and happily ever afters!

Prologue

"We're almost there, Mom," Summer James called over her shoulder, as she danced along the broken sidewalk, dodging tall weeds growing from the cracks.

Rachel watched her slender daughter and wished she had a fraction of the energy that Summer exhibited this October morning, but her tired steps were no match for the bouncy strides of her long-legged daughter. "Slow down just a bit, honey."

"Are you okay, Mom?" Summer scrutinized her mother's face.

Rachel hoped the makeup concealed the sallowness of her skin. She wouldn't be able to keep the truth from Summer much longer. She'd have to tell her soon, but not today.

Anxiety replaced the excitement in Summer's voice. "We don't have to go shopping if you need to lie down."

"I'm fine, honey. The fresh air's good for me." Rachel smiled fondly at her daughter. "Besides, today's special. It's not every day that my daughter becomes a teenager!"

Summer's grin returned at the word *teenager*. She linked arms with her mother, and they laughed together as they continued on, enjoying the crunch of brown leaves underfoot.

"I think you're obsessed with these earrings. Are you sure you don't want a stereo instead?" Rachel teased.

"Oh, no! I've wanted them since the first day I saw them. They're incredibly beautiful cabochon rubies set in gold filigree. Why, they're already antiques! They'll be heirlooms to be passed from generation to generation."

Rachel chuckled. "That sounds like something from one of those books you're always reading."

Summer blushed. "Well, the card in the window said cabochon rubies. I looked cabochon up, and it means they're rounded off on top instead of cut in angles."

"They sound awfully expensive. Are you sure they're only seventy-five dollars?"

"That's what the tag on them said last week. It just seems a miracle that no one has bought them and they've been there since last Christmas and here it is my birthday and they're on sale and I have the money!" Summer rushed on, "And ruby earrings are an important gift, just right for an important birthday!"

"There's that talking book again." Rachel laughed as she pushed open the door to Time After Time Antique Jewelry.

An immaculately groomed woman, her dark hair in a sleek chignon, looked them over, from their windblown hair to their sneaker-clad feet. Rachel smoothed her sandy hair into place and tucked her white shirt into the waistband of her worn jeans.

Summer dragged her mother to the counter. "Ma'am, we'd like to look at the cabochon ruby earrings in the window, please."

The woman glanced at Rachel, then back at Summer. She arched a dark brow and said, "They're rather expensive, my dear. Most of our merchandise is."

Rachel stiffened, pink stained her sallow cheeks, but before she could say anything, Summer chattered, "I want them. I've saved my baby-sitting money since I first saw them."

The woman sighed and pursed her lips. "Very well, but I

don't think a child like you could possibly have a hundred and fifty dollars from baby-sitting."

"A—a—hundred and fif . . . fifty dollars?" Summer blanched. "But I thought the tag said seventy-five dollars!"

The woman held the small velvet box in front of Summer's face. "That's seventy-five dollars *off*. They were originally two hundred twenty-five dollars."

"No." Summer raised stricken eyes to Rachel. "Oh, Mom!"

"I didn't think you'd have that kind of money," the woman said.

"Just a moment. I'd like to look at them," Rachel commanded, her hand outstretched.

"Perhaps there's something else you'd like to see. We have some moderately priced costume jewelry."

"No, we're only interested in these earrings." Rachel took the velvet box from the woman and opened it. Summer was right. The earrings were beautiful. Small red stones, surrounded by lacy gold, glowed with hidden fire. She held one up to Summer's ear, her heart breaking at the anguish in her daughter's green eyes. Poor baby! She had worked so hard, saving every penny that Mrs. Garcia paid her for watching her two kids after school. Rachel had thought Summer would forget about the rubies, but that hadn't been the case. Jewels lasted forever, she thought with a sad smile, unlike people.

"We'll take them," Rachel said, reaching into her worn canvas purse for the money, leaving only a ten-dollar bill in her wallet for groceries. "Give the lady your money, Summer."

Summer whispered, "Mom, I don't need them. Truly I don't. They're just a passing fancy."

"Everyone should get their heart's desire once in a while,

9

especially on their birthday," Rachel whispered back, smiling.

On the way home, Summer stumbled over a break in the sidewalk. Misery colored her voice. "Why did you do it, Mom?"

"Maybe I liked the shock on that snotty woman's face when I told her we wanted them." Rachel grinned, not regretting the impulsive decision at all. She wiped her damp forehead, dismayed at how little energy she had these days. With a tug on Summer's hand, she pointed at a bench at the bus stop. "Let's sit and rest a bit."

"Are you okay?" Summer asked. "Oh, Mom, we should never have wasted our money for these stupid earrings. We should have spent it on another doctor, a private doctor."

"I'm fine, Summer. I just need to rest a little. And quit agonizing over this. That money doesn't matter a bit. I want you to enjoy your rubies." She stroked the blonde wisps from Summer's forehead. "Sometimes we have to ignore common sense and go with our heart. My heart told me you wanted these earrings, and I wanted to give you something that you could keep forever." Rachel turned away so Summer wouldn't see the tears that filled her eyes.

"Mom, I love you." Summer snuggled against her mother's shoulder. "Every time I wear the earrings, I'll think of you."

"And I love you, honey." Rachel cleared her throat. "Besides, I don't mind eating peanut butter sandwiches for the rest of the month, do you?" She tugged Summer's ponytail.

"No." Summer took Rachel's work-worn hand as they rose. "When I grow up, I'm going to be rich," she vowed, "and we won't ever have to worry about money again. We'll live in a mansion and have a maid and beautiful clothes, fancy cars, and all kinds of jewels. You can have a greenhouse like you've always wanted. And no one will ever look down their nose at us again."

Rachel hugged Summer to her, wanting to hold on and never let go. Oh, my baby, who'll take care of you when I'm gone? "I'm going to enjoy living on easy street," Rachel lied, swallowing her tears.

One

The arid Texas wind lazily tossed grains of red dust at the windows of the small frame house.

Summer paused in her packing. The scratch of sand against glass abraded her nerves as much as it did the exterior of the paint-blistered bungalow. Me and my big mouth, she thought with a grimace as she risked a glance at her best friend. For once, Annie Redmond seemed completely at a loss for words.

Summer's nerves and emotions conspired against her, causing her hands to shake. Cold air pouring from the vents of an air-conditioner perched in the middle of a trio of old-fashioned windows did little to stop the perspiration from forming beneath her arms and on her forehead.

"You are crazy, Summer Louise James!" Annie enunciated each syllable emphatically, her innocent blue eyes incredulous.

Summer sighed; too bad Annie hadn't stayed silent. "Yeah, crazy like a fox," Summer muttered. Ignoring her best friend, she concentrated on packing away all her new cosmetics.

"Oh, no! Crazy like you need to be put in a mental institution!" Annie flopped onto the end of the bed, her feet nervously tapping out a rhythm on the hardwood floor. "You are absolutely certifiable."

Summer rolled her eyes. Why wouldn't Annie at least try

to understand? If she'd known her best friend was going to react with such horror, she'd never have told her about The Plan. Glumly Summer studied the streaks of bright light that sneaked into the room when air from the top vents of the air-conditioner buffeted the roller shade above. For a moment those were the only sounds in the bedroom—the hissing air and the rhythmic flap of the sun-yellowed shade.

"Summer, please, talk to me?" Annie wailed.

Summer's hands stilled. Softly she said, "I've talked to you for the last hour, trying to make you understand." She shrugged; the white halter dress tightened over her full breasts. "My mind is made up. There's nothing you can say or do that will change it."

Annie sprang from the bed and grabbed the eye shadow palette from Summer's hands.

"Annie, give me that!" A scowl marred Summer's perfectly made-up face. "If I'd known you were going to carry on so, I'd never have confided in you." Summer made a grab for the colorful powders, but Annie whipped the case behind her back.

"Summer, just listen to me," Annie said hurriedly. "What you're planning is totally insane! Why, just look what you've done to yourself!"

Summer's spine stiffened and her head snapped up. Perhaps her first impression when she'd seen herself in the mirror at Monsieur Claude's salon had been accurate. Maybe she really did look like a streetwalker! She shook her head in denial. The book said men liked blondes—the blonder, the better, she argued mentally. Annie just didn't understand.

Summer sank onto the bed in the spot Annie had vacated. "What do you mean? I haven't *done* anything to myself."

"What do you call ruining your beautiful hair? And painting your face so you look like a . . . a . . . bleached-blond raccoon? And look at those claws you've got glued to your finger-nails!"

Summer studied the long, scarlet-lacquered nails. Gingerly she touched the carefully arranged layers of hair, then rose to peer into the cheap mirror nailed to the closet door. She still found it difficult to recognize the woman who looked back at her.

Four carefully blended shades of eye shadow colored her eyelids. Chocolate brown lined her upper eyelids; emerald lined the lower. Crimson lipstick colored her full lips. Two shades of blusher emphasized the high cheekbones in her oval face.

"Perhaps it is a little too much for daytime," Summer conceded, a frown marring her forehead.

Annie snorted and paced quickly, her steps gathering speed with the words that poured from her. "And just look at all the money you've spent on clothes and this expensive luggage. And why did you throw away all that money on that old clunker your grandmother left you?" She tossed the eye shadows on the bed.

"Because the book said that men with money appreciated classic cars. Since I couldn't afford an expensive set of wheels, I had to work with what I had. I figured that a classic Chevy in mint condition would be better than my old Toyota."

"You're right there." Annie guffawed. "That Japanese rust bucket you drive to school would be a dead giveaway to your millionaire."

"I spent almost five thousand on the Chevy, so quit calling it a clunker. It's an antique car—and worth every cent I put into it. Why, you can sell a fifty-seven Chevy convertible for a pretty penny in today's market!"

"Well then, you ought to sell it, because it sure as heck

won't get you all the way to Houston without breaking down."

Summer's frown deepened. She'd worried about that herself. Most of the money she'd spent on the car had been on cosmetic restoration. The mechanic had warned her that the engine needed an equal amount of work, but she'd had to cut corners somewhere.

Staunchly she denied Annie's charge. "I had it tuned up and a new muffler put on. It sounds fine."

"It may look great and sound good, but it wouldn't start last week, remember?"

"So it's a little cranky sometimes."

"Cranky? You really are nuts! You have an answer for everything, but all your answers are merely rationalizations."

"Annie, if you're just going to stand there and nag me, then you can leave." Summer glared at her friend.

"I'm sorry. I don't mean to be a pain, but I'm worried about you. Maybe you need a rest. My God! You've worked two jobs every summer since I've known you. And for what?" Annie glanced around the shabby room. "I wondered what you were doing with your money. It was obvious you weren't spending any on fixing up this house you inherited from your grandmother."

Angry spots of color deepened the red on Summer's cheeks as green fire flashed in her eyes. "You're right, Annie, I have worked hard. I needed money for something more important than this old house. I needed it to create a secure future for me."

Annie stared at her friend from the top of her blond head to the red-painted nails of her toes, peeking through the straps of high-heeled white sandals. "And this is your future?"

Doubt filled Summer. If she could make Annie understand, perhaps her confidence in The Plan would strengthen. She spoke slowly, searching for the right words. "Annie, you don't know what it's like to have nothing. To be at the mercy of the world because you're poor." Summer paced with quick, jerky steps.

"You had parents who took care of you, sent you to college. Then you married Wayne right after graduation. He'll make sure you never want for anything. Why, you don't even have to teach if you don't want to. You could quit Neubauer Elementary tomorrow."

Summer whirled to a stop. The words seemed ripped from her soul. "But I come from nothing. My mother and I had nothing and no one." Summer's fist struck her palm, emphasizing each word. "Everything I've got, I worked damn hard to get. I don't want to struggle every day of my life. I want security."

"But, Summer—" Annie began.

Summer broke in, "You don't know what it's like to eat oatmeal day after day after day and then have nothing when the oatmeal is gone. Or what it's like to be the butt of everybody's jokes because your clothes always came from the Salvation Army." Summer stared at the faded roses on the wallpaper, seeing instead the dusty artificial flowers at her mother's grave.

"You'll never know what it's like to see somebody you love die because there's no money for the kind of medical care you take for granted." Summer choked on the bitter memories. "I'm not ever going to be poor again." Her lips trembled. She pressed them together, controlling herself with an iron will.

"But you're not poor. That's in the past. You're college-educated with a good job. Maybe being a school librarian here in Red Rock doesn't pay much, but you're young and have more than enough for your needs." Annie patted Summer's shoulder.

"And what happens if I lose this job and can't get another? Or if I have a major illness? Or I'm disabled in an accident?"

"So that's what triggered this!" Annie exclaimed, her face a picture of distress. "That wreck you were in last year!"

"I realized I'd been fooling myself. There's no security when the only thing standing between me and poverty is a job."

"But, Summer, if you'd taken the money that you've spent on this—" she waved her hands to encompass Summer's body "—and on all these sports you tried to learn—why, you could have had a sizable savings account. You could have invested it."

"But I did invest it, Annie, in myself." Summer spoke with quiet conviction.

Annie groaned. "Turning yourself into a—a—man-trap and taking off for Houston to snag a millionaire isn't my idea of investing. You should have put your money in . . . in . . . mutual funds, or something," she grumbled.

"Hasn't it occurred to you that if I had a head for business, I'd have majored in accounting or something besides library science?" Summer asked, exasperated with Annie's continued arguments.

Annie smiled reluctantly. "You've got the brains if you'd just apply yourself."

"This is what I want, Annie. Please understand," Summer pleaded. Reaching out to Annie, she hugged her shorter friend. "Trust me on this. I've got to try."

"Okay, I see your mind is made up," Annie conceded. "Just don't try to impress any millionaires with your golf game," she joked gruffly.

"Well, perhaps I'd better limit my golfing to keeping

score and driving the cart."

"Yeah." Annie snorted. "Wayne said he never played anybody before who took seventeen strokes on each hole."

"Hey! I wasn't that bad!" Summer grinned and picked up the eye shadow box and placed it in her makeup case, glad that Annie seemed to accept her decision.

Annie sat on the bed again. Her smile faded. "All kidding aside, you really won't reconsider?" she asked gently.

"Annie, look at me." Summer twirled around in the middle of the room. The rippled mirror reflected a wavy image.

Resigned, Annie said, "Okay, okay. You've got all the right equipment. In that dress, you look like an adolescent male fantasy come to life."

"I've gone too far to back out now." Summer ticked off on her fingers the expenses she'd incurred. "There was the work on the car, the expenses of bonding my teeth, and the contact lenses. Why, all this makeup and the lessons on how to put the gook on my face cost almost as much as the contact lenses. My claws, as you call them—" Summer waved her fingers around "—cost forty dollars initially, then twenty dollars every two weeks to maintain."

"You'll poke your eye out if you're not careful," Annie muttered, studying her own short, unvarnished nails.

Summer twirled again. The circle skirt of the white cotton halter dress whirled about her pale legs. "Then, of course, as you've pointed out, my clothes, accessories, luggage, and lessons—dance lessons, tennis lessons, golf lessons! Lessons ad infinitum! And subscriptions to *Architectural Digest*, *Forbes*, *Cosmopolitan*, *Bon Appétit*, and *The Wall Street Journal*."

"I used to think you were the best-read person I knew. If I'd known you had some crazy idea about hunting down a rich man to marry, I'd have . . . Well, I don't know what I'd have done, but I'd have done something!"

"I wanted to be able to converse with wealthy men. It said in—"

"Yeah, I know, that stupid book that inspired you. *How to Marry a Rich, Rich Man!*" Annie rolled her eyes. "What a ridiculous title. Just wait until I get my hands on Janie Prather. I'm going to wring her neck for giving you that book when you were recuperating from the wreck. I hope you don't regret the day you ever read that dumb book."

"I won't." Summer stuck her chin out stubbornly. "I've followed the book as nearly as possible, even though, I'll admit, I didn't succeed at everything."

"Yeah," Annie snickered, "like golf."

"Right. I thought Wayne was going to strand me on the course the day I played with you two."

"He thought about it, but I talked him out of it."

"Then I spent over a hundred dollars on having my hair styled and lightened."

Indignantly Annie shook her head. "I can't believe any stylist in his right mind would have changed your hair. It is— was—a beautiful color."

Summer snorted. "I'd hardly call dirty blond beautiful."

"You were the only one who ever called it dirty blond."

"Actually, Monsieur Claude tried to talk me out of it, but I insisted," Summer confessed. Her lips twitched as she remembered his horrified expression. "But you have beautiful hair, no?" The owner of the Dallas salon had stated indignantly.

"No, you're right, I don't!" Summer had replied, steadfast in her decision to be as blond as possible.

Confused by the negatives, Monsieur Claude had shaken his head. "Thees language ees like American women— impossible!"

Though Summer had worried about being a "bleached blonde" with the attendant problem of dark roots, she'd ignored her misgivings because the book that had inspired The Plan insisted that men preferred blondes. So she'd said good-bye to her dark honey tresses and endured the smelly concoctions that took her hair a couple of shades lighter. Though she didn't much like the color, she adored the layered cut Monsieur Claude had said would work wonders with her thick mass of wavy hair.

She tossed her hair over her shoulders in a gesture she'd been practicing for days. Annie groaned. "Save it for the millionaires, please!"

Summer laughed, filling the room with the musical sound. "At least I didn't have to have breast implants."

Annie laughed. "Yeah, that would be like forcing ice on the Eskimos. And you'd probably have done it despite the risks, as obsessed as you are."

Thank heavens for small blessings—no, make that large blessings—Summer thought as she remembered her posture and pulled herself up to her full height of five feet ten and a half inches. Standing erect with shoulders back, she willed herself not to feel self-conscious about the thrusting breasts that had been the bane of her existence since ninth grade.

Summer continued, "I've spent thousands, Annie. Every penny I didn't need for subsistence. I've got too much invested to back out now. Not just money, but the last year of my life."

Summer paced. "I've worked days, nights, weekends! I've taken lessons—studied till I couldn't keep my eyes open. Every penny has gone into The Plan. I've lifted weights, jogged, and done aerobics when all I wanted to do was collapse. Everything I've done has been in preparation for this."

"You make this sound so cold-bloodedly simple. How can

you imagine going to bed with someone for money?"

"That's not what I'm doing," Summer protested. "I intend to marry—not just take his money and run."

"You're just prostituting yourself for one man instead of several."

"You're wrong, Annie. I intend to be a good wife if by some chance this works. I'll be faithful. He'll never regret marrying me. Besides, I'm not going to hop into bed with anybody until after I'm married."

"Summer, you are so naive! Do you think that a man in this day and age is just going to fall in love with you, propose, and then wait until after the wedding to sample your charms?"

Summer had tried not to think about that aspect of it. "Well, yes, I guess."

Annie hooted. "Now I know you're a hopeless innocent."

Summer knew that Annie was right. She had little experience sexually. The memory of the awkward fumbling she'd endured from her college sweetheart still left her embarrassed.

"Actually, I have thought about this." Summer cleared her throat and walked over to fiddle with the air-conditioner controls. "I realize that sex is part of marriage. I'm sure I can go through with it when the time comes."

"Go through with it? Let your Auntie Annie give you a word of warning. One of these days you are going to meet someone, and the last thing you'll think about, when it comes to sex, is how to go through with it."

"And what makes you think you're such an expert? You told me that Wayne is the only man you've ever been with."

"Because I have experienced passion, my dear innocent," Annie stated smugly.

Summer snorted. "You're making entirely too much of

this. I'll work out the details as they happen."

"You make it sound like some kind of business transaction. What happens if you get some guy so hot and bothered, he doesn't want to postpone the consummation?"

Summer's lips thinned. "I'm sure I can handle any over-the-hill playboy if it comes to that."

"So you're aiming at an older man, huh?" Annie grimaced.

"The book said most men with big bucks are over fifty, so that's what I anticipate."

"Looks like you've got all the answers. What happens if you fail?"

"I have no intention of failing." A thread of steel laced through Summer's voice.

Annie stood and faced her. "What if you get hurt?"

"How can I possibly get hurt?" Puzzled, Summer frowned.

"What if you fall in love with your millionaire and he doesn't love you back?"

"That's hardly likely. I don't want his love, just his fortune," Summer answered flippantly.

"So you say." Annie shook her head. "What I think you really want is love. You're starving for it! You never knew your father, and your mother died when you were young. My goodness! Your grandmother didn't even acknowledge you except in her will! You're a textbook case! You need—"

"That's enough!" Summer cut her off. Raising her hands as if to stop a physical onslaught, she continued, "Annie, you're my dearest friend in the world, but that's all the analysis I can take for one day."

"One of these days, you're going to explode, carrying all that hurt around inside of you."

"Yeah, well, not today. Today I'm leaving for Houston."

Summer snapped the makeup case closed. "Come on, Annie. Wish me luck, because I really want this. Maybe money doesn't buy happiness, but it can buy security. It's as simple as that."

Resigned, Annie shrugged her shoulders. "If you're set on this harebrained scheme, then do it. Get it out of your system. Just don't get hurt."

Summer laughed at Annie's dour blessing. "Thanks, Annie; I don't know what I'd do without you." And she meant it, she thought, with a fierce rush of love for her friend.

Filled with renewed energy, Summer walked to the nightstand and picked up the dog-eared copy of *How to Marry a Rich, Rich Man*, by Tiffani Devereax and placed it in her tote bag. She had to take the book with her. When she held it, she could believe her dream was achievable.

Annie picked up the garment bag and the makeup case. Summer draped the strap of a small white leather purse on her left shoulder, the tote bag on her right, lifted the two matching cordovan leather pullman cases, and followed Annie from the room.

In silence they walked across creaking wood floors and out the back door to the turquoise convertible parked under a rust-stained aluminum carport. The morning breeze ruffled Summer's hair. She glanced skyward. The day promised to be another scorcher. Classic car or not—driving without air conditioning in Texas in the summer was not her idea of fun. She hoped cruising with the top down would keep her cool enough to prevent perspiration from ruining her hair and makeup.

After everything but her handbag was stowed away, she slammed the trunk and turned to Annie. "I just want to check the house one last time. I'll be right back."

Summer needed to say a solitary good-bye to the old

house that had sheltered her since she'd arrived in Red Rock to claim her inheritance and her first job as school librarian.

The routine of checking each detail calmed her nerves. The front door was locked—not that crime was a very big problem in this dusty county west of Fort Worth.

When she turned off the air-conditioner in the bedroom, the silence unnerved her. Not even a faucet dripped in the old-fashioned hall bathroom. Everything was neat and clean, if somewhat dilapidated.

For once, the shabbiness dismayed Summer. Well, she vowed, when she had married, she'd restore the house. Perhaps use it as a vacation cabin, she thought as she locked the back door.

"Don't worry about anything," Annie said, "just be careful."

Summer hugged Annie, then tossed her purse onto the front seat before sliding beneath the big steering wheel.

"I'll call you in a week," Summer promised. She backed out the gravel driveway but stopped before pulling onto the highway and stared at her house, seeing it clearly for the first time. Dismay filled her at its run-down condition. The Texas sun had blistered away the white enamel long ago and faded the paint on the shutters until it was hard to tell if they'd once been blue or gray. The front porch sagged. Half-dead blades of Saint Augustine grass masqueraded as a lawn while perennial red verbena struggled through the weeds in what had once been flower beds. The area around Red Rock had been ignored by the fickle summer storms that flooded the neighboring counties, so a fine coat of red dust clung to every object—living and inanimate.

Summer closed her mind to the past and gunned the engine. Gravel pinged against the undercarriage of the car until she got out onto the asphalt country road. She slid the shift lever into drive and headed for Houston.

The wind whipped her hair about her face. A long day of driving in the hot Texas sun lay ahead of her. Then she'd know if all the planning, all the money and time she'd spent on herself, were worth it. I just hope I don't lose my nerve, she thought, gripping the steering wheel.

Two

Harding Bennett Carson muttered a string of obscenities that would have shocked his genteel mother had she heard him. In fact, knowing the iron-willed matriarch of the family, he knew she'd have wanted to wash his mouth out with soap—regardless of the fact that he was thirty-two years old and six feet two inches tall. Irene Harding Carson had never let something like age or size stand in the way of disciplining any of her five children.

Ben thought about his mother, waiting for him in Houston. She was really going to be ticked at him this time! Especially since he had missed last year's July reunion.

"Aw, hell! Start, damn you!" He gave the ignition key a vicious twist. The engine of the silver Jag whirred but didn't oblige. Ben slammed the heel of his palm against the leather-wrapped steering wheel. "Dammit!"

He'd been speeding along the blacktopped road, singing along with Travis Tritt and enjoying the quiet countryside, when the engine had died. No amount of pleading or cursing would make it start again.

Frustration boiled within him. He ran long fingers through his thick ebony hair and leaned his forehead against the padded steering wheel. Motionless, he sat in the comfortable leather seat a few minutes more, but the steadily increasing heat forced him to make a decision. He'd have to leave the car. Soon the interior temperature would be well over a hundred degrees.

With a sigh, he swung the car door open and stepped onto the sticky asphalt. Intense heat enveloped him in its smothering embrace. Perspiration instantly beaded his forehead. With a monogrammed handkerchief, he blotted his tanned face. The crisp square of linen wilted instantly.

Vainly he searched for fencing or a mailbox, but as far as he could see, there was nothing to suggest anyone lived close. Just my luck, he thought. Stranded in the middle of nowhere.

Ben shrugged out of his jacket and tossed it onto the car seat. No use taking it with him. Though he'd never hitched a ride before, he was quite certain that hitchhikers didn't need the dress-for-success look. He rolled up the sleeves of his ivory silk shirt three turns, revealing dark hair sprinkled liberally over muscled forearms. He stared at his new car, then angrily slammed the driver's door. He hadn't even had the damn thing a week yet!

There was no use in peering under the hood at the marvel of machinery that powered the expensive luxury car. After all, he barely knew a spark plug from a radiator.

When he was growing up, Cecil Johnson had always taken care of the many cars driven by the members of the Carson family. Although Ben had hung around the garage as much as Cecil would allow, dogging the former stock car racer's footsteps and hanging on his every word, he'd never learned a thing about the internal combustion engine from the taciturn man. The only thing he had picked up from the grizzled mechanic was an appreciation for what Cecil considered the finest offerings from Detroit.

Even after he'd moved away from home, deserting Houston and family for Dallas and Janine, he'd never had occasion to open the hood of any of the cars he'd owned. They'd always run perfectly. In the event his car needed servicing or maintenance, he merely dropped it off at the nearest dealership.

Maybe he'd been lucky, he mused with a shrug of wide shoulders, but he'd never had any problems with the various foreign-made sports cars he owned. Until now.

Ben pressed the security alarm pad on his key chain. A quiet electronic hiccup sounded from within as the security system armed itself. He stared at the car his dad had warned him a month ago not to buy.

"It'll be in the shop more than in your garage," his dad had said. "Buy American, son! Do your part to decrease the trade deficit," Big Ben had argued. "Get yourself a nice top-of-the-line Caddy or even one of those little Corvettes."

That his father would disagree with his choice of cars was a given. Big Ben had voiced the same objections when Ben bought his first car, a hot red Porsche. And then, as now, Ben had disregarded his father's opinion because his dad thought anything made in another country could never be as good as something made in the U.S. of A.

Ben grinned ruefully. Maybe his dad had been right—this time. And would he enjoy saying, "I told you so!" But that didn't bother Ben nearly as much as it would have a year ago. Hell! His dad had been right about the car—and about Janine.

What the hell! The car was still a gorgeous hunk of gleaming metal. Ben admired the deep-luster paint as he stepped away from the Jaguar. He raked his hands through his hair again.

If only I'd waited for the defective cellular phone to be replaced, he mused, I wouldn't be in this predicament. The installer had said he'd get to it as soon as possible. But Ben had never been noted for patience. And the installer had a busier schedule than most executives Ben knew. Suddenly everyone in Texas wanted to reach out and touch someone—while in their car.

He shrugged his shoulders, acknowledging responsibility for his current situation. He hadn't wanted to wait another moment before seeing Dallas in his rearview mirror. Thoughts of home tantalized him once he'd made the decision to go to Houston. So he replaced thought with action.

Obviously I should have thought more, Ben reflected, but he'd wanted to end his self-imposed exile immediately. He'd spent too much time licking his wounds and then playing the singles scene—trying to erase Janine's memory with the women who flocked to succeed her. And there had been many women—gorgeous brunettes and redheads. But no blondes. After Janine, he'd lost his taste for sexy blondes.

Disgusted with his train of thought, he bestowed a good hard kick to the left rear tire of the recalcitrant vehicle. The electronic siren shattered the quiet of the countryside, scattering mockingbirds and crows from the nearby trees.

Ben grinned. His mood lifted. "That'll teach you, you overpriced bucket of bolts." A dimple popped out at the left corner of his mouth as he turned and swaggered down the potholed country road. Hands thrust in his trouser pockets, he whistled cheerfully.

According to the map he'd looked at this morning, this farm-to-market road intersected with a service road to the interstate. It should be no more than a mile or two from here, he reasoned.

Again he regretted the impulse that had led him to leave the interstate. The side trip had been fruitless since the parcel of land he'd been interested in had severe drainage problems. The previous week's rains had all but put it underwater.

As he walked, his thoughts returned to the circumstances that had brought him to his present situation, the phone call from his mother. Though he'd tried his best to avoid the family as much as possible, his mother had done her best to make that impossible. Oh, he'd talked to his parents and his sisters on the phone and had seen them if they came to Dallas, but he hadn't set foot in the house where he'd grown up since his divorce. No, even since before that, he remembered. The last time he'd been there had been Christmas two years ago. He winced as he recalled the screaming fight Janine had engaged him in that day.

She'd been tossing back tumblers of Scotch as if they were water and had slapped his nephew when he'd spilled cherry punch on her ice blue satin dress. She'd cursed the child, him, and everyone else within earshot before he'd succeeded in hustling her from the room. He shook his head as he thought again of the two miserable years he'd lived with money-hungry Janine. The painful memories kept pace with him during his walk.

Life with Janine had grown steadily worse. Divorce hadn't healed the pain. With each passing month, his cynicism had hardened. A few months ago he'd realized he'd lost his taste for everything. Business coups offered no fulfillment. Sexual conquests held no pleasure. Ben snorted. Hell! There was no conquest when women flocked to you! His lips curled in disdain. His dark good looks—and his money, he thought with brutal honesty—ensured his desirability. He'd finally quit trying to guess if the woman in his bed was after his body or his money.

After two years of punishing his parents for being right about his ex-wife, he'd decided to forgive them. He hoped they could forgive him for being an immature jerk.

Even before his mother had called to gently coerce him into attending the annual reunion, he'd been thinking about moving back to Houston. He needed a change. The commercial real estate company he'd built in Dallas, which had made him his first million, no longer thrilled him. He found his thoughts returning to his hometown—to the excitement and friendliness of Houston. He thought often of his family, now scattered in every direction. His parents and sisters, who laughingly embraced life.

Each day he found it harder and harder to go through the motions. Some days he thought he'd scream from sheer boredom. Nothing excited him anymore—not Dallas with its New York pretensions, not his work, not even the women he slept with.

Then there was the night he'd gone home with a woman he'd met at a nightclub. He frowned as he remembered how she'd tried to get him in her bed. He'd been bored. For the first time, he simply wasn't interested enough to make the effort.

He'd realized then that his life was empty. Oh, sure, he had friends, but that wasn't enough. He needed someone to care if he lived or died.

Impulsively he'd decided this trip to Houston was the perfect solution for what ailed him, the need to mend his fences and get back to his roots. Possessed by those twin forces, he'd acted. And this was the result, he thought in disgust.

Just a mile or two, Ben thought again, wiping his perspiring brow. No problem. Ben inhaled deeply, enjoying the scent of the evergreens. His ears, more attuned to the sounds around him now, picked up the buzz of insects and the rustling of the underbrush that signaled small animals nearby.

A mile or two! Why, he ran more than that many evenings at The Fitness Center on Forest Lane. He glanced at his feet. Of course, he didn't run in Italian loafers—new ones at that. The gleaming leather seemed a bit tight. Wistfully he thought of the comfortable running shoes in his closet at home. Why didn't I at least stop to pack a bag?

Time seemed to slow to a snail's pace. The pavement, wet-looking in spots where the sun had melted the asphalt, burned through the thin soles of his shoes. Not a breath of wind swayed the tall weeds on either side of the road, and the tree line stood a little too far away to shade the lane.

The silk shirt clung to him, and perspiration trickled down the waist of his tan tropical-weight wool slacks. His skin felt as if it were being turned into beef jerky in the Texas sun.

An hour passed, and Ben's mood steadily declined. The road stretched endlessly from one hilltop to the next. He limped along in his Italian loafers, trying not to put pressure on the blister that had formed on his right heel.

He began to wonder if he'd read the map wrong or had made a mistake about his location. Maybe he was twenty miles from the interstate, not two, he thought in dismay.

He'd tried walking in the patch of green beside the road, but millions of mosquitoes had risen from their hiding places in the weeds, deciding he was lunch. Recent rains had caused a population explosion among the thirsty little bloodsuckers. The annoying pests, coupled with the spongy black mud that threatened to suck the shoes from his feet, sent him back to the blistering road. As hot as the asphalt was, Ben decided, it was preferable to being eaten alive.

Unfortunately, now that the mosquitoes had discovered him, they were reluctant to let him go, plaguing him unmercifully, even biting through his sweat-drenched shirt. "Damn!" he muttered as he slapped one that was trying to make a meal of his right cheek.

Perspiration soaked him to his underwear. He knew he must have hundreds of insect bites all over his body, and his hot, swollen feet felt as if they were crammed into shoes too small for his five-year-old nephew to wear. Any minute he expected the seams of the shoes to burst. In short, he'd never been so miserable in his entire life.

Where the hell was the interstate? His frown deepened. A short while later, he crested a small hill and froze, staring at the ribbons of gray concrete less than a quarter mile away.

I must be getting old, he thought, picking up the pace to a limping jog until he reached the service road. He gazed at the interstate highway that connected Houston to Dallas. He'd never seen anything so beautiful in his entire life, he thought, scratching his arms vigorously.

The southbound lanes lay farthest from him. First he'd have to cross a strip of land that looked like a lake of green Johnson grass. He groaned; more mosquitoes. Then he'd have to sprint like an Olympic runner across the two northbound lanes and negotiate another verdant median before reaching the half of the freeway that led south to Houston.

After what he'd been through? No problem, he thought, and stepped onto a patch of green. Immediately he sank up to his ankles in gooey, surprisingly cold, mud.

"Damn it to hell!" With a few more choice expletives, he succeeded in freeing his feet and sloshing across the deceptively green jellylike area between the service road and the northbound traffic lanes. When he reached the shoulder of the busy highway, black mud encased what had once been exquisite glove-leather Italian loafers. He stomped his feet, trying to shake off some of the mud, but it clung like thick black glue.

Cars and trucks traveling well past the speed limit created gusts of hot air against his grimy skin. He waited for a huge semitruck to pass, then he darted across the road, reaching the other side as a compact car, horn blaring, rocketed past him.

Fifty feet of what, on closer inspection, could only be

described as swamp separated him from his goal. He stepped onto the boggy ground. Mud oozed and sucked hungrily at his shoes. A black cloud of mosquitoes appeared as if by magic and attacked every exposed inch of skin.

Hands flailing at the flying carnivores, shoes squishing with each step, he slowly made his way across the field. Traversing the muck felt like jogging in blackstrap molasses, though not nearly as pleasing to the nose. With each heavy step, he cursed his abandoned car, his shoes, and his impulsiveness.

Just then he stepped into a hole, onto a rock hidden beneath the muck. His right ankle turned. His arms thrashed the air trying to maintain his balance, but to no avail. Ben fell like a loblolly pine sliced by a chain saw.

Though he tried to break his fall, mud still coated his body and painted his face. The smelly black stuff covered his soiled shirt and the ruined trousers. Stunned, with the breath knocked out of him, he lay unmoving for long minutes.

As soon as his breath returned, he muttered every profane word he'd ever heard, most of them learned at Cecil's side. The aroma was nearly as bad as the slimy texture, he thought, wrinkling his nose. With an effort of will, he pulled himself to his feet and tried his ankle. Not too bad. Just a little painful. He could walk on it, he decided.

"This has got to be the worst day of my entire life," he groaned aloud as he hobbled across the rest of the muddy field to the edge of the highway.

Dispiritedly he stuck his thumb in the air. He hoped—prayed—some good Samaritan would take pity on him. Privately he doubted it. If his looks didn't scare everyone away, his smell would. His shoulders sagged in despair.

Half an hour later, Ben admitted defeat. No one had even slowed down. Even men driving pickups sped by. They must think I'll pollute their truck bed, he thought with a furious scowl.

Efforts to wipe off the mud merely smeared it around. The scalding sun dried the smelly mess, hardening the black slime until Ben felt encased in a putrid suit of dirty armor.

When the classic Chevrolet convertible topped the rise, Ben stopped and stared in disbelief. It looked so much like the old one his dad and mom had when they'd gotten married, the car his dad had given him when he turned sixteen, that he almost forgot to stick his thumb in the air.

Much to his surprise, the car slowed. Elated, Ben grinned at the woman driver and ran toward the car.

Suddenly the car lurched ahead and raced away, but not before Ben got a good look at long, creamy legs beneath billowing white skirts. Dark glasses and wind-tossed blond hair couldn't hide the horrified expression on a very pretty face. Her image seared onto his retinas.

Stunned by the sense of betrayal, Ben scowled and shook his fist at her. Torn between wanting to pull every bleached hair on her head out by the dark roots and wishing he'd had another moment to gaze at her incredibly long legs, he began walking again. He couldn't get her out of his mind. He swore out loud at her arrogant behavior.

Damn! She must really think she's hot stuff, he fumed. Racing around in that old convertible, dress blowing in the breeze up to her waist, smiling and teasing the men she passed on the highway. She'd better be careful or she may get more than she bargained for, he thought. Surely the bleach hadn't killed all her brain cells. She must have more sense than to pull that trick too often.

He devoted his energy to walking and lifting his thumb. Several cars passed before a battered white pickup filled with Mexican laborers topped the rise and lumbered toward him.

The driver slowed and, with a shout and a grin, beckoned to Ben.

"Hey, man, thanks!" Ben shouted exultantly, and jumped over the tailgate of the truck when the vehicle had slowed enough. He grinned his thanks to the workers in back and waved at the driver through the rear window. The old truck was better than any limo he'd ever ridden in, he thought with a happy grin, settling against the side of the truck bed.

Though the workers were as dirty as he, they didn't smell nearly as bad, he noticed. They smiled at him but gradually began inching as far away from him as possible.

After a few abortive attempts at conversation, the only word of which he understood was *Centerville,* he decided to imitate the tired laborers by closing his eyes against the glare and trying to sleep.

Unfortunately, the only thing he saw behind his closed eyes was white. White blond hair. White, startled face with red, pouting lips. A sexy white dress blowing in the breeze. White thighs. Surprised at the jolt of lust that hit him, he shifted uncomfortably and tried to think about the car she'd been driving instead. Ben recalled how delighted his dad had been when he'd given the old Chevy back after buying the Porsche.

No matter how hard he tried to force the blonde from his thoughts, her image teased his mind ruthlessly. So the mysterious blonde was sexy. So what? Judging by her behavior, she was a tease. Could be as bad as Janine.

His dad used to say, pretty is as pretty does. Ben had never thought much about what that meant, but he'd learned. Janine had taught him a lesson he'd never forget. She had exemplified the cliché. Never again, he vowed silently, would he get tangled up with a faithless woman like his selfish ex-wife.

I'm old enough to think with my head instead of what's inside my pants, Ben thought. But he couldn't help wonder what she looked like without the dark glasses. He tried to think of other things, but he kept seeing those luscious long legs and that mane of hair whipped by the wind.

Three

When Summer reached Centerville, a small town north of Houston, she decided to stop. After half a day under the broiling sun, she'd realized she'd made a serious error in driving with the top down on her car. I should have planned the trip for night, when it's cooler, she thought, glancing at her heat-reddened face in the rearview mirror. Every bit of exposed skin felt—like a boiled lobster.

Not only could I have been spared the unmerciful sun, but I'd also have avoided the truckers, she thought with a grimace. It seemed as if the driver of every eighteen-wheeler in the state had blasted his air horn as he'd passed her. She'd begun to cringe each time she'd seen one of the diesel behemoths barreling along the freeway, coming up behind her.

She'd longed to stop before at one of the public rest areas, but like most women who traveled alone, she avoided the rest stops if there were only a couple of vehicles to be seen.

Summer approached a street lined with fast-food restaurants. The tree-shaded parking lot of a Dairy Queen drew her like an ice floe in the Antarctic attracts penguins. Gratefully she pulled into the shady spot and turned off the engine. Stretching her arms over her head, she winced at the movement that tightened the fabric of her dress against her skin. She felt light-headed and a little nauseated. A headache pounded between her eyes. The day had been so hot, she wouldn't have been surprised to see her artificial nails melt.

Summer longed to splash her burning face with cold water, but knew her makeup—what little remained—would smear and run. She couldn't very well arrive at the hotel with mascara tracks down her face.

She half stumbled into the restaurant, luxuriating in the blast of cold air that greeted her. Perhaps if she stayed here a while, she'd feel better, she thought. How foolish to drive with the top down under the blistering Texas sun! The increased air flow might have felt good, but her skin was going to pay the price for that ventilation, she knew, worried belatedly about blistering and peeling.

In the rest room, she bathed her red arms and spread water-soaked paper towels on the deep vee of skin exposed by the plunging halter neckline. With a moan of pleasure, she splashed her face with cold water—to heck with her makeup, she decided. When she looked in the mirror, she almost laughed at the clown face peering back at her. Streaks of black mascara striated her sunburned face. She remembered the old joke from her childhood. *What's black and white and red all over? A sunburned zebra!* That's exactly what she looked like, she thought with a wan smile.

With shaking hands, she cupped water and held it to her face. Soaking more paper towels under the running water, she tried to spread them on the tops of her shoulders. The sudden cold on her burning skin caused a chill to shake her body.

Gradually she felt a little better. Summoning her energy, she took mascara and lipstick from her purse and repaired her makeup as much as possible.

Tiredly she used a short plastic pick to get the tangles out of her hair. Then she slid her sunglasses to the top of her head to serve as a makeshift hair band.

"Good golly! You're cooked, lady!" The chunky,

brown-haired girl behind the counter said loudly.

"Yes, I know. It's not bad as it looks," Summer lied.

"Even if it's half as bad, that's bad enough!" The girl looked Summer up and down, from her burning face to her raw shoulders and arms, to the deep neckline of her dress.

"Good golly! Even your feet are red! You know ma'am, as fair as you are, you should use sunscreen."

Summer rolled her eyes to the ceiling. "Just give me the biggest cola you've got, with a ton of ice."

The girl grinned and complied, placing a forty-four-ounce vision of crushed ice and soda in front of Summer moments later.

Summer murmured her thanks and walked to one of the red vinyl booths. Sipping the chilled drink, she decided nothing had ever tasted so good. She slid gingerly into the booth. The plastic seat felt like ice against her blistered back. Chills rippled across her skin. Determined to ignore her discomfort, she stared out the window.

An ancient white pickup truck pulled into the gas station across the street. Summer's mouth dropped open as she recognized the man who jumped from the back of the truck bed. It was the bum from the interstate—that filthy hitchhiker! He grinned and waved at the driver, who slowly pulled away. So he'd found someone to pick him up.

Fascinated, Summer couldn't pull her eyes from him. How could anyone get that dirty? she wondered. He spoke to the service station owner, who nodded his head. Then he walked over and picked up the water hose, turned it on, and held the nozzle over his head.

Wistfully she watched the water gush over him. I bet that feels good, she thought. He moved the nozzle, concentrating the spray on the muddiest patches on his clothes. He took his time spraying himself clean from top to bottom, even taking his shoes off and directing the stream of water inside them. The impromtu shower refracted the afternoon sunlight into a rainbow. Summer stared at the man standing in the rainbow he had created. He drank thirstily from the stream of water. Then he turned off the hose and shook himself like a dog. Water droplets flew from his shiny black hair and his body.

Summer's mouth felt as hot and dry as a desert. She groped for the straw in her icy soda, gulping her drink as she watched him take his shirt off. She fanned her face with the napkin. Had the air-conditioner in the restaurant suddenly started blowing hot air? She couldn't seem to cool off.

Her eyes devoured his sleek body, admiring the ripple of muscles, the wet bronze skin. The muscles in his shoulders and arms bunched as he twisted his shirt, wringing the excess water from it. She sucked in her breath.

"Good golly! Have you ever seen such a hunk in your life?" Summer reluctantly looked toward the counter girl, whose mouth hung open in awe. I hope I don't look that enthralled, she thought. Determined not to look at the man again—hunk or not—she walked to the counter. "I'd like a hamburger and curly fries—make that a large order, please?" Summer studied the girl's name tag. "Debbi? Debbi?"

She heard the swift inhalation from the jeans-clad girl who shared this moment with her. Surrendering to her voyeuristic desire, she followed Debbi's line of sight. Summer's green eyes caressed the man's broad chest, covered by a mat of dark hair that tapered narrowly to his waist. His trousers, heavy with the weight of water, hung low on his hips, revealing a trim waist and a band of white skin above the band of sodden cloth.

Her heart thudded heavily and a warmth pulsed low in her body. What more could she see if he were closer? She watched as he wrung out his socks. Then he removed the belt from his trousers, coiling it neatly and placing it in a wet shoe. His hands went to his trousers. Summer caught her breath. Surely he wouldn't take his pants off in front of God and everybody! Uneasily she wished the silly little girl who worked here would tend to the grill and peel her eyes from his bronzed body. As for Summer, wild horses couldn't have dragged her away from the scene across the narrow street.

His fingers moved. Summer strained to see. Suddenly his trousers gaped at the waist, only the closed zipper keeping the soggy pants from pooling at his feet.

"Good golly!" Debbi breathed reverently.

Summer waited, breath suspended, eyes glued to the scene. Good golly indeed, she thought. What a body! She gripped the paper cup and waited. Disappointment replaced anticipation when he turned and headed for the rest room. A sigh escaped Debbi's lips.

Irritated by her own response and by the young girl's reaction, Summer jerked her eyes from the window. The noisy slurping that signaled her cup was empty sounded amplified in the sudden silence.

"Oh, did you want something, ma'am?" Debbi asked, reluctantly turning away from the window.

Summer repeated her order to the girl, who seemed oblivious to her annoyance. After getting a refill on her large drink, she returned to her seat.

Restlessly her eyes darted to the service station. When would he come out? Disgusted with herself, she rose from the booth and walked over to the jukebox to make a selection. She stood for several minutes reading the list of songs, surprised when she found a listing for Perry Como's "Catch a Falling Star." With a smile, she dropped in a quarter and punched its number.

"Ma'am, your order's ready!" Summer smiled gratefully

at the girl and picked up the tray. Minutes later, she realized how hungry she'd been. The nearly naked wet male across the street fled her mind as she bit into the charbroiled hamburger. She closed her eyes in delight.

Twirling a fry in ketchup, she casually glanced out the window, but the man was nowhere in sight. Likely he'd moved on once he'd got his pants wrung out. No matter how many times she told herself she was being silly to react this way to a man, a stranger, she couldn't stop thinking about him—about how he'd looked with water dripping from his nearly naked body.

Why, Annie would laugh herself silly if she could see how foolish I'm acting over some nameless man! Summer shied away from putting a name to what she felt when she'd looked at him standing bare-chested under the hose spray. Ruthlessly she slammed the door on her thoughts. Men were a means to an end—wealthy men, she reminded herself.

Minutes later, the door to the restaurant opened, letting in a furnace-hot blast of moist air. She looked up and there *he* was—every tanned, wet inch of him, exuding power and sexuality in equal measure. Up close, he seemed even more male —his muscles larger, his skin more tanned, his features more chiseled.

Summer shivered, recalling his raised fist as she'd sped by. What if he'd come in here looking for her? What if he'd been aware of her watching him earlier? She cringed at the thought.

Swallowing, she felt the food lodge in her throat. After several swallows of soda, it slid down to land like a stone in her stomach. She hoped he wouldn't notice her. She tried to slide down in the booth while still keeping an eye on him. He'd finger-combed his hair, she noted. The dark curls lay damply against his forehead. She had a crazy desire to brush the curls away from his face. Would his hair feel silky sliding between her fingers?

His clothes looked better in the sense that they weren't covered with mud, but they were still a sorry mess, much-wrinkled from the twisting and wringing. Still, that was an improvement from before. He wore his wet, rumpled clothes with a natural grace and style, though his shoes squeaked with each step. Summer hid her smile behind the large paper cup she sipped from.

"Miss, could I have a large cola with lots of ice?" he asked Debbi.

His voice, a hint of a drawl in the deep tone, suited him perfectly, she decided. And so polite to a mere counter girl, Summer thought in surprise.

"Yes, sir!" the girl replied with a simpering grin. Summer had an insane desire to tell her to throw herself on someone her own age.

The man smiled back at the girl. Summer was surprised the girl didn't melt into a puddle at his feet. She watched as he pulled all the change from his pockets.

"That'll be a dollar five, sir."

Dark red suffused his face. With an audible sigh, he said, "It seems like I don't quite have enough. Sorry. Could I just have a cup of ice instead?"

"Oh! I'm sorry, but it will be almost the same, because I have to charge you for the cup." The girl sounded genuinely distressed.

"Oh. Well, then. Do you have a phone I could use? The one at the station across the street was out of order."

"Sure. No problem." The girl grinned, seemingly happy to oblige him in any way possible.

Summer's heart went out to the handsome man who must be down on his luck. She knew what it was like to have only a few coins. To not have enough for a cold drink when you were practically senseless with thirst. To have to miss meals. Though he didn't look like he'd missed any meals, she thought as she remembered his body—as nearly perfect as she'd ever seen.

Poor man, she thought. Before she allowed herself to reconsider her actions, she dashed to the counter and ordered the drink he'd wanted and paid for it, telling the girl to give it to him when he finished on the phone.

Ben called the dealership first. As usual, his name commanded enough respect that they were only too willing to make arrangements to pick up the car and him. He interrupted their profuse apologies and assurances and told them he'd call them back if he needed a ride back to Dallas.

The next call he placed was to Tracey, the oldest of his four sisters. Perhaps it was an omen, Ben thought. He got a recording of his brother-in-law Ryan's voice on the answering machine informing him that the Millers were out at the moment. With a sigh, he decided to just go back to Dallas with the tow truck, so he left a message telling them that.

Before he could call the dealership back, someone tapped his shoulder. He turned and saw the teenaged girl who'd flirted with him at the counter.

"Here's your soda." She thrust the drink at him.

"Hey, no, I couldn't let you pay for this."

"Good golly, I didn't." She giggled and blushed.

"Then who did?" His brows lifted in question.

"The lady over there."

He looked where she pointed and got another shock. Today must be the day for them, he thought, staring open-mouthed at the woman in the booth next to the window. The sexy blonde from the interstate! For a moment, anger at her earlier teasing actions flared to life. What did she want now?

45

To bait him because he had no money?

"Thanks," he muttered to the girl, taking the drink. He'd never imagined he'd see the woman again. Automatically he appraised her and decided with regret that she was even better-looking than he'd first thought. Even with her pale skin an alarming shade of red, she tempted him.

Oh, yeah. She tempted him—big time. His anger changed to heat of a different kind. His eyes traced her curves and flowed down her long legs to high-heeled sandals. Yep. He'd been right about something else, too. She was trouble—in capital letters.

For a moment, he considered refusing the drink, but then his common sense asserted itself. He was thirsty, and, he acknowledged with a grin, beggars can't be choosers. Millionaire or not, with sixty-seven cents in his pocket, including the quarter he'd found on the rest room floor across the street, he was a beggar for the first time in his life. This condition of being without funds—without means of any kind except his wits—was distinctly odd. As odd as this entire day had been, he thought with a wry twist of his lips.

Thoughtfully he sipped the cold drink as he observed the blonde across the room. He remembered his panic in the rest room across the street when he realized his wallet wasn't in his trousers pocket. The image of him placing his wallet in his inner coat pocket rose before him. As did the memory of tossing his sport coat on the car seat.

He was broke, with no identification, no credit cards, no transportation. His first alarming thought had been, how was he going to get to Houston or back to Dallas? Here he was, a millionaire in his own right, with sixty-seven cents to his name. His clothes were ruined, his sunglasses were lost in the mud, and his Rolex was cracked. At the top of his list of complaints, though, was the fact that he was hungry and thirsty.

With characteristic thoroughness, which he'd unfortunately not utilized since deciding to hightail it to Houston yesterday, he analyzed the amazing predicament in which he found himself. An insane idea took root. Could he survive on his own? Without his name and his fortune to precede him? Just depending on his wits? Mentally Ben played around with the crazy idea. Mud and mosquitoes notwithstanding, he'd made it this far on his own, hadn't he? How far could he get just on his native intelligence?

Not for the first time, he wondered what it would be like to approach the world as an ordinary person—not as Harding Bennett Carson, born with a silver spoon in his mouth and a bankbook in his hand. He'd always privately deplored the cushion his name and money provided. Maybe it was time to find out if he was as smart and resourceful as he thought.

Just then his eyes collided with startled green ones. He sucked in his breath as her eyes roved over him, then jerked back to his dark-fringed brown eyes. His body tightened in desire. Maybe it was time he found out if women found *him* attractive, or his money. He smiled at the woman and saluted her with his cup.

He wouldn't have thought it possible for her skin to turn redder, but he knew she was blushing. He nodded imperceptibly. So she wasn't as jaded as she appeared. Oddly, that pleased him. His smile widened. Her eyes darted away like a frightened fawn.

His thoughts returned to the insanity he contemplated. What would it be like to be an ordinary man? Would this luscious blonde be interested in him if he were a truck driver or a carpenter instead of one of the state's most eligible bachelors? Damned if he knew why, but suddenly he wanted to find out.

Mortified, Summer studied the half-eaten burger and rapidly cooling fries in front of her. Her thoughts were in a whirl.

She hadn't been able to help herself. Her eyes had seemed to have a will of their own. Her rational brain had lost control of them. That was the only excuse she had. She hadn't been able to keep her eyes off him. She'd stared as if willing him to notice her. And he had! She saw him move from the corner of her eye.

Resolutely she vowed, I will not look at him again. I will not look at him again.

"Thank you for the drink, miss."

Summer shivered as if he'd drawn his fingertips across her skin. Breathlessly she whispered without meeting his eyes, "You're welcome."

With a start, she realized he was sliding into the seat opposite her.

"You can't sit here!" Panic bloomed in her at his nearness. She couldn't breathe with him so close.

"Why not?" he asked, grinning at her discomfort.

"Well, because, because I didn't ask you to." Briefly her eyes met his. That was a mistake, Summer thought, recognizing the frank interest in his velvety brown eyes. Her eyes darted away.

"But you bought me a drink."

"But that doesn't mean I want you to sit with me!" Summer's heart pounded as if she'd run all the way to Centerville.

"Oh, the drink was charity."

"No! I just felt . . ."

"Sorry for me?"

"Yes, I mean, no! Not exactly. I just wanted to help out. You seem kind of down on your luck. Perhaps I should have minded my own business," Summer regretted her impulse. Why didn't he leave? She glanced at him, trying not to stare at his hard male nipples clearly revealed by the wet cloth of the shirt. His body seemed so big . . . so . . . so . . . male. Summer glanced at his hands, large and well formed. She swallowed the lump in her throat. Overpoweringly male.

"No, ma'am. I appreciate your kindness. I guess I'm not used to someone lending me a helping hand." His brown eyes twinkled. He slurped his drink and closed his eyes. "Oh, that is so good," he declared.

Summer couldn't help but smile. "Yes, I know what you mean. Like a breath of fresh air."

"Yeah, it's a hot day to be traveling."

Summer thought about him hitchhiking along the freeway and felt sorry for him all over again. He seemed like a nice enough person, not frightening at all, she mused, just tired and broke. Maybe he was like her, heading toward the unknown, lonely and kind of scared. Maybe he was going to Houston for a job. The recession hadn't hit there as much as in other large cities.

"You really got cooked in that convertible. Why didn't you put the top up?"

"Well, my car doesn't have air conditioning. I thought it would be cooler driving with the top down." She held her arm up and looked at it. "I hope it will turn brown," she said hopefully.

"Don't count on it. You look like maybe, beneath that bleach job, you're a natural blonde. You probably always burn rather than tan."

Summer bristled at the phrase "bleach job," but her ire dissipated when she realized he was just speaking the truth— but he didn't have to be so blunt, she thought. Worried, she studied her arms. It would be almost impossible to attract a millionaire when she looked like a candidate for a burn clinic.

"Where are you headed?" he asked after another pull on his drink.

"Houston." Summer picked up a french fry but paused.

49

How long had it been since he'd eaten? she wondered. She pushed the dish toward him. "Would you like some?"

She heard his stomach growl. "Yeah, I guess I would." He poured a little puddle of ketchup on the side of the dish and dipped a fry in it.

Summer took a bite of her burger, feeling uncomfortable eating it in front of him. Should she offer to get him one? What was the protocol for dining with penniless strangers you'd just met? she wondered.

"My name is Ben Car—uh—Ben Carr. What's yours?" he asked between fries.

"Summer James."

"Well, Summer James, pleased to meet you."

"Same here, Ben Carr."

He nodded, a smile suddenly breaking across his face, and stuck his hand across the table at her.

Summer smiled, and placed her smaller, softer hand in his big brown one. His hand was warm, his grip firm. Her heart pounded at the sensation of his skin against hers. Quit being silly, she scolded herself.

"I'm going to Houston, too," he said, picking up another fry.

"Business or pleasure?"

"Maybe a little of both. You?"

"Just business," Summer answered without smiling.

He nodded. "Would you consider giving me a ride?"

Summer choked on the french fry. Wildly she shook her head. "No!" A paroxysm of coughing shook her.

"Are you all right? I'd pound you on the back, but your skin's so red. . . ."

Summer held her hands up to ward him off. She managed a weak "I'm fine."

"I'm an honest, law-abiding citizen. After all, you don't go

50

around buying drinks for every bum you feel sorry for, do you?"

She managed a weak response. "No, but—"

"Look, I'm not a bum. My car broke down back on a farm road. I walked over to the interstate but tripped and fell in the mud. That's why I looked so horrible when you passed by."

"Hey, I'm sorry about that. I wasn't teasing you. I have never picked up a hitchhiker. I was just so stunned by your appearance . . ."

"That you had to slow down for a closer look," he finished with a grin.

Summer couldn't help grinning back at him. "Something like that."

"I finally got a ride here after you passed, but they were only going this far. I've got to get to Houston. It's really important. My family always has a big July reunion. I've kind of been at odds with them for a couple years, so I haven't seen them for a while. I promised my mom I'd be there this year."

His persuasive voice pulled at Summer's resolve. "Gee, Ben, I'd like to help, but . . ."

"Summer, I really need your help," he pleaded. Earnestly he looked into her eyes. "You were right before when you said I seemed down on my luck. I need to get to Houston because I've got a . . . job interview! I can't afford to miss it! Won't you help me?"

Summer wavered. He really needed her help. But every newspaper story she'd ever read about serial killers who preyed on innocent travelers on the highways played through her mind.

"I'd show you my identification, but I left my wallet in my sport coat in the car. That's why I don't have any money."

Summer wanted to tell him he didn't have to make up stories to cover his being broke. She was certain his wallet was in his pants pocket. As certain as she was that the wallet was also empty. Gently she said, "I see." She'd let him salvage his pride if that's what he wanted to do. Sometimes pride was the only thing that kept a body going. "I've never picked up a hitchhiker before. . . ."

"Hey! I'm not a hitchhiker now. I'm the guy you're sharing your table and your meal with." He swirled another french fry in the ketchup then plopped it into his mouth.

Summer stared at his mouth. Her eyes jerked to his when he spoke again.

"Hear me out before you decide. I swear you have nothing to fear from me. What if I can guarantee your safety? Give you insurance? Would you give me a ride then?"

"Well, I guess so, but I don't know how you can do that," she stalled.

"We can give the counter girl your license plate number, name, and address. Even do the same to the man across the street at the service station. They can take my picture with you, for all I care. That way if anything happens to you, they'll come after me. You'll be perfectly safe, I swear."

Summer shook her head. "I don't know. I've just never done anything like this before." Maybe it would be a good idea to have someone help her with the driving. It was getting late, and she didn't feel very well. And he needed her. And he seemed so nice. But if he's so nice, part of her argued, why does he make you feel so jittery and nervous?

"I'll even leave my fingerprints, my parents' names and address, with them."

"Well . . ."

"Come on, be a good Samaritan one more time. Besides, you look exhausted, and you're blistered pretty bad. I could help out by driving and let you rest."

Summer thought about her pounding headache. She

feared there might be some truth in what he said. She had to get to Houston or she might chicken out completely.

"Well . . ."

"Miss, miss, could you come over here?" Ben waved at the chunky girl.

Debbi scurried over to them. "Yes, sir?" She beamed at him and batted her eyelashes.

"This young lady is picking me up. I'm going to travel to Houston with her. Take a good look at me so she'll be assured you can recognize me in the event something happens to her."

The girl giggled.

Embarrassed, Summer raised a hand to protest his light-hearted treatment of her and the situation.

"I've got an even better idea, Debbi. Give the lady your phone number. If she hasn't called you by, say, eight o'clock this evening, you call the sheriff and tell him about this."

He arched his eyebrows and asked Summer, "Satisfied?"

Trapped by his fancy maneuvering, Summer nodded her assent. She pushed away the rest of the burger. What had she agreed to? she wondered.

Ben stared at the cold burger a moment, then asked, "Are you going to eat that?"

"Why don't I order you one?" Summer asked dryly.

"No, no, this is fine. I don't think I could wait for one to cook."

Summer pushed it toward him. "Help yourself." She watched him wolf it down and finish off the fries. When Debbi, giggling and making breathy comments to Ben, dropped a slip of paper on the table directly in front of Ben, Summer grabbed it and dropped it in her purse.

A few minutes later they walked out to Summer's car.

"Let's get this top up first," Ben said, wrestling it up and locking it into place.

"Now, before we leave here, let's find a store where you can get some ointment and a soft towel or sheet to lay across the seat so the vinyl won't stick to you."

"You certainly like to take charge, don't you?" Summer frowned, irritated at his taking over.

"Yeah, it's one of my worst faults." Ben grinned, opening the passenger door for her. "My sisters call it bossiness."

"Well, I call it irritating," Summer snapped, slipping into the passenger seat. Let him drive, she thought. I don't care. At the moment she was more concerned with her declining health, which threatened her ability to carry out The Plan. She felt worse with each passing minute.

Ben slammed the door and walked around to the driver's side. "Hello, baby," he murmured as he slid behind the wheel.

Summer groaned. "Don't tell me. You're a car freak?"

"No, not really, but an old friend of mine named Cecil Johnson, who knew everything there was to know about cars, taught me to appreciate a beautiful piece of machinery when I see one."

Summer heard the affection in his voice as he went on to quote statistics about her Chevrolet convertible.

"My dad had a car like this when he proposed to my mom. He kept it for sentimental reasons and gave it to me as my first car."

The story appealed to Summer. She could picture a long-haired, teenaged version of Ben driving around in a car older than he was, probably with a cute cheerleader seated next to him. Smiling at that image, she asked, "Do you still have it?"

"No, I gave it back to my dad when I bought my first new car." Ben shifted into reverse, raced the engine a little, and, grinning at Summer's frown, pulled sedately from the lot.

Summer thought about his parents, who probably subsisted on Social Security and drove an ancient Chevy like hers. She and Ben had a lot in common, she thought, smiling sympathetically.

Four

Luckily, Centerville boasted a well-stocked supermarket. In addition to a pink floral sheet, Ben found a pair of cheap canvas sneakers. He lifted his eyebrows at Summer in question. She shrugged her shoulders, then nodded. She knew the wet loafers must be rubbing his feet raw.

At the health-and-beauty aisle, Summer watched, amused, as Ben read the labels on several medications before selecting an anesthetic spray. When he selected a bottle of name-brand aspirin, she shook her head and pointed to the generic bottle. Ben spent a few minutes reading the two labels. "Well, learn something new every day," he muttered, tossing in the plastic bottle of no-name aspirin.

They proceeded on up the aisle. Ben pitched a tube of anti-itch mosquito bite ointment into the cart. Before they made it to the check-out stand, he'd added a bag of oatmeal raisin cookies, a package of white cotton T-shirts, a bag of white athletic socks, some white cotton briefs, a pair of sunglasses, and a jar of macadamia nuts.

Summer's amusement changed to annoyance with each new item. He took a lot for granted, she thought. If they'd stocked shirts and slacks, he'd probably have bought a set while he was at it. "Just who do you think is paying for this?" she finally asked.

"You're the money man—uh, lady," he replied with an

unrepentant grin. "Oh, I'll pay you back as soon as we get to Houston."

"You bet you will. In the meantime, I don't think macadamia nuts quite fit into your budget." She removed the jar and placed it back on the shelf. "How about some peanuts?" She smiled sweetly as she placed the economy-size house brand in their cart.

Nothing seemed to ruffle his feathers. For some reason she couldn't figure out, he acted as if everything she did and said was hilarious. As she'd expected, he laughed and agreed to the cheaper nuts. For somebody broke and without wheels, he certainly seemed to be in a buoyant mood.

"Wow! You're loaded," he said when he glimpsed the thick wad of bills in her wallet as she paid for the items at the check-out.

Summer snapped her purse closed. "And you're nosy!" For a moment she entertained the disquieting thought that he might have a larcenous bent after all, but just as quickly, she discarded the thought. Instinctively Summer knew she had nothing to fear from him.

He grabbed a brown paper bag in each arm and motioned for her to lead the way. He looked exactly like one of the sixth graders at school, Summer thought, eagerly carrying his favorite girl's books. That thought brought her up short. He's not a kid, and you're not his girl, she reminded herself. But that thought depressed her.

When they reached her car, he ripped open the package containing the sheet, shook the crisp pastel material, and spread it over the seat.

"I can't believe I had to pay twenty dollars for a sheet!" Summer grumbled as she eased into the passenger side.

"Do you always gripe about every penny you spend?"

Summer studied his face to see if his words held sneering

recrimination, but he just looked curious. "There's nothing wrong with being conservative with money. Maybe it's a habit you should develop, especially since you are currently unemployed."

"That's right. I forgot."

"How can you forget something like that?"

"Money's not that important to me," Ben replied.

"Usually the only people who say that have so much money, they don't have to worry about it," Summer muttered.

Ben wadded up the packaging from the sheet and crammed it into one of the bags and then removed the top from the can of sunburn spray. "Here, lean forward and let me spray you with this."

She obliged, lifting her hair from her neck and presenting her back to him. After a moment, she turned to see why he hesitated. Her eyes were caught by the flare of heat in his dark eyes. Surely her heart must have stopped beating for a split second. Why else would she feel as if the earth tilted on its axis? Then his eyes dropped and she was uncertain of what she'd read in his dark gaze. Confused, she turned her head away and waited for him to apply the medicine. The seconds seemed to become hours. Then she heard the quiet hiss of the aerosol as he misted her back with the soothing anesthetic spray. She sighed in pleasure, forgetting everything but the cooling spray on her burning skin.

"That feel good?" he whispered.

"Ummm, yes, thank you." Summer smiled slightly.

"Let it dry a little before you lean back."

She wondered at the strain she heard in his voice. Summer opened her eyes and glanced at him, but he turned away and busied himself removing his ruined shoes, replacing them with soft socks and the cheap sneakers they'd bought. When he shrugged out of his shirt, she closed her eyes. She didn't think she could pretend to be nonchalant while he changed shirts.

Eyes still closed, she settled against the fabric-draped seat and leaned her head back. The quiet rustling of fabric teased her ears. Her wretched imagination supplied the mental picture of what he looked like without a shirt. Summer heard the hiss of the spray can again and jumped when the cooling balm landed on her shoulders and throat and between her breasts.

"You're as jittery as a cat. Do you feel okay?"

"Yes," Summer mumbled, embarrassed. Afraid he could see what she was thinking in her eyes, she kept them closed. The spray on her fiery skin felt wonderful. She heard the soft hiss again, then felt the pads of his fingers gently spreading the white foam onto her face. At the touch of his fingers, her traitorous brain called forth the image of him shirtless in the deluge from the hose, sodden trousers riding low on trim hips. So this is how his hands felt—incredibly gentle. How would those hands feel stroking her in other, more sensitive places? Just the thought of his hands sliding down her arms, around the curve of her waist, over her hips, made her weak. What is wrong with me? Summer wondered, frightened at the intensity with which she wanted the fantasy to come true.

"There. That should do for now." His breathing sounded raspy to her ears, as harsh as his voice. The gentle drawl was noticeably absent.

Lazily she opened her eyes. Beads of perspiration dotted his forehead. She longed to reach up and wipe the moisture away. Taking the coward's way out, she murmured, "Sorry my car doesn't have air conditioning," then closed her eyes. She had to fight this weakness, Summer decided. "You were right. The sheet feels a lot better against my back than vinyl. Even if it did cost twenty dollars."

Ben cleared his throat and started the car.

"You know, I don't even know you. You're a total stranger." Summer spoke aloud the words she'd been thinking.

"I know what you're thinking. You don't want me driving your car, but I think you've had it for today. I'll get us into Houston before night."

That wasn't what she was thinking, but Summer had no intention of enlightening him. "Actually I'm grateful that you plan to drive the rest of the way. I'm just going to close my eyes and think cooling thoughts. Like winter in Texas with an ice storm snapping tree branches. A blue norther dropping the temperature thirty degrees within a few hours." Summer tried desperately to keep her thoughts off the man seated next to her, but after Ben got the car back on the interstate, she yielded to her curiosity. "Tell me about yourself, Ben Carr."

Ben gripped the steering wheel and tried to still the clamor of his body. He tried to mentally review the report on the structural integrity of an old house in Dallas that he had considered buying with the thought of renovating it. It was no use. His blood still pounded through his veins like a jackhammer.

Thank God her eyes were closed, or she'd really be in a panic, he thought, willing the hardness to go away. He had a feeling she wasn't as free and easy as he'd originally thought. She seemed a little too proper. A lopsided grin flashed across his tanned face when he glanced at her. Like the way she had tucked her skirt beneath her legs so it wouldn't blow about. He knew she must be suffering in the heat.

He'd had to exert every ounce of willpower he possessed to refrain from kissing the back of her elegant neck or the spot between her breasts where the vee of the dress met the tight cummerbund waist. He breathed deeply. For the first time in months, he felt alive—really alive! Not just going through the motions. His eyes strayed from the highway again to caress the curve of her breasts. He wanted to unsnap the gathered material behind her neck and slide the white fabric from her shoulders until it fell to her waist. Blood pounded through his veins. He shifted uncomfortably on the hot seat. He felt almost dizzy with the effort of denial. This is ridiculous, he snorted. Quit acting like a horny teenager, Carson, he exhorted mentally.

"Ben?" Summer's voice interrupted his fantasies.

"Hmmm?"

"I asked you to tell me about yourself."

"Oh, right. What do you want to know?"

"The usual. Where do you live? What kind of work do you do? Are you married?" The nonchalance of her voice didn't fool him for an instant. Ben recognized feminine interest when he heard it. Pleased that she was as interested in him as he was in her, he answered, "I live in Dallas now, but I grew up in Houston. As far as work, well, let's just say I've been heavily involved in real estate for the last couple of years. And I'm not married now. I corrected that mistake."

"Oh. I'm sorry. I didn't mean to bring up bad memories."

"It's in the past. Over and done with." As he said it, he realized the words were true. "I think I knew it was a mistake when I married her, but God! She was beautiful. Really beautiful—pale blond hair and a fantastic body. I thought she was the greatest thing since sliced bread. She really seemed to love me—just me!" He glanced over at Summer and saw the sympathetic expression on her face. For the first time, he wanted to talk about Janine.

"What happened?" Summer asked softly.

"The usual. I was in love with her, but she wasn't with me. The only thing she was interested in was what I could give her. She just married me for my money," he said without thinking.

"I didn't know construction workers commanded such good salaries." Her brow wrinkled in confusion.

"Construction worker?" Bewildered, he didn't understand where she'd got that idea.

"You said you were in real estate. I thought that was just a fancy way of saying you built houses—or office buildings? Did you mean you sold real estate?"

Oops, Ben thought. "Oh yeah. You're right, and it was buildings. Glass towers for nine-to-five executives." That was true in a way, he rationalized, realizing that he'd started a lie that was growing by leaps and bounds. "What about you, Summer?"

"Oh, I grew up in Fort Worth, went to school in Arlington at the University of Texas. Then moved to this little place west of Fort Worth. I'm sure you've never heard of it. Red Rock?"

"Are *you* married?" She didn't wear a ring; he'd checked automatically. He didn't mess with married women. He knew too well how it felt to be on the receiving end of betrayal.

Her voice flat, unemotional, she answered, "I'm not married now, but I hope to be within the next few months."

Ben's heart clenched. Engaged. His smile faded. "Just who is the lucky guy?" he snapped, confused by his own reaction.

"I don't know yet," Summer murmured, drowsily.

Ben swerved to pass a horse trailer drawn by a pickup. "What do you mean, you don't know?" He glanced over at her.

"What?" Summer roused and opened her eyes.

It would be easy to drown in those green depths, he thought, pulling his eyes back to the highway. True green eyes were so rare, but she had them—shining emeralds, fringed by thick black lashes. He wondered what shade of blond her hair really was.

Summer straightened. "I think that's enough conversation. Why don't you turn your attention to the road?"

"I asked you who the lucky guy was," Ben persisted.

"Oh, uh, no one you know," she stammered, squirming against the seat.

Ben eyed her curiously. Most women loved to brag about their fiancés.

They drove in silence for a while, busy with their respective thoughts. The afternoon sun seemed hotter than ever. The closer they got to Houston, the worse the traffic got.

Ben eyed Summer. She didn't look too good. White splotches intermingled with the red of her face. He thought about pulling over. "How are you feeling?" Concern colored his voice.

"Truthfully, not so good."

"Do you want to stop?"

"No, I just want to get to the hotel. Keep going."

"I forgot to ask, where are you staying?"

"The Claremont, downtown."

Ben's eyebrows raised. He whistled in surprise. "You have reservations at the Claremont? Nice place."

"I hope I live to see it," Summer groaned, pressing her forehead.

Ben tried to distract her by asking about her family. With surprise he learned she'd never known her father. "Do you mean he died before you were born?"

"No," Summer replied, her voice cold and unemotional. "He never married my mother. Apparently he came from one of the best families. That's all I know. My mother was young and in love. He used her and then dumped her when she got pregnant."

"So your parents weren't married? That's nothing to be ashamed about."

"I'm not ashamed," Summer replied fiercely. "I could never be ashamed of my mother. She took the money they'd given her for an abortion and used it to pay for my birth. She loved me enough to give me life." Summer fought tears. "As for my father, I don't even know his name. My mother would never tell me, and it's not on my birth certificate. I could pass him on the street and not know who he was."

Ben reached over and placed his hand over her fisted hands. "I'm sorry, Summer."

Summer's laughter had a brittle edge to it. "My best friend Annie says I'm a textbook case of the poor little orphan."

"Is your mother no longer alive?" He wanted to hold her and take away the pain he heard in her voice when she replied.

"No, she died shortly after my thirteenth birthday."

"What happened then? Did you go live with relatives?"

Summer's voice became colorless, flat. "I had no relatives. I went to live at the Tarrant County Home for Children. My mother had been an only child, and her parents had disowned her when she got pregnant out of wedlock. I never knew either of my grandparents."

Ben's heart nearly broke at the bleakness in her voice. He glanced quickly at her, wishing he could pull her into his arms. Shocked, he tried to imagine not having anybody—being raised by strangers. Ever since he could remember, he'd lived surrounded by the noisy, sprawling Carson and Harding families. He still had two sets of grandparents, his parents, four sisters, and a multitude of uncles, aunts, and cousins. Even though he'd been apart from his family, at his choice, he knew they loved him and would do anything for him if he but asked. "How did you happen to move to . . . Red Rock, is it?"

"I got a scholarship to college, and I worked. Just before graduation, a lawyer called me. I'd inherited my grandmother's estate. My mom's mother had always known about me."

Outraged, Ben asked, "You mean, she knew about you, but ignored you?"

Summer gave a bitter laugh. "That's about the size of it. She knew about me, but I never knew she existed. My mother never talked about her or my grandfather. When they kicked her out, she decided never to look back. I used to ask questions, but it upset her so much that I finally stopped."

"God! I'm sorry. You must have had a hell of a time growing up." He imagined her as a little towheaded girl with braids, all alone in the world.

"Oh, well, she made up for it in the end. She left me her house when she died, and this car."

"That could never make up for it," Ben disagreed. "So that's why you moved to Red Rock?"

"Yes. I applied at the school district. If I could get a job there, I could live rent-free and save most of my salary."

"And that's important to you? To save money?"

"One of the most important things in the world."

This time Ben understood her frugality a little better.

Summer forced a laugh. "So there you have the sad but true history of the poor illegitimate orphan girl." She looked at Ben, and said brokenly, "Don't you dare feel sorry for me, Ben Carr."

Ben acted as if she hadn't spoken. "What do you teach?"

"Actually I don't teach. I'm the school librarian."

Ben looked her up and down. "If you don't mind my saying so, you don't look like a librarian."

Summer laughed. "That's because you didn't see me during the school year with my hair pulled back in a barrette, glasses instead of contacts, and ankle-length dresses with sensible shoes."

Ben laughed with her. He had a million questions he wanted answered, but didn't know how to ask them. Just thinking about her alone—so terribly alone—brought forth every protective instinct he'd ever had. Funny. He'd never felt that way about Janine,

"Does your fiancé teach at your school?" he probed, wanting to know about his unknown competition. *Competition?* The word echoed through his head, startling him with its implications.

"Enough about me. I'm boring—just a country girl from Red Rock. Tell me about you. It must be exciting living in Dallas. I had my hair done at a salon in Dallas that I'd read about in the newspaper."

Privately Ben thought anybody who had messed with her long mane of hair should be horsewhipped. But wisely he decided not to say anything. He remembered the stony look she'd given him back at the Dairy Queen when he'd commented on her bleached hair.

"Living in Dallas isn't very exciting. Any place is what you make it, and I haven't made much there."

"How long have you lived there?"

"A few years. I had a falling out with my parents over my choice of wife." He glanced at her. "It took me a little longer to grow up, I guess. They were right about her, but I hated to admit it, so I left. Moved to Dallas and haven't darkened their door since." His blithe words didn't conceal the hurt.

"So now you're going to bury the hatchet?"

"Yeah. Janine is history." He thought of what it had cost to get rid of her. "I'm ready to take my medicine like a man."

"I'm sure it won't be that bad."

"You're right. My mom and dad would never say, 'I told you so,' to my face. In fact, my dad would probably punch anybody's lights out who tried." He laughed.

"It must be wonderful to have such unconditional support from a family," Summer said wistfully.

He nodded. "Yeah. They drive me nuts sometimes, but when push comes to shove, they're always in my corner."

Six o'clock came and went. The sun hung noticeably lower in the sky now. Ben wondered how Summer would react when he asked her to drop him at the Carson mansion in River Oaks. He frowned. No, he didn't think he'd do that. He wanted a chance to get to know her better without his money and his name interfering. He'd never met anybody like her before. She intrigued him. It was amazing that she had turned out as sane as she had with her background. She didn't seem bitter or mad at the world.

What should he do? he wondered. Continue with this charade? Tell her the truth? He couldn't decide.

Summer studied his profile as he drove along, left arm resting on the window frame, brown hand grasping the big steering wheel. The hours they'd spent together had flown. He really was the nicest man she'd met in a long time. The only man, Annie would have reminded her sourly. Oddly, Summer felt at ease with him, more so than with most men she met. She'd told him about her background, and she'd never shared that with anyone except Annie. He had listened without offering platitudes.

Though she hadn't told him much, she knew Ben had sensed the loneliness and rejection she had endured as a child. There hadn't been pity in his eyes like in the eyes of the social worker who had sat opposite her at the small dinette table almost twelve years ago.

Mom's old cuckoo clock had ticked loudly in the tiny kitchen. Summer had tried to focus on the rhythmic tick, tock, repeating the sounds in order to force out thoughts of death, thoughts of life without Rachel.

The sound of children playing in the street and talking about the police and ambulance that had come and gone from the small house on Lantana Street drifted through the open windows of the house. The officials filled out their forms and took Rachel James away. Summer wanted to ask the lady who sat at the scratched kitchen table if poor people had funerals.

Scared, Summer pleated the hem of her denim skirt between nervous fingers. What was going to happen to her now that Mom had died? That hot, choked feeling closed her throat again. She blinked the tears back. Bravely she repeated to herself what Brother Sledge at the nearby Baptist Church had said. Mom wouldn't suffer anymore. She was in a better place now than she'd ever known. Of course, Summer thought, looking around, most any place was better than the roach-infested shack they'd lived in since Mom had got too sick to work.

"Are you all right?" Ben's hand covered hers, stopping her from nervously pleating the hem of her white skirt.

Summer blinked rapidly and smoothed her skirt out. She looked at Ben. There was no pity in his dark eyes, just concern. She forced the hurtful memories away and focused on him.

Poor guy! He hadn't complained a bit. Divorced, unemployed, and estranged from his family. He'd had it rough also. How long had he been out of work? Had he got his tan and his muscles from working out in the sun, building skyscrapers? Exactly what did he do? she wondered. Electrician? Carpenter? Plumber?

Summer couldn't picture him doing any of those things. He just didn't seem to be the type. And his nails were clean and well tended. He must have been unemployed for quite some time.

A sad voice reminded her it didn't matter who he was and where he was going. She would never—could never—see him again after today. He definitely didn't fit The Plan. Walk away now, she admonished herself, aware of how her initial attraction to him had deepened. Just think of him as a gorgeous face and body. Still, she couldn't pull her eyes from his sculptured profile. When she thought he wasn't looking, she studied him intently beneath her dark lashes.

Her headache worsened with each mile. When they reached Spring, her stomach started knotting. Cold sweat popped out on her body. She breathed deeply, trying to fight the impending sickness. Her stomach seemed to swell and turn over. Her headache was twin hammers in her temples. "I don't feel very well," she gasped.

Ben studied her tense face. "Uh-oh." His eyes searched the service road. At the next exit, he pulled from the freeway, entered the far right lane, and pulled into the parking lot of a seafood restaurant.

Summer bolted from the car, reaching the grassy plot next to the parking lot before falling to her knees. Miserably she retched into a bed of white begonias. Ben held her hair from her face and spoke soothing nothings to her. He looked around at the surrounding businesses before helping her up. "Can you walk?"

Summer nodded, humiliated by what had happened. Tears filled her eyes. Though her legs shook, with his hand gently cupping her elbow, she made it to the car.

He drove a short distance down the service road before turning in to the parking lot of a budget motel.

"What?" Summer mumbled from where she huddled miserably on the seat.

"I'm going to get you a room and put you to bed. You're too sick to go any further."

"No," Summer protested feebly. "I have reservations at the Claremont in downtown Houston. I have to arrive before eight because the room's not guaranteed."

"You're not going anywhere, lady. It'd take another hour and a half—maybe longer with the road construction up ahead—to get you into a bed at the Claremont. I'm tired and you're sick. You won't make it another hour."

"I will. Just go away. Give me my car keys. I'll drive myself."

"Like hell you will! You have two choices—a bed here or a bed at the nearest hospital emergency room."

"You big bully," Summer started, then grabbed her stomach with one hand and the door handle with the other.

"That settles it," Ben declared as he watched her lean from the car. She moaned piteously but didn't succumb to the nausea this time. He grabbed her purse and gathered Summer close, nearly carrying her toward the motel office.

"I can walk by myself!" Summer tried to make her voice stern, but it sounded like the dying request from a terminal patient.

A rather small, balding man held the door open for Ben. "Looks like your wife is kind of sick. Oooh." He sucked air over his teeth. "What a sunburn!"

"Yeah, she's cooked, all right." Ben didn't bother to correct the man's assumption about his relationship with Summer.

"Good thing you stopped. A soak in a tepid tub will do wonders for her," the little bald man declared brightly. "I've got a nice double on the ground floor." He busied himself filling out a form and getting a key, then had Ben complete the paper.

Ben wrote his name and asked Summer for the license plate number of her car. He awkwardly fished in her purse for enough money to cover the room rate. "I don't suppose there's a restaurant here at the motel?"

"No, sorry. But the diner next door will prepare a carryout order for you."

"Thanks," Ben replied, "I don't think she'll feel like going out for dinner tonight."

"Room one-eighteen, Mr.—" the manager squinted at Ben's signature "—Cars—"

"Carr, Ben Carr!" Ben almost barked at the manager.

"Oh, yes, sir." The manager studied Ben's card again, then handed the key to him and hurried to open the door for them.

As soon as they got outside, Summer hissed, "You registered for only one room! You let that sweet little man think we were married. You sleazy sneak. You degenerate. You—you—you! You're crazy if you think I'm going to sleep with you!"

"Shhh. Save your strength. Besides, I haven't asked you to sleep with me. In case you haven't noticed, you're not particularly desirable right now." He balanced her as he inserted the key. "You ought to be thanking me for taking such good care of you. God! But you're a real handful, lady."

"Let go of me!"

"No, you're staying here."

"You don't understand. I need to . . ." She nearly jumped out of his arms, then stumbled to the bathroom. He held her hair again as she knelt over the toilet. "Oh," she cried, "I just want to die."

Five

Shame filled Summer—as galling as the nausea that churned her stomach. Sitting on the cool tile floor of the bathroom, she leaned weakly against the cold porcelain of the bathtub, eyes closed against the disgust that must be in Ben's eyes.

"Here, this will help." Ben's voice was as gentle as the hands that swabbed her feverish face and throat.

Oh, the wet cloth felt wonderful, she thought. The only thing in the world she wanted at that moment was a cool bath and a bed. But she didn't have the energy to draw a bath.

"Lean forward," Ben softly commanded.

She complied. He pulled her long hair up in a one-handed ponytail and stroked the back of her neck and gently sponged her sunburned shoulders. Before she knew what he was doing, he had unfastened the neck of the halter dress. She felt each side of the dress slide free. Clumsily she caught the cloth, shielding her breasts from his eyes.

"What do you think you're doing?" she muttered weakly.

"I'm making you more comfortable. Now, be quiet." The soothing cloth stroked from her hairline, down her back, to the waist.

Though she sat stiffly, alert to any impropriety he might make, she didn't argue with him. What he was doing felt too good. He gently blotted the tender sunburned skin. When he quit, she softly protested the loss of the coolness.

"I need to wet the cloth again," he soothed. When he

brought the cloth back to her, he leaned beyond her and turned on the spigots of the bathtub, adjusting the water until it was tepid.

"Lean back against the tub if you can stand the coldness so I can put this cloth on your forehead. That'll make your headache feel better."

With the fight drained out of her and her spirit too weary to argue, Summer did as he commanded. Again he was right.

"I'm going to put you in the tub, then go get your things from the car."

"You're not putting me anywhere!" Summer's outrage lent her strength.

"Don't argue with me. Save it for when you can give a good effort to it." He slid the shoes from her feet, tossing them into the bedroom. Angry red marks crisscrossed each instep where the sun had reached the pale skin of her slender feet.

The next thing she knew, Ben was pulling her to her feet. She stood like a rag doll while he unzipped the waist of the dress. "Hey, just a damn minute, Ben Carr!" Summer gathered her scattered wits; holding the bodice of her dress to her breasts, she used her other hand to push his hands away.

"Now, Summer, I'm just trying to help." He spoke quietly as if calming an upset child.

"If you want to help, then get out of here."

He hesitated. "Look, you've spent the entire day with me. You should have realized I'm not the kind of guy to take advantage of a sick woman."

"I don't care if you're Mother Teresa in drag. I'm not taking my clothes off in front of you."

For a moment, she thought he'd continue arguing, but he conceded with a grin. "You sure you'll be all right?"

Summer drew herself up. "Of course. Despite the evidence to the contrary," she said haughtily, "I'm not some wimpy woman who's apt to faint in my bath. Now, get out!" She gave him a little push.

He held up his hands in defeat. "Okay, okay. I'll get your bags and the other stuff from the car." He stopped in the doorway and said, "Just do me a favor to set my mind at ease; don't lock the door in case you need help. Promise?"

"Yes! Sure! Just get out!" As soon as he'd cleared the doorway, Summer slammed the bathroom door and turned the lock defiantly.

"You sure are hardheaded!" Ben yelled through the door.

And you're too solicitous, too tender—and desirable—for my own good, Summer thought, tiredly letting the dress drop. She stepped out of the puddle of white fabric, removed her half slip and the lacy bikini panties. With a quick twist, she turned off the rushing water, and gingerly stepped into the bathtub. She wished she had some baby oil to put in the water. Her skin needed moisturizing. The water slid deliciously over her body as she lay back and closed her eyes.

What a day! She tried to block out all thoughts of the miserable day and of sexy Ben Carr and tried to concentrate on her goal. The Plan. She visualized herself walking through the hotel lobby and bumping into a handsome, wealthy man who had a broad chest with a mat of dark hair—or shopping at the Galleria and meeting a heartstoppingly gorgeous man who had dark, wavy hair and velvety brown eyes. Her eyes flew open as she realized who she'd pictured in her fantasies.

I'm losing my mind, she thought in disgust. I've only got two weeks to make this work, so I'd better concentrate on meeting an eligible man instead of thinking of Ben Carr. Summer sighed. Once I drop him off in Houston, I'll forget him. Then I'll start making the rounds of places where I'm sure to meet some eligible men. Maybe I'll be lucky and meet someone immediately. If all else fails, I can always crash that big charity ball next week.

Sleepily she soaped herself, then tiredly splashed away the suds. She'd make some definite plans in the morning. No use worrying about her sunburn tonight. Like Scarlett O'Hara said, "Tomorrow was another day." She'd feel better tomorrow. After all, she certainly couldn't feel any worse, she thought, wincing.

When she got out of the tub, she'd call the Claremont and see if they would hold her room until tomorrow. Summer yawned widely. Too bad the day had turned out the way it had. She wouldn't be able to make the eye-popping entrance she'd planned. Most men really went for the retro look of a sexy blonde in a convertible, according to the book.

As an afterthought, she remembered she had to call Debbi what's-her-name in Centerville. Otherwise, the cops would be out after Ben. Summer smiled. Maybe with a threat like that, she could keep him away or make him go away and leave her in peace.

Drowsily her thoughts turned to Ben Carr. She warmed from the inside out thinking about the way his eyes had looked her over in the Dairy Queen. Too bad he wasn't suitable, she thought with a pang of regret. But even if he had money, men like him weren't marriage material. Even with her limited knowledge of men, Summer knew he had to be the kind of man women made fools of themselves over. When she closed her eyes, though, that knowledge didn't stop her from remembering the feel of his slow hands against her skin.

Ben leaned against the bathroom door a few minutes before going to the car. He heard the water lapping against the sides of the tub and imagined it sliding over her ivory body. His hands trembled. He looked at them and remembered the way her skin felt when he'd stroked her. The way her dark lashes lay against her skin. His breath sounded harsh to his ears as he pulled himself away from the door. His body ached to press against hers. What was wrong with him? She was just a woman like any of a hundred others out there, right?

When he opened the car trunk a few minutes later, he stared in surprise at the expensive Italian designer luggage. Summer had great taste in luggage. The cases were a twin to the ones in the storage room of his condo. Ben frowned as he unloaded the car. How could a librarian in a public school afford this luggage? For that matter, how had she afforded the dress she had on? He hadn't needed to see the label when he unzipped it to know who the designer was. He shook his head. It didn't add up.

Maybe she wasn't a librarian, he thought, remembering the way she had looked when he'd first seen her. A beautiful, sexy woman who drove an expensive antique car, and bought clothes that cost more than she could make in a month's time as a school librarian, had to have income from some other source. Ben didn't like the direction of his thoughts. But once the idea insinuated itself in his mind, he couldn't banish it.

What could the source of her funds possibly be? His eyes hardened to chips of obsidian. What indeed? The insinuation burst into full bloom. Ben set each piece of luggage down next to the car. With an oath, he slammed the trunk and gathered everything up. Arms full, he stalked to the room.

He argued with himself mentally. She could have a second job. She could have inherited money along with the house and the car. She could have taken a loan out. He dropped the bags next to the bed. None of the arguments eased the ugly suspicion. No matter how hard Ben wrestled with the thought, he could not exorcise it. What kind of business could bring her to Houston? What kind of business would a woman who looked like an expensive call girl be involved in? Tutoring? He snorted. Not likely. And, he remembered, she had reservations at the Claremont, something else out of a librarian's price range. What kind of business indeed?

And he'd begun to think of her as an innocent despite the way she dressed. Ha. The joke was on him. The more he thought about the inconsistencies in her life-style and her background, the surer he was about his suspicions. What an act she was putting on! Was it all for his benefit? For the first time, he wondered if perhaps she'd recognized him. Though he kept a low profile, his photo had appeared in some of the Dallas newspapers. She could have seen it and be playing some kind of seductive game with him. He shook his head. No, that was too much coincidence.

Ben stared at the bathroom door. What was she up to? Why act so damned modest? Maybe she liked to play games? Well, he could play with the best of them. He'd had plenty of practice. How dare she act so demure! He scowled, thinking of her selling herself to anyone who had her price.

He paced, waiting for her to come out so he could tell her what he thought of her and her business in Houston. His anger grew with each step. The thought of her with other men turned his stomach. He felt like putting his fist through the wall. In fact, he thought, the hell with this. Why am I getting so upset over a woman I hardly know? It's not as if I have designs on her. Liar, he charged, running his hands through his hair.

Hell! I'll just call Tracey and ask her to pick me up. Better speak to Ryan, he decided. His brother-in-law wouldn't give him the third degree the way Tracey would. Out of habit, he glanced at his watch, scowling when he saw the cracked face and the hands that hadn't moved since early afternoon. With a muffled curse, he sat on the empty bed and reached for the phone.

The bathroom door opened abruptly. Ben turned, and his heart shifted into overdrive. Even with her face washed clean of makeup, she was beautiful. Summer, wrapped in a fluffy white towel, stood in the doorway, braced with either hand gripping the wooden facing. Water dripped from her hair. "Ben," she whispered, and swayed.

Ben dropped the phone and leapt to her side, scooping her up into his arms as her knees gave way. He held her gently, aware of her burned skin, careful not to scrape his shirt against it. An incredible tide of feeling washed over him as he held her.

Summer leaned her head against his chest and whispered, "I feel like such an idiot for being so weak. This is awful. All my plans will be ruined if I don't get to feeling better."

Reminded of her business, he stiffened. "Well, your back isn't as badly burned as your shoulders and face. That shouldn't put too much of a crimp in your plans." Resolutely he denied the tenderness that threatened to swamp his senses. He fought against the pleasure she aroused in him just being in his arms, pressed to his body.

He walked to the foot of the king-sized bed and set her down none too gently. With quick, economical movements, he turned back the covers, and bowed at the waist to Summer. "Your bed, *madam.*"

Summer didn't understand his sarcasm or his sudden coldness. During the time it had taken her to bathe, he had changed from a caring, solicitous companion to a cold, cynical stranger. No, she thought, that wasn't right. When he'd lifted her into his arms, he'd been warm and gentle, but she'd watched the play of emotions across his face, seen the tenderness replaced by iciness.

His coldness made Summer want to cry, but she swallowed the tears as she had so often in life. Quickly she scooted up the bed, hesitating before crawling beneath the covers. She didn't want to sleep wrapped in a wet towel, but she didn't want to remove it and sleep naked either. In a quandary, she looked at the suitcase that held her nightgowns. She didn't have the energy to unpack them. And she didn't want to ask him to do it either. How silly, she thought, feeling tears slide down her cheek, that this can reduce me to crying.

"What's the matter?" Ben asked, eyeing the tears.

"Nothing." Summer tried vainly to keep from snuffling but lost the effort.

"Summer, what is it?" Ben looked stricken. He sank onto the bed beside her, his thumbs catching the tears that trickled down her cheeks.

Summer wanted nothing more than to lean against him and have him comfort her. She shook her head. "It's silly. I guess I'm just tired. I need a nightgown, but I'm too tired to get it. I didn't want to ask you because you suddenly seemed so hostile."

"Which case?"

Summer pointed to the larger of the two. "Please?"

With a curt nod, he opened the case and rooted through the silky gowns and other lingerie. He pulled out a diaphanous gown of ivory silk. He held it to the light and frowned.

Summer hoped her sunburn concealed her blush. She had forgotten how transparent her new nightclothes were.

He walked over slowly and dropped the gown in her lap.

"Would you turn your back?" she asked in a voice so low, he had to strain to hear.

"Lady, you don't have anything I haven't seen before."

Summer gasped at his crudeness. Anger erased the tears from her eyes. What was wrong with him? How dare he act so —so mean! Especially after having been so sweet and considerate to her earlier. Why, he must be crazy to have such mood swings! She looked him defiantly in the eye. He shrugged and turned his back. She eyed his broad shoulders warily, then hastily removed the towel, dropping it to the side of the bed, and pulled the nightgown over her head. "Ohhh," she moaned.

"What's wrong?" he demanded, swinging around in time to see the gown drift over perfect breasts.

Summer yanked the covers to her chin. "Nothing. It just—it just hurts having anything touch my skin."

Some of the stiffness seemed to leave him. "Yeah, I guess it must."

Silence fell between them, but their eyes studied each other cautiously.

"Want me to put some more of that stuff on your sunburn?"

She trembled at the thought. The medication would soothe, as would his hands. Yet his touch could well be her undoing. She was more vulnerable than she'd thought. No, she'd better not let him touch her again, she thought; then, to her consternation, she heard herself say breathlessly, "Yes, please."

He sat on the edge of the bed. She slowly lowered the covers, keeping the fold around her breasts. Just then, someone knocked on their door. Summer jerked the covers up to her neck. Her startled eyes questioned Ben.

He shrugged his shoulders and walked to the door. Peering through the peephole, he saw the night manager. "Yeah?" he called through the door.

"Mr. Carr, it's Bud Kazinski, the night manager. I thought you might like this for your wife's sunburn."

Ben ignored the dark look from Summer at the words "your wife" and opened the door. "What is that?"

"Oh, it's a few leaves from my aloe vera plant. I'm something of a horticulturist." Even the top of Kazinski's bald head blushed. "Aloe vera is great for treating burns of all kinds. I've peeled the pointy things off and split the stalks so that the flesh is exposed."

Ben unwrapped the foil and saw three oozing green, spear-shaped leaves. "What do I do with it?"

"Just rub the flesh over the sunburn periodically. You'll be amazed at how quickly it works. Much better than any cream or ointment. It should keep Mrs. Carr from being red tomorrow and maybe from peeling."

"Oh. Well, thank you, that's very kind of you."

"You're very welcome," Kazinski bobbed in place. "Hope the wife is better tomorrow."

Ben nodded and closed the door.

"How dare you register us as Mr. and Mrs. Carr." Summer's angry hiss drew his attention to her huddled figure.

Irritation bubbled in his voice. "I didn't. I just put my name. I guess he jumped to the conclusion."

"I imagine so with you dragging me around like a sack of potatoes!"

"Look, do you want to argue or do you want me to treat your sunburn?"

Reluctantly Summer decided to shelve the argument for now. "I want you to treat my sunburn," she mumbled. "I've got to look good as soon as possible."

"Oh, yeah! Why? Turn over." He pulled the slender straps of satin from her shoulders and smoothed the aloe plant over her shoulders, arms, and back.

Summer murmured appreciatively.

"Turn over onto your back now."

Obediently Summer sat up and turned to face him.

He stroked the aloe vera plant over her face, neck, and shoulders, edging down to the sheet she held to her breasts.

His breathing grew ragged, but Summer didn't notice. She had all she could do to keep her eyes fixed at a point beyond his shoulder. She prayed he couldn't tell how her blood pounded through her veins. Her breathing was as ragged as his.

"Does that hurt?"

"No," she whispered. Not nearly as much as the longing she felt growing inside her for him to continue touching her.

When he stroked the fleshy part of the plant across the curve of her breasts, her eyes drifted closed and she let her imagination have full rein. Her heart hammered in her chest. Surely he could hear it, she thought.

"Turn over and I'll do your back again," Ben said.

Sluggishly Summer lay down and rolled over, sighing blissfully at the soothing balm he applied to her back.

"Why do you need to look good as quickly as possible?" he badgered her.

"What?" she murmured.

Ben repeated the question.

"For The Plan," she mumbled sleepily. "I can't afford to waste any time. I only have a couple of weeks to accomplish my goal."

"What is your goal?" Ben whispered, taking advantage of her relaxed state.

"To get married, of course," Summer answered.

Shocked, his hands stilled. "Married to whom?"

"I don't know. Whoever I meet that qualifies."

"Summer, what in the name of all that's holy are you talking about?"

"What?" Summer opened her heavy eyes. She'd almost been asleep.

"What is this plan and this goal that you're talking about? You sound like you plan on marrying a total stranger."

Uneasily Summer came awake. "Just forget what I said, Ben. I was half-asleep."

"No, I don't want to forget it. Now, tell me what you mean."

Summer had an uneasy feeling he wasn't going to like it or understand it any better than Annie had.

"Well, you know the business I said I had in Houston?"

He nodded.

"Well, the business is—that is—what I'm trying to do . . ." She searched for words. Suddenly she was too embarrassed to tell him. What would he think of her?

"Just spit it out."

She turned over carefully, pulling the covers to her neck. "It's really very simple." She tried for a matter-of-fact tone. "I came here to find a husband—one with money."

Ben's mouth fell open. "You what?" he choked.

"Look, you don't have to make it sound like some crackpot idea. I've thought and planned this very carefully."

"You have?" He crossed his arms and stared at her. He looked as if she'd announced that she'd come to meet aliens from outer space.

"Yes." She stuck her chin up. "I have planned, studied, and groomed myself to meet wealthy men and to marry one."

"And just how are you going to do that?"

"Well, if you want to hunt moose, then you go to where the moose are. I want to find a man with money, so I'm going to where the wealthy shop and play and work."

"I see. Assuming you meet a man, just how are you going to ascertain that he has money? Are you going to ask to see a financial statement before you go out with him?" Cold humor glinted in his eyes now.

Was he laughing at her or sneering? she wondered uneasily.

83

Haughtily she replied, "Of course not. I know what to look for in a wealthy man. I think I'll be able to recognize a man with money when I see one by the clothes he wears, his jewelry, the car he drives, et cetera."

"Et cetera?" He was definitely laughing at her, she decided. "So you think you can recognize a wealthy man just by looks, huh?"

"Why, certainly. You could do it, Ben, if you knew what to look for. Like hands. Rich men have soft, pampered hands."

Suddenly Ben burst out laughing. "You think so."

"I know so." Summer wanted to punch him.

"What if I told you I was rich?"

"You? Please don't make me laugh."

"You don't think I have any money?"

Summer laughed. "Ben, if you had any money, you wouldn't be hitching rides on the interstate."

"But I told you my car broke down."

"Sure. What kind of car?"

Ben hesitated. "What if I said a new Jag?"

Summer laughed. "Ben, Ben, Ben. Men who drive new Jags are not nearly as young as you."

"Oh, you think old men are the only ones who can afford them?"

"Well, no. I'm sure some young rich men can, but they usually go for flashier cars. And just look at you." She waved her hand at his clothes. "Those clothes you've got on look like they came out of the bin at the Salvation Army—no offense, but you asked."

Ben grinned as he looked down at his ruined clothes. "I've got to admit you're right. They do look like rejects."

His grin was infectious. "So Summer James, mild-mannered school librarian from Red Rock, is here on safari. I hate to ask, but is that why you wore that ridiculous dress today? Bait?"

"In a manner of speaking, yes. And that dress was not ridiculous. It's very similar to the one Marilyn Monroe wore in *The Seven Year Itch.*"

He snorted. "It was ridiculous to wear something like that riding in a convertible all day."

"Well, you do have a point there," she conceded.

Ben mused on the information. "Tell me a little more about this plan of yours."

"Well, I read this book *How to Marry a Rich, Rich Man*—"

Ben hooted with laughter. "You mean there is really a book with that title?"

"Oh, yes. The author was on all the talk shows about a year ago. I saw her when I was recuperating from an accident. And a friend of mine gave me a copy of her book as a get-well present."

"So what did you learn from this literary epistle?"

"Go ahead and laugh, but it changed my whole life. It showed me how to get the kind of life I wanted."

"How? By selling yourself?"

"I'm not selling myself," she nearly shouted. Calmer, she said, "I'm just using all my assets—my brain and my body—to get what I want."

"And what is it you really want, Summer?"

"Security. A life of ease and comfort. I don't ever want to be hungry again or to feel afraid." Aware she'd become too serious, she brightened. "Because of the book, I'll have that."

"Haven't you ever heard that money doesn't buy happiness?"

Summer snorted. "Haven't you ever heard that if money doesn't buy happiness, you must be shopping in the wrong mall?"

He laughed. "No, I hadn't heard that. So the hair, the dress, the car? All to fulfill some image in a book?"

She nodded. "I made myself over just like the book said."

"Into a bimbo?"

"No! Into the kind of woman who'd appeal to a wealthy man!"

Ben lifted a silky lock of her hair. "But you must have been beautiful before. What all did you do to change?"

Summer told him about the lessons, the hair, the teeth, the contacts, the exercise.

Ben stared incredulously at her. "So you truly mean to prostitute yourself?"

Summer tossed her head, pulling the lock of hair from his hand. "You're as bad as my friend Annie. I'm not prostituting myself. I'm bettering my lot in life. Look, I'm smart, but not a genius. The only edge I have is my face and body. I made a few minor changes to make me more marketable."

"Marketable, hell! Dress it up any way you like, but you're still packaging and selling yourself, exploiting yourself."

"Well, it's better than being exploited by someone else!" Summer shrugged her shoulders. "Look, what difference does it make to you? We'll never see each other again after tomorrow."

"You're right. It doesn't make a bit of difference to me." Ben stood. "I'm going to get something to eat. Do you want anything?"

Just you, Summer mused, but squelched the thought immediately. Though she had little appetite, she thought she'd better eat something. "Yes, please. A sandwich or maybe some soup. Anything. And a big soda. I'll make a couple of phone calls while you're gone," she said.

His brow raised in question.

"To the Claremont to ask them to hold my room."

"Ah, yes, I see. Stay in a hotel frequented by rich men."

"Look, just go eat and leave me alone. I don't need your comments. I had enough of that from Annie just this morning."

"Yeah? Well, you should have listened to her." He started for the door but stopped with his hand on the doorknob. His shoulders slumped. "I'll need some money," he said quietly.

"Hand me my purse and I'll give you some."

"Put it on my tab," he said. "By the way, don't forget to call little Debbi at the Dairy Queen. I wouldn't want to find my picture at the post office next week."

Summer regretted arguing with Ben. He'd been more than kind to her, but his comments rankled. What did he know of anything? Of her, or her life or her needs? He was nothing but a stranger—a moody stranger whom she'd known for less than twenty-four hours. A stranger with a voice that made her think of silk sliding over her body. A stranger with hands that seemed to set her nerve endings on fire. A stranger whose nearness threatened to destroy everything she had worked for.

She called Centerville first and told a giggling Debbi that she had arrived in Houston and was just fine. After the hotel said there was no problem in holding her room, Summer breathed a sigh of relief and relaxed. While she waited for Ben to return, she closed her eyes, thinking she'd rest awhile. At least her skin felt better. The aloe had really worked.

Ben walked through the humid night. Probably be a storm tonight, he thought, glancing at the night sky, not surprised to see clouds obscuring the stars.

His protesting stomach reminded him he'd had little to eat that day. The food at the diner was surprisingly good. Real chicken-fried steak—not that processed patty kind—with thick cream gravy and a man-size order of fries. The red-headed waitress winked at him as she refilled his coffee cup for the third time. Ben pretended not to notice.

The order of chicken noodle soup and a grilled cheese sandwich was ready for him when he paid the check. He stopped at the soft drink machines on the way back to the room and got a couple of cans of cola.

Ben entered the room softly when he returned. Summer had fallen asleep with the bedside lamp on. He set the sodas and the container of food down and went to fill the ice bucket.

Fifteen minutes later after a much-needed shower, he pulled on a pair of the new briefs and a T-shirt. He refused to slip into the stiff, wrinkled slacks until he had to in the morning. He turned out the bathroom light and walked to the bed.

Amazingly, considering her outrage at sharing a room with him, they had not got around to discussing sleeping arrangements. He sighed, remembering the crazy conversation about her looking for a rich man to marry. It went against his grain to even think about it.

The king-sized bed was large enough that they could keep their distance from each other. It's not as if I'm trying to take advantage of her, he reasoned, sitting on the edge of the bed. Why, if she knew who I was, she'd probably be all over me. The thought depressed him. She'd be just another woman who wanted what he represented—not him, the man.

If he had called Tracey before now, he could be in their guest room or even at home in his old room instead of in some cheap motel on the freeway with this woman who threatened to drive him crazy.

He glanced over at Summer. He always prided himself on his honesty with others and with himself. What he'd done today, withholding the truth from her, went against his nature. He'd intended to tell her tomorrow who he was, but how could he now, when he knew her plans? And honesty forced him to admit that he had this insane desire to protect her from herself and her crazy plan. She was so naive. He hated to think about her getting hurt. And she would if she persisted in this scheme.

Quietly he smoothed the sheet and folded it down around her hips. Though it was pure torture looking at her lying there with her luscious body highlighted by the diaphanous gown, he knew it was better for her sunburn to be uncovered as much as possible. His eyes lingered on her full breasts, barely concealed by the thin silk.

He ran his hands through his hair. It was going to be a hell of a long night. He grinned; even if he didn't have such strong scruples, she was too tired and sunburned for anything besides sleep. Of course, her *plan,* he thought with a twist of his mouth, probably precluded her messing around with a man she considered a peon.

He leaned down to stroke her hair away from her face. Frowning, he noticed it was still damp and snarled. She must have fallen asleep without combing it. Calling himself six kinds of a fool, he smoothed her tangled hair away from her forehead. She stirred but didn't wake.

Satisfied he'd done everything he could for her, he checked the thermostat and turned out the lights, then settled himself on the other side of the bed. He removed the T-shirt, tossing it to the foot of the bed. What a strange day it had been, he thought. Though bone-tired, he couldn't sleep immediately. He kept thinking of the woman next to him. Eventually his body calmed, but his mind busily contemplated her wild plan.

So she could spot a rich man at twenty paces? She was so

naive, she'd get hustled and bedded by some of the barracudas who ran with the moneyed crowd before she knew what hit her. The woman needed a keeper. She'd proved that today. He might as well fill that position. Satisfied with his decision and looking forward to what promised to be an unusual week, he fell asleep within minutes.

Six

Thunder woke Summer shortly after midnight. A small scream tore from her throat as she jerked awake.

"Shhh. It's just thunder. A storm blew in." A strong hand clasped hers in the dark.

Grateful for the human contact, Summer controlled her frightened breathing and tried to shake the tentacles of the bad dream from her mind. "I was dreaming," she murmured, gripping his hand. She felt the bed dip as he turned on his side to get closer to her. Rather than feel intimidated, she felt safe. Slowly her muscles relaxed.

"Want to talk about it?"

She shook her head, then realized he couldn't see her in the dark. "No, it was dumb. Silly of me to be frightened by it." In her dream, a wretchedly old man with saliva running from his mouth had been chasing her. She shivered with disgust at the moment in her dream when he'd grabbed her and pressed lips that felt like parchment against her mouth. You're being ridiculous, she chided herself.

Ben squeezed her hand. "Better now?"

"Yes, thank you." He started to move away. "Please, talk to me a little," Summer pleaded. A thunderclap followed by lightning caused her to jump.

Ben rolled closer to her. His hand moved to stroke her hair, pulling his fingers through the strands. "How's the stomach now?" His hands continued stroking her silky hair, marveling at the texture.

"Not too bad." Summer's eyes drifted closed. "Tell me about your wife." The question surprised her as much as it did him.

"My ex-wife, you mean." He toyed with a curly lock of hair. "It was four years ago. I'd never really been in love before. In fact, I'd worked so hard trying to excel at school that I hadn't had much time for anything else. Then after school, I was going to save the world. I wanted to build houses for the underprivileged."

Summer heard the cynicism in his voice. Sympathetically she clasped his hand and squeezed it.

"It didn't take long for me to find out that there aren't any easy answers to problems that have taken generations to create." Ben sighed deeply. "Janine was on a slum tour doing token charity work. To use an old cliché, I fell for her like a ton of bricks. I thought her concern and interest in what I was doing was genuine."

Summer wished she could gather him into her arms. He was still hurting. The darkness enclosed them until she thought they were the only two people in the world.

The words came slowly as if he were trying to explain to himself as well as to her. "Boy! Was I wrong. Even before the wedding, she started her campaign to have me stop playing around and do some *prestigious work,* to use her words. I was so blind to everything but her that I let her lead me around by the nose."

"It's natural to want to please the woman you love," Summer argued, making excuses for Ben.

"Maybe. But it's unnatural to betray everything you believe in. People trusted me to help them. In the end, they thought I was just another do-gooder, exploiting them for my own reasons."

"You must have hurt a great deal."

"I was all mixed up. Part of me wanted to please her. Part of me resented what she wanted me to be. Through it all, no matter how she turned my life upside down, I couldn't get over wanting her."

Summer decided she loathed Janine. "What happened to end it?"

"I began to see beneath the veneer of sexuality. I think maybe I didn't love her that much. Hindsight tells me it was infatuation. She had a way about her that drew men like bees to honey. The only trouble was, she wasn't always satisfied with just attracting men. I found out she spent almost as much time in other beds as she spent in mine."

"Oh." Summer didn't know what to say. How could a woman do that to Ben? How could a woman prefer any other man to Ben? She traced circles on the back of his hand.

"To make a long story short, I came home early from a business trip. When I caught her, I'll never forget how she acted—almost relieved. Evidently she'd decided she'd spent enough time with me. Since she expected to make out quite well with half of everything I had, she told me she wanted out."

"Oh, Ben, that's awful." Summer wanted to cry. Did Ben see her as another user like Janine? How could she condemn Janine when she intended to do the same thing? No, Summer denied, I'd never do that to a man. Once I marry, a bargain is a bargain. But she found little in her mental arguments to hold herself from the contempt she felt for Ben's ex-wife. Remorse filled her. "Oh, Ben, I'm so dreadfully sorry."

Ben leaned over Summer. He was just a shadow in the night. She knew he was going to kiss her. She ought to protest. She should stop him. But she couldn't think of a good reason to do so. If only circumstances were different, she thought sadly, waiting for his kiss. A tear trickled from her eye.

His lips touched her cheek gently. Ben brushed at the salty tear. "Hey, what's the matter, Summer?"

"Nothing. I'm just tired," she lied, shattered by his tenderness. Feeling like a miserable, rotten manipulator—just like his ex-wife—she moved away from him until she lay on the edge of the bed. How had she gotten so involved with him?

"Go to sleep. Tomorrow you'll feel much better," Ben said, moving away. After a moment, he snapped, "You'd better move over before you fall off the bed."

Summer heard the hurt in his voice but didn't try to explain her actions. Long after she heard Ben's relaxed breathing, she lay awake. She was hypersensitive to his long frame sprawled beneath a sheet, mere inches from where she lay. He breathed deeply, without snoring, his body relaxed and at ease, one leg bent, arms sprawled overhead.

Lightning flashed, lighting up the room. Of their own volition, her eyes traced the lines of his body. He was beautiful, she decided, her eyes lingering where the sheet concealed his lower body. How could he sleep when she lay next to him, sharing a bed with him? Her cheeks flamed as she wondered what it would be like to lie beneath him.

Summer closed her eyes. One day with him, and I can't keep my eyes or my thoughts off him. I've got to get rid of him as quickly as possible, she decided. I must not forget why I'm here, she reminded herself. To find a rich man to marry. Not some poor out-of-work laborer—no matter how gorgeous he is. I could have got someone like him at home. Though a small voice told her there was no man nearly this sexy in Red Rock. Toward morning Summer finally drifted to sleep, only to dream of Ben's eyes seducing her, his hands caressing her, his body loving her.

Groggily Summer awoke shortly after dawn. Easing out of bed, she padded to the stack of suitcases, carrying the large case and her makeup bag to the bathroom. Surely she'd feel better if she showered and dressed. She'd also be better able to confront Ben and send him on his way.

When she looked into the bathroom mirror, she thankfully noticed that the intensity of the sunburn had faded. I guess Mr. Kazinski was right about the healing effects of his aloe vera, she thought, studying the dusky red of her cheeks. The skin was still a bit tender, though, but another day and she should be all right as long as she stayed out of the sun.

That's all right. I'll work the hotel today and the Galleria tomorrow. The country club can wait until the following day, she decided with relief. It was going to require tremendous guts on her part to crash the most elite golf course in Houston. The reprieve would give her time to build up her courage.

The shower restored her energy. She styled her hair and artfully applied the expensive cosmetics. Shaking wrinkles from the cotton knit pants suit, she enjoyed the softness of the fabric against her skin. A long pink T-shirt skimmed her thighs, and the narrow-legged slacks with the elastic waist were comfortable. White wedge-heeled sandals completed her ensemble.

Summer eased open the door and stepped out, trying to be quiet in case Ben was still asleep. She didn't want to confront him just yet.

"Good morning." Ben's lazy voice startled her.

"Oh, I thought you were still asleep."

"No. I see you've been up awhile." His eyes glanced approvingly at her.

"Yes. I'm finished in the bathroom if you'd like to, uh, you know."

"Thanks." He hesitated, eyebrows lifted inquiringly.

"Do briefs bother you?"

"Oh!" Summer whirled, feeling ridiculous considering she'd shared a bed with him last night, but her imagination ran riot as she heard him fling the covers back. She gulped. "I'll just tidy up while you get ready."

"Sounds fine. I'll hurry. I'm starving," he said.

Summer couldn't help herself. She watched him from the corner of her eye. Thankful that her blushes could be attributed to her sun exposure yesterday, she sank onto the bed with a deep exhalation when she heard the bathroom door close. She covered her eyes with shaking hands but couldn't obliterate his image.

He sang in the shower, she discovered. Sang very badly, she thought with a smile. Tunelessly he bellowed an old Willie Nelson song. With a grin, she stood and smoothed the covers on the bed, then packed her things and placed the bags by the front door. She saw the bucket of melted ice and the sodas he'd bought her the night before. A container from the restaurant next door held congealed soup and a cold cheese sandwich. How sweet, she thought. Only Annie had ever catered to her before.

A half hour later, Ben exited the bathroom, clean but looking for all the world like a pirate, or a biker, she thought with his day-old growth of beard and the rumpled trousers. His bronze chest drew her eyes like a magnet to steel. "Uh, would you like to borrow my razor?" she asked.

"That would help. I hate to embarrass you at the restaurant and the hotel."

Summer's smile slipped. "The hotel?"

"Yeah. I figured I'd get you checked in later, then be on my way."

"You don't have to do that," she answered, handing him a pink razor.

He took the razor and looked at it. "I guess you shaved your legs with this?"

"Of course. Why?"

"You'll see." He walked back to the bathroom but left the door open. Hesitantly Summer walked to the doorway to watch him.

"I've never seen a man shave before," she said nervously.

"Really?" He looked at her in disbelief. "Have all your male friends had beards?" He splashed his face with water and lathered soap onto his hands, then spread it over his cheeks.

She turned her head away. "I don't really have any men friends."

His mouth dropped open. He looked her up and down. "You don't expect me to believe that!"

"Believe what you like." Their eyes met, and time seemed to stand still.

He turned slowly from her and looked into the mirror. He stroked the razor down in a swath from his sideburn to his chin. Summer watched, fascinated, as he removed the stubble from his face.

"Ouch!" he said. A tiny spot of blood appeared on his throat.

"Oh, you've cut yourself."

"It's nothing. There'll probably be plenty more little nicks to match it."

"The razor seemed fine when I shaved my legs."

"I'm sure. I've found it's best not to use the same blade on your face that a lady uses on her legs." He grinned.

"I guess you have plenty of experience using ladies' razors." She cringed at the snide tone in her voice.

"A bit," he admitted, finishing up. He rinsed the razor and dried it before handing it to her.

Summer didn't know why she was upset. It stood to reason anybody who looked like him should have lots of women. "Shall we go eat?" She picked up his shirt from the doorknob and handed it to him.

His hand enclosed hers, and she dropped the shirt. "Sorry." They both reached for it at the same time, nearly bumping heads. Summer felt the hair on her arm stand up.

"You smell good," he murmured, bringing his face close to hers.

"You smell like soap," Summer whispered breathlessly. She swayed closer to him.

Abruptly he stood. "Let's go, I'm starved." He extended his hands to pull her to her feet.

Summer jerked up, ignoring his outstretched hands. Feeling like a love-sick child, she walked away from him to the door.

"You look like pink cotton candy in that outfit," he said as he followed her. "Good enough to eat," he whispered into her ear as he reached beyond her to open the door to the room.

Dismayed by her reaction to his words, his body, everything about him, Summer walked through the door without replying.

Ben propped open the door with the heaviest suitcase while he ferried out the other luggage. After stowing everything in the trunk, he took her elbow and walked her to the restaurant.

The smell of freshly brewed coffee sharpened Summer's appetite. After they were seated in a booth in the no-smoking section, Summer realized how very hungry she was. The last time she'd really eaten had been at Centerville, when she'd nibbled on french fries and a hamburger.

"Oh, I think I want one of everything."

"Make that two," Ben agreed. "You must be feeling better."

Then ended up ordering fried eggs, hash brown potatoes, bacon, biscuits, and fresh fruit. Gratefully they sipped the steaming coffee the waitress brought.

"Now, let's talk about this plan you've got," Ben began.

"I don't think there's any point in that. You'll just make fun of me again."

"No, I won't. I really want to hear about it. I've never met anybody who had such ambitious goals. When did you conceive of this campaign?"

"I don't want to talk about it."

"Why not? Surely you're not ashamed to trick some poor schmuck with more money than brains into marrying you?"

"See? I knew you wouldn't understand. Just because I'm being rational and realistic, you think I'm heartless. I'm not tricking anyone into anything. I'll tell him I'm not rich."

"You will? When?"

Summer fidgeted with her coffee cup. "Before the ceremony," she mumbled.

Ben guffawed. "As you walk down the aisle?"

Summer slammed her cup down. "Look, all I'm doing is using certain tactics to meet wealthy men. I'm not coercing them or twisting their arm. After I meet them, what happens next all depends on how attracted to me they are."

"Oh, they'll be attracted, all right. Let me give you a hint, though. Don't sleep with them until after the wedding. Because that is the ultimate thing you have to sell. Why buy the cow when the milk is free?"

"There's no need to be crude!" Summer wanted to slap his smirking face.

"Sorry. I just get a little tired of all you women chasing a man because of what he's got or who he is. They used to call

99

women like you gold diggers."

"What's the difference in all you men chasing a woman just to find out what she's like in bed? You men don't even look beyond the size of a woman's breasts. What do you call men who do that?"

"Macho?" he asked with a grin.

"Is that what you really think?"

"No, I'm just kidding. Look, maybe you've got a point."

"You're darn right I do. Men have always exploited women, but if a woman turns it around, then she's a gold digger or worse."

Ben nodded and held up his hands in surrender. "You've got me convinced. I'll help you any way I can."

"Wha—what?"

"I said I'll help you. Where do we start? What's our game plan?"

"Oh, no. I don't need your help."

"Sure you do."

Summer shook her head. "No, I can do this on my own."

"Now, Summer. You've never been to Houston before, whereas I was born and reared here. I know the place like the back of my hand, including where all the rich people live."

The waitress served their breakfasts, and conversation ended while they ate hungrily and appreciatively.

Ben polished off the last bit of eggs. "As I was saying," he pressed on, "I have some contacts among the wealthier families, so I could get you introductions and admittance to certain places you'd never be able to go."

"You can?" Summer asked, curious despite herself. "How do you know these people?"

"Well, I went to school with some, and others have worked for companies I've been involved with."

School? He must mean college. She remembered his comments last night about working so hard in school. She wondered if he had earned enough credits to graduate, but she didn't ask. She didn't want another reason to admire him or to feel sorry for him. It would be best for both of them if she kept him at arm's length. But his offer for help might prove valuable if she was serious about pursuing The Plan. Summer frowned. Of course she was serious, wasn't she? "Well, maybe you could show me around today," she conceded.

"We'll get you checked in to the hotel, then I'll give you the grand tour."

"Okay, I agree, but what about your family, Ben? Will this interfere with your reunion party?"

"My family?"

"Yes, the family you just had to see? You were desperate to get here. Remember? Won't they expect you today?"

"Oh, uh, right. I'll call them from the hotel."

"I can drop you at their house before I go to the hotel."

"No! That is, they'll be at work, and I don't have the key."

"Oh, I kind of thought the way you talked that they were retired." Another misconception, she thought.

"No, not completely. My dad can't stand to sit around and do nothing."

After leaving the restaurant, they walked to the office to check out and to thank Bud Kazinski for his help and kindness.

Summer felt odd hearing him call her Mrs. Carr but was too embarrassed to correct him. Maybe this was the nineties, but she wasn't used to sharing a motel room with a man.

"Too macho to let a woman drive, huh?" Summer asked as Ben opened the passenger door for her.

He just grinned and walked around. When he turned the key, only a clicking sounded.

"Oh, no." Summer groaned. "I was afraid of this."

"What's wrong with it?"

Summer stared at him in amusement. "You don't know much about cars, do you?"

"Nope. Sure don't. If I did, I might have been able to get mine running yesterday."

"It's the starter solenoid," Summer answered, opening her car door. "If you'll open the trunk and the hood, I'll see if I can get it fixed."

Ben complied and watched curiously as Summer removed a small hammer from the trunk.

"I might not know much about cars, but I do know you don't use a hammer on the engine."

"You turn the key when I say to." Summer ignored his comment and walked around to the front of the car.

"You got it."

She tapped on the solenoid with the hammer. "Try it now."

He turned the key, and the engine fired. Summer slammed the hood, put the hammer back in the trunk, and closed it. "You know even less than you thought, don't you?" she asked with a smirk.

"How did you do that?" he demanded.

"Sometimes a little tap or a push or bounce will get it going. I don't know the mechanical explanation for it. I just know it works."

"Well, I'll be damned. What did you call that?"

"The starter solenoid."

Within minutes they were back on I-45 south, headed into Houston. The morning sun promised another unmercifully hot day. Wind whipped tendrils of hair from Summer's bun. Unaccountably, Summer felt marvelous—despite the sunburn and everything else. She realized part of that was because she enjoyed being with Ben. They drove along and she floated with the feeling.

The traffic got even more congested after they reached the Greenspoint area. "This is worse than Dallas," she declared as they sped along toward the downtown skyline.

"Oh, I don't know. I guess I've always been used to this. To me, it's easier to find your way around Houston than Dallas."

A panicky feeling hit Summer. Houston was so much bigger than Dallas. What made her think such an insane plan would work? Why, she'd probably get lost and stay lost for a week! Summer's stomach filled with jumpy butterflies.

"What's the matter?" Ben asked, glancing at her.

"A little stage fright, I guess."

"Well, don't worry." He squeezed her hand again. "I'll be here to help you every step of the way. We'll find you a millionaire or my name's not Ben Carr." He laughed.

Summer wished she could truly take Ben up on his offer to be her friend, but she couldn't allow it. He disturbed her too much. She had to get rid of him somehow, if only he weren't being so friendly and charming.

Ben pulled up to the Claremont. "Your future awaits!" He got out of the car and flipped the keys to the valet. Ben bowed at the waist and held his arm out to Summer.

She couldn't help but laugh at him. So what if he looked like somebody she'd picked up off the highway? she thought, lifting her head regally. She placed her hand on his arm and allowed him to escort her into the hotel.

Ben hung back in the shadows while Summer completed checking into her room. They entered the elevator behind the bellman. The glass enclosure rose swiftly to the fourth floor. Neither she nor Ben said anything as they walked to the door of her room. They stood aside as the bellman gave instructions on operating the electronic card lock.

"Well, this is it." Summer stood in the doorway, blocking Ben's entry. She refused to listen to the voice inside that mourned his leaving.

"So it is," he acknowledged with a grin.

"I guess I'll see you later. Don't you have to go visit your family or something?"

"Right you are. But I get the feeling you're trying to brush me off. You wouldn't be planning on giving me the slip and then avoiding me if I tried to call or come up here, would you?"

"Don't be silly. Why would I do that?"

"Of course, we have an agreement, don't we?" he asked.

She flinched under his scrutiny. Was he psychic in addition to being gorgeous?

"And you always keep your word, don't you, Summer?"

She sighed and gave it up. "Yes, we do have an agreement, though I don't know why it's important to you. And yes, I do always keep my word."

"Good. Now that we have that settled, let me step inside a moment so we don't have to discuss this business in the hall."

"Okay." Summer moved aside to let him enter the room, following a step behind him. "Oh, my goodness," she breathed as she walked into the room. "Have you ever seen anything so beautiful?"

"Yes, I have," Ben replied, his eyes on her.

She blushed. "Ben, we need to get something straight, right now." Summer looked around at the bellman, who was stacking her luggage on the rack by the closet. When he finished, she discreetly slipped him several ones.

"What else do we have to settle?" he asked.

She ignored Ben's amused expression. "I want you to understand that I'm here to find a husband, a wealthy husband. I like you, Ben, but you're wasting your time coming on to me."

"Well, it's my time, right?"

"Seriously, Ben, don't think I'm going to . . ."

"To what? Sleep with me? Fall in love with me?"

"Well, yes. I'm going to be a good wife, a faithful wife, to whomever I marry."

"Hadn't you heard that rich people are corrupt, Summer? They sleep around and have no interest in fidelity? Their only interest is in accumulating wealth? Isn't that what you think?"

"Perhaps I have thought that before, but I'm not going to do that. I've never slept around." She blushed. "What I mean to say is, I don't want you to get hurt."

"Well, that's kind of you," he mocked. "I appreciate your warning. I don't think you have anything to worry about."

"Oh. Well, good." She fought the dismal feeling that arose in her from his casual rebuff. Aloud she asked, "Friends?"

"Friends!" Ben held his hand out. They shook. "I'll call for you in a couple of hours for lunch, okay?"

"Sure." She nodded. With him gone, maybe she could scope out the hotel and see if there were any likely prospects hanging about, she thought defiantly.

Ben rode the elevator down to the pink marble lobby and walked over to the concierge's desk.

"Mr. Carson, I thought that was you." The concierge eyed Ben's clothes.

"Hello, Albert. I wonder if you could do me a favor."

"Certainly, Mr. Carson, anything you want."

Ben thanked Albert for sending someone out for toiletries and clothes, then walked over to the check-in counter, where he picked up the card to the suite reserved by his father's company.

When he got to the suite, he first checked on the Jag at the

Dallas dealership, then called a local Cadillac dealer and arranged for a new Allante to be delivered.

Later he called his parents. They were so delighted to find he'd come on to Houston instead of returning to Dallas after his car had broken down that they didn't even complain about him staying at the Claremont suite instead of coming home.

Relaxing in the whirlpool bath, he thought back over the last twenty-four hours, picturing Summer in his mind and remembering their conversations. The woman was infuriating. At first he'd thought she and Janine were two peas in a pod, but her sympathy last night had been genuine. Remembering her soft voice in the dark, he grew hard again. It had been all he could do to keep from rolling atop her, but he'd never have broken his word to her by taking advantage of her.

So the little fortune hunter wanted to be his friend? That was fine with him, he thought, grinning lazily. He'd settle for being friends with Summer—for now—until she gave up her ridiculous plan to find a rich man to marry. Until then, he decided to keep his identity secret. He wanted her in his bed, but only if she came freely, without thought of what she could gain from him.

They'd be friends—and lovers. His blood heated at the thought. He just hoped he'd be able to take the frustration until then.

Seven

Summer examined the elegant room. A hunter green paisley covered the walls, with the pattern repeated on the bedcover. Sunshine streamed through ivory sheers hung between heavy green velvet draperies. Her feet sank in the plush ivory carpet as she walked to the window. Eagerly she opened the sheers. A view of skyscrapers thrusting into a brilliant blue summer sky took her breath away. The sidewalks teemed with people scurrying along.

Delighted, she smiled. She'd arrived. She'd done it! With Ben gone, ambition returned and excitement filled her. Humming to herself, she unpacked her cases and hung the expensive clothes away. In the bathroom, she freshened her makeup and took a few minutes to smooth her hair. When a knock sounded at her door, she sighed. Ben had returned.

"Did you look to see who was here?" Ben demanded sternly when she opened the door.

"No, I knew it was you."

"Look, Summer, you're not in Red Rock. Houston can be a dangerous place. Especially hotels! Use the peephole next time. Even if you think it's someone you're expecting."

Summer frowned. "Okay, okay. I'm not totally stupid, you know."

"Well, then, quit acting like it."

Her face froze in displeasure. "Who made you my keeper?"

"You did when you asked me for help."

"I did not ask for your help. You volunteered it. Why don't you unvolunteer and just go away?"

"Nope. I never back out of a bargain." He grinned. "Maybe I came on a bit strong, but it's just out of concern for you."

"People always say that when they lower the boom on you."

He lifted her chin gently. "That's no way to act to your partner. Let's kiss and make up."

Before she could move, he'd pulled her to him and covered her startled lips with his own. Stunned, she couldn't think, could only feel. She marveled at how warm his lips were and how they unraveled all her goals and ambitions when they pressed against hers. When the tip of his tongue traced the line between her lips, she reacted as if scalded.

"Ben! What do you think you're doing?" Aghast, she pulled away from him, ignoring her traitorous body, which wanted to melt into a puddle at his feet.

He released her immediately and sauntered toward the door. "Come on, let's get a move on." He held the door open.

Summer wanted to reprimand him for his forwardness, but he had already walked out into the hall. She grabbed her key card and handbag and rushed after him. How could he act as if the kiss meant nothing when it devastated her senses? She tried her best to match his air of nonchalance.

"Don't do that again," she said coolly.

"You act like you've never had a friendly kiss before." Summer thought about that. Actually she hadn't had too many kisses, friendly or otherwise. Was it just a friendly kiss he'd given her? She'd hate to be on the receiving end of a passionate one if it was. "Well, just remember what I said. I'm not interested in an affair with you."

"And remember what I said. I haven't asked you!" He took her elbow and ushered her into the elevator. When they reached the lobby, he led her to the revolving door.

"I thought we were going to have lunch here."

Ben placed his hand at the small of her back to guide her into the revolving door. "I borrowed a car from someone I know here so I can show you the town. I thought we could stop someplace for lunch. Houston has a lot of great restaurants."

Summer frowned. "There's nothing wrong with my car. We could have gone in it."

He held his hands up. "There's nothing wrong with your car. It's a gorgeous hunk of metal but has no air conditioning. If we're going to spend the day observing Houston from a set of wheels, I insist you don't risk another sunburn."

Summer couldn't argue with that. She could, but she decided it probably wouldn't do any good.

Ben led her to a beautiful gold Cadillac Allante parked in the circular drive. He opened the door for her.

Summer's mouth dropped open. "Ben, where did you get this?"

"Oh, I have a friend who works at a dealership here." Summer stroked the gleaming metal. The car was the most beautiful thing on four wheels that she'd ever seen.

"What's the matter? Don't you like it?" He grinned.

"Not like it? Oh, it's beautiful. And you borrowed it?"

"Of course." He nudged her. She slid onto the gold glove-leather seat.

Ben grinned at her as he slid beneath the steering wheel. "Don't look so shocked. It's just a car."

"Oh, it's too beautiful for words. The seats are so soft. And that cold air feels heavenly." Summer laughed.

"You can't live in Houston without air conditioning."

He told her how to adjust the seats, and Summer spent the next few minutes playing with the electrical controls, raising and lowering the seat, tilting it just right, inflating the lumbar support in the seat back.

While she did that, Ben watched her with a smile of pleasure lighting his tanned face. He played with the seek-scan button on the radio's electronic tuner until he found a country station.

"Comfy?" he asked.

"Divinely comfortable," Summer answered with a smile. He was the sweetest man! She looked at his mouth, remembering the feel of it against hers. With a blush coloring her face, she glanced away, hoping he hadn't noticed.

"You ready to track the rich and famous to their lairs?"

"Sure," Summer said. She hated the way he talked about her quest. "Lead on, Mr. Carr."

As Ben drove, he explained about the different freeways encircling the downtown area. "Now that you're oriented," he said, "we're going out to Memorial and to River Oaks."

"I guess everyone has heard of River Oaks."

"Seems that way sometimes," Ben muttered under his breath.

"What did you say?"

"Nothing." He drove along and answered the questions that tumbled out of Summer by the bushel.

"I've never seen anyone who was as curious as you."

"Well—" Summer blushed "—I've never been anywhere except Dallas and Fort Worth, so I'm easy to intrigue."

Ben laughed. "That's okay. It's an unusual experience to find someone so enthusiastic about everything."

"You must hang out with a pretty jaded crowd if my naíveté fascinates you so much," she said dryly.

"That's probably truer than you know."

Ben turned onto Kirby and drove at a snail's pace while Summer ogled the mansions. Her gasps of delight came in a steady stream. "Oh, my! That has to be the most beautiful of all!"

Ben followed her pointing finger and shifted uncomfortably.

"Ben, do you know who lives there?"

"Uh, I think that's the Carson place."

"Wow! I've never seen such beautiful roses. Look! There's someone out there spraying them."

Ben quickly slouched down so the woman wielding the pump sprayer wouldn't see him.

"Do you think they have an eligible son?" Summer joked.

Ben fidgeted. "Uh, I, uh, think they do, but he doesn't live in Houston anymore."

Summer looked at him. "Ben, are you all right? You look kind of strange."

"Guess I'm just hungry."

"Oh, I forgot. We haven't eaten. I was so excited about the car and then so interested in the city that I forgot all about lunch." She laughed. "What time is it?"

"About three. Why don't we stop and get a burger or something, then have an early dinner?"

"Dinner?"

"Well, Summer, you probably won't be able to make contact with anyone today. And I'm sure all the rich men have plans for the evening, so why not spend the evening with me? I'll show you some real fun."

"Sounds good; I don't feel like getting all dressed up tonight anyway."

"Well, gee, I don't know when I've overwhelmed a woman so much," Ben said dryly.

"Don't pout." Summer grinned at him. "I would like to at

least hit the Galleria today if that's all right with you. We can eat first, though. I'll buy—and I won't even add it to your tab," Summer stated magnanimously.

"Anything you say, Miss Money Bags."

At the first Bennigan's, he pulled into the parking lot. They ordered burgers and fries. Ben had a beer, and Summer decided recklessly to have a frozen margarita.

Ben lifted his stein to her. "Here's to the most beautiful librarian I know."

Summer laughed delightedly and warmed under his sensual looks. She couldn't resist flirting with him just a bit. "I bet I'm the only librarian you know."

"You're a very intuitive young lady!"

"And you're too handsome for your own good, Ben Carr. I bet you've got a girl in every port, or whatever the construction worker equivalent is. Admit it." She waved her margarita glass to punctuate her laughing statement.

"Well, you hit the nail on the head. I have to admit I've been known to be rather liberal with my affections the last couple of years."

Summer quit laughing. "I've never been loose with anything. I've often thought there must be something wrong with me. I'm so out of step with the times." She glanced up, then dropped her eyes. Her fingers twisted the straw wrapper around and around.

"What do you mean?"

"I've never done anything. I hear other girls talking, and it seems that they've all had romances and affairs, and I just—haven't," she finished lamely.

Surprise filled his voice. "You must've had relationships?"

Ill at ease, Summer tried to change the subject. "What's next on the agenda?" She didn't want to reveal how terribly naive she was. Ben seemed so much more worldly than she. If he found out how sexually inadequate she was, he'd laugh at her, just as Steven had. Memories of his hot, sweaty hands pulling at her clothes in the dark depressed Summer. She'd been so stupid to fall for a jerk like him, but she'd been so flattered that one of her professors was attracted to her. Her college sweetheart—what a joke!

She took a gulp of her drink, cleared her throat, then said, "Well, shall we go to the Galleria now?"

Ben just looked at her for a few minutes, calmly sipping his beer. Then he answered, allowing her to change the subject. "I thought we'd go look at the River Oaks Country Club, then drive through Memorial Park and then over to the Galleria."

When they were back in the car, he kept up a running commentary complete with gossipy trivia about every place he showed her. Summer couldn't remember ever having so much fun before. He was a walking, talking guidebook.

When he wasn't talking, his eyes watched her, seeming to be looking into her soul. He seduced her without saying a word. Summer found herself watching his hands, remembering the feel as they stroked along her skin when he was tending her sunburn. Every nerve ending in her body felt as if he were touching her whenever his brown eyes flicked over her.

At six o'clock they parked in the Galleria lot and went inside the huge indoor mall. Summer tried not to gawk at the elegant boutiques on each level, with an ice rink in the center of the building. Ill at ease in this arcade, where the very air seemed to smell of money, Summer asked Ben to wait for her.

"Why can't I go with you to shop?" he argued.

"Because."

"Because why?"

Exasperated, Summer stamped her foot. "Because I didn't come here to shop. I'm here to meet men. So I don't want you watching me like a dog with one bone."

"Meet men here? What are you going to do? Walk up to some stranger and ask to see his stock portfolio?"

"No! Just go away," she wailed, aware of people looking curiously at them.

"How about if I just follow at a discreet distance? Maybe I could pick up some pointers. If you're successful, I might decide to look for some rich woman to support me."

Angered by this statement, Summer turned her back and walked away. She breathed deeply trying to calm herself, and tried to remember everything the book had said about scoping out the "game" in up-scale stores. She sauntered to the men's department of Lord & Taylor. Casually she strolled around, stopping to look at silk ties. She nearly gasped aloud when she saw the price tag protruding from an ugly silk tie that looked like a dead trout. From the corner of her eye, she saw a man approach. Ugh. Bald. Well, she thought with a sigh, she'd expected that.

When he said, "pardon me," she turned her most brilliant smile on him.

"May I help you with the ties, miss?" he asked. His face looked as bored as his voice sounded.

"Uh, no, thank you." Summer blushed and walked away.

When she heard snickering behind her, her head snapped around. She hurled an angry look at Ben, who stood at a rack of Hawaiian print shirts. He seemed to be unsuccessfully trying to stifle his laughter.

Summer's eyes narrowed and she hissed at him. "Go away!" Then she flounced off. She spent another half hour browsing through men's accessories, aware of Ben, who followed, grinning like an idiot, about twelve steps behind her. The only men she saw were either incredibly old or were accompanied by women. She began to doubt the wisdom of the book, which said department stores were good places to meet men. Maybe they were, but you might have to stake them out every day for a month to get lucky.

Just when she was about to give up, she spotted a likely-looking fellow. Blonde, spiky hair, younger than Ben, more her age, and dressed in a monogrammed shirt. The gleaming gold watch on his wrist might be a Rolex. She stood still and stared into space, assuming a pose that said, *approach me,* she hoped.

He looked at her and smiled. She smiled back. She heard Ben clear his throat. He stood at a display of silk boxer shorts. From the corner of her eye, she saw him hold up a pair of yellow shorts festooned with red poppies. She wished he'd just disappear. He eyed the shorts this way and that as if trying to decide whether to buy them. He held them up across his waist, looked at her, and wagged his eyebrows inquiringly.

Summer wanted to strangle him. The man was still walking toward her. Her heart hammered in panic. She placed her hands behind her back and leaned nonchalantly against the end display, not even noticing what it was. He paused at the display where she stood and picked up a packet and studied it. Should she say something to him or let him speak first? she wondered anxiously.

"Excuse me, miss?"

Summer gazed into his eyes. "Yes?" she asked breathlessly.

"Do you have these red-striped ones in a small?"

"I beg your pardon?" Her puzzled eyes fell on the pair of men's bikini briefs he waved at her. Summer jerked upright. "I don't work here," she snapped. All Summer could hear was Ben's loud guffaw of laughter.

"Oh, I beg *your* pardon." He walked away.

Mortified and blushing to the roots of her hair, Summer

whirled on Ben. "What are you laughing at?"

Ben laughed even harder, slapping his thigh. He finally managed a weak, insincere apology.

"Just be quiet. You're embarrassing me to death!"

He wiped tears of mirth from his eyes and walked over to her. Still laughing, he draped his arms around her. "Honey, if that's the kind of advice that book offered, you'd be better off taking out a want ad."

Summer pushed him away. "Get off me, you laughing baboon."

"No, it's hyenas that laugh; baboons just kind of grunt."

"Oooh!" Summer ground her teeth in frustration and stomped away.

Ben trailed behind her, still chuckling.

Summer tried again in three other stores before giving up. Maybe all the eligible rich men were out of the country, or else the author of the book hadn't known what she was talking about.

"Hey, cheer up! Come on, let's get out of here and have some fun. Not that it hasn't been entertaining." He grinned and tried to take her arm.

She was so upset with him and with her failure to make one connection that she shook him off. Grumbling, she followed him to the car.

"Would you like to drive?" he asked.

Summer, who had been spoiling for a fight, was mollified by his offer. "Could I?"

"Sure."

They drove onto the busy 610 loop. He directed her to head south. Summer loved the responsiveness of the car. When she lightly pressed the accelerator, it leaped ahead. She laughed. "I feel like I should have on a pair of leather driving gloves."

He smiled at her. "I'll have to get you some."

"Oh, right, I'll need them when I drive the Autobahn." He directed her to the Astrodome. Summer raised her eyebrows in question, but he just directed her to a parking area.

"Come on, I'm going to show you some real entertainment." He tugged her along and they followed the crowd.

"When you said real entertainment, I had no idea you meant a baseball game!" Summer sat in the seat Ben pushed down for her.

"Hey, this isn't just a baseball game. This is The Show! As far as I'm concerned, one of the greatest shows on earth. The Astros are having a fantastic season this year."

"I've never been to a ball game before."

"You, my dear, have led a sheltered life." They settled into their seats.

"Maybe so," Summer agreed, looking around. "Gosh, there's more people in the Dome than in the whole county where I'm from."

"Looks like maybe forty-five thousand here tonight."

He looked through the netting that protected their area from wild balls. "Do you know anything about baseball?"

She arched an eyebrow. "I'm American, am I not?"

He grinned. "What does that mean?"

"You know as well as I that if you grew up in this country, you absorb by osmosis that three strikes and you're out, four balls and you walk, and all that other stuff."

"So you played when you were a kid, huh?"

She nodded. "One family I lived with had two little boys who wanted to grow up to be just like Nolan Ryan. And next door to them was a family that had five kids—three boys and two girls—so between all of us, we had two makeshift teams. We played every afternoon." She grinned fondly at the memory.

"How long were you with them?" he asked quietly.

"Until Mrs. Seldes got pregnant again. They simply didn't have room for me. They were my last foster family. From then on, I lived at the home. I always regretted having to leave." She sighed. "We had such fun—almost like a real family."

"Well, then, you are just a novice. Let me explain the finer points of RBI, ERA, and other terms unique to The Show."

Summer batted her eyes at him and simpered, "Oh, you mean there's more to it than hitting home runs?"

"Pay attention, librarian, and learn something."

Summer studied him as he explained terms and told stories about so-and-so doing such-and-such. She didn't know if she'd remember a pitchout from an infield home run, but she had a feeling she'd always remember the enthusiasm in his voice as he shared something he adored with her. Excitement colored each word as he told of seeing legendary Nolan Ryan pitch a no-hitter, of their win against the Giants in 1986. He described how confetti had rained from the Dome ceiling and people had hugged and kissed total strangers in their excitement.

Summer pictured it in her mind. Especially the kissing part. He said something she couldn't hear over the noise level. She learned toward him. His dark eyes captured her green ones. He leaned closer; his mouth was mere inches from hers. She still didn't hear what he had to say because all her attention was concentrated on his mouth. Wondering how his lips would taste. Wondering how his tongue would feel trespassing into her mouth. Her breathing quickened to match her soaring pulse rate. As if in slow motion, she watched his head move closer to hers. She looked askance at him. The teasing smile had left his face. He leaned toward her. She was amazed at the shock of feeling that coursed through her. A heavy pulse began low in her belly. Anticipation stole the breath from her body.

His lips brushed her cheek as he leaned close to her ear to repeat what he'd said. Her eyes drifted closed. She didn't care if everyone in the Astrodome watched. His lips touched the lobe of her ear. A thrill like a jolt of electricity coursed through her, making her shiver with desire. When he touched the curve of her ear with his tongue, she knew she wanted more. She turned her head to bring her mouth to his. Just then the crowd roared. The people seated all around them leaped to their feet. Summer jerked away. If only it could be Ben, she thought.

He took her chin in his hand and turned her face toward him. They ignored the thousands of screaming fans. "What are you thinking?" His voice was quiet, yet she heard his words.

"Oh, nothing important." She licked her dry lips and swallowed. "I was just wondering why you weren't rich."

For a second he didn't say anything. "Maybe I'm rich in other ways," he whispered, his eyes seducing her.

She closed her eyes and swayed toward him, wanting him to kiss her again even though she knew there was no future with him.

"You are so beautiful."

"The most beautiful librarian you ever met?" She tried for a lighthearted tone.

"The most beautiful woman I've ever met."

"No, I'm not."

"Don't be modest."

She waved her hand. "I'm not. I'm fairly realistic about my looks. I know I'm above average but not really beautiful. I've just learned to make the most of my assets."

As if the game were the most important thing in the world, she stared at the brightly lit field. Ben kept silent, and pretty soon Summer relaxed enough to actually see what was happening on the diamond. To her surprise, she found herself caught up in the excitement. Ben bought her a huge foam mitt, emblazoned with ASTROS, that fit over her hand. Whenever the Astros did something the crowd approved of, Summer thrust the giant "hand" in the air. She laughed more than she'd ever laughed in her life. "This is fantastic. I love it!" she declared during the seventh-inning stretch.

"Well, maybe one of these days you can own a piece of a ball club," he teased.

"Maybe so," Summer agreed with a laugh. She looked around. For the first time, something odd struck her. "These are awfully good seats, aren't they?"

"Sure are."

"How did you get tickets for them at the last minute?" She frowned. "We didn't stop to buy tickets, come to think of it."

"Oh, that. Well, uh, I knew a guy who knew a guy who had season tickets. I just called around to see if they were being used tonight."

"You have the most incredible luck!"

"Ben? Well, I'll be damned if it isn't Ben Car—"

"David!" Ben jumped up. "David, what a surprise!"

Not a very pleasant one, Summer thought, judging from the dismay on Ben's face. She looked at the man who stood in the aisle pumping Ben's hand and slapping him on the back. He looked over at her and smiled. She smiled back.

"Aren't you going to introduce me to this vision of beauty, you son of a gun?"

"David, Summer. Summer, David."

David reached across Ben and took Summer's hand in his. He brought it to his lips, disregarding Ben's sour expression. "As beautiful as a summer day!"

Summer smiled. What nonsense! "I'm happy to meet you, David."

"I'm enchanted to meet you, sugar, but that introduction left a little to be desired. I'm David Blackwood, attorney at law."

"And I'm Summer James."

David stepped past Ben and settled into the empty seat on the other side of Summer. "Well, Miss James, what are you doing with this reprobate?"

"Why, Mr. Blackwood, I'm learning the finer points of baseball."

"Well, sugar, I know more than he does about the subject. I played professional baseball a few years ago."

Ben snorted. "You were in the minors, Blackwood. And it was fifteen years ago if it was a day. Don't you need to go back to your seat?"

"Ben, Ben, I'm wounded. I haven't seen you in—how long? A year? And you treat me this way. Don't you want to drink a cup of kindness for old times' sake?"

"I'll settle for another beer," Ben said tersely.

"Ben," Summer remonstrated. What had changed his lighthearted mood? She tried to make small talk, but Ben just looked daggers at David while David flirted shamelessly with her. He was so brazen about it, she had to laugh, and found herself enjoying his company almost as much as she'd enjoyed Ben's. Maybe I have been lonely, she thought. At least Annie thought so. That may be the reason Ben appeals to me so much.

Discreetly she studied the clothes David wore and noted the Piaget watch on his wrist and the gleaming leather shoes. Everything about him shouted money. And he was a nice guy, even if he did enjoy needling Ben. When he asked her to lunch the following day, she didn't hesitate to accept.

Eight

By the time the Houston Astros defeated the San Francisco Giants, Ben was steaming. He'd endured Summer's flirting with David, barely hanging on to his temper. But David, the low-down, miserable cur, had come on to Summer like gangbusters. Ben could tell by the laughing glances thrown his way that his old friend saw Summer as just another competition between friends. Couldn't David see Summer was more than that? fumed Ben.

With the game over, Ben saw his chance to lose David. He had to get Summer away from David before his friend let something slip—like Ben's real name and status. With the crowd clogging the aisles, Ben grabbed Summer by the hand and pulled her along.

"Hey, wait a minute. Ben, slow down. We lost David." Summer looked over her shoulder, trying to locate David in the sea of faces.

"Good!" Ben muttered with a heated look.

"What?"

Ben halted and whirled to face her, his grip moving from her hand to her shoulders.

"I heard you make a date with that puffed-up Romeo. He doesn't need to see you again tonight. I'm sure, by now, he knows where to find you tomorrow."

"Yes, he does. But you're being awfully rude. After all, he's your friend."

"Some friend! And anyone would think he was your long-lost soul mate." Ben batted his eyes and said in a falsetto, "Oh, David, you're so funny. Oh, David, you're so charming. I'd love to go out with you." He ignored the fire that leapt to her eyes.

"You're being ridiculous," she replied. "At least I didn't act like a spoiled brat who doesn't want to share his toys."

"No, you acted like the available woman you are. Why don't you just hang a sign around your neck that says, 'For sale to the highest bidder'?"

Summer sucked in her breath. "You're obnoxious, Ben Carr."

"Oh, right, I forgot. You need to specify that those below the poverty level need not apply."

Summer swung her hand. Ben caught it before it made contact with his face. She jerked to free her hand, but he tightened his grip. Unmindful of the people who poured around them like water in a stream around two flat rocks, they stared into each other's eyes. Fire met fire.

Then he saw something shift in her eyes. He knew desire shot through her body just as it did through his. He felt the trembling begin in her hand. His eyes darkened. He wished he were a million miles away, on a desert island with her. Anywhere but in the midst of this noisy mob. He released her wrist, his hand sliding up her bare arm to her shoulder, up the length of her neck to cup her cheek.

Her eyes slid shut and she swayed toward him. Yes, Summer, fall into my arms. Into my bed, he thought, getting even harder at the prospect.

"Ben! Hey, Ben! Summer! Over here!"

The moment shattered. Ben groaned as he recognized David's voice. Summer's eyes snapped open. She jumped away from Ben.

David loped up to them. "Just wanted to confirm our lunch tomorrow, Summer. I'll meet you in the hotel lobby at noon."

Summer smiled wanly and cleared her throat. "Yes, that's fine, David. I'm looking forward to it."

"Ben, call me in the morning. Maybe we can do lunch while you're in town." He pointed his index finger with thumb aloft at Ben and made a clicking sound.

"You can count on it, Blackwood," Ben said with narrowed eyes. Just wait till I get through with you, he thought.

"I'd like to take you home," David said to Summer, "but I came with someone else," he apologized.

"Who is she?" Ben asked.

"My sister," David answered blandly. "You remember her, don't you, Ben?"

Ben grunted. David's sister hated baseball and wouldn't be caught dead at a game. Aloud he said, "Summer came with me, so she'll leave with me."

"Yep, you're a fine gentleman and a credit to your upbringing." David grinned and gave a little salute to Summer. "See you tomorrow."

Summer and Ben didn't say a word all the way to the car. He knew what her intentions were, so why was he acting like the wronged party? She had enjoyed the evening until her unsettling argument with Ben. Even the innocent flirting with David had been fun, not arousing. With Ben, though, one look and her bones melted. And when he touched her, she forgot about her goal and her dreams. She'd have to make sure she didn't let him touch her, she decided.

The more she thought about the whole situation, the more dismayed she became. Her innate honesty forced her to recognize that the more Ben had scowled, the more she'd flirted with David. He'd been jealous! And she had played on that fact. She'd sensed the undercurrents but hadn't stopped to analyze the scowling looks he'd directed at David.

She disliked her desire to make Ben jealous. How immature of her! After all, why would she want Ben to be jealous of David? She shouldn't and wouldn't care that Ben felt possessive of her, because that would mean that she cared too much about him.

I don't care, she thought, it's just . . . lust. But thinking about him touching her started her blood pounding. She shivered remembering the feel of his hand sliding up her arm. Each moment had been an eternity. What would have happened if David hadn't intruded, if they hadn't been caught in the middle of a crowd but had been alone, in a quiet room? The question bothered her as much as it excited her.

Ben had insinuated himself into her life in such a short time. He made her laugh and nearly made her forget her reason for coming to Houston. She had to get back on track, even if it meant giving up his company. Besides, she had a feeling she represented just another notch on his bedpost. He didn't mean anything by his interest in her. Even if he met her requirements for a prospective mate, he wasn't interested in her hand in marriage, she thought dryly, only in other parts of her anatomy.

Silence hung like a heavy curtain, separating each of them with their private thoughts. The city skyline, breathtaking in its cloak of darkness that obscured the urban decay along the freeway, held no appeal for Summer.

"I'm sorry if I was out of line," Ben offered, his eyes fixed on the traffic ahead.

"Me, too. I shouldn't have been so quick to take offense." Summer smiled tentatively. "Truce?"

"Truce." Ben smiled at her, making her forget all the sane, sensible reasons why she shouldn't get involved with him.

When he directed that smile at her, her insides turned to mush.

Arriving at the hotel, he bypassed the driveway that led to the lobby and took the next one for the parking garage.

"What are you doing?"

"I think we should go inside and put an end to this."

Her heart sank. All the way from the car and up to her room, she gathered the courage to bid him good-bye. She rehearsed the words as he escorted her to the door of her room.

"Ben, I think you are right. I think we should end this."

"Let's go inside." He held his hand out for her card.

Reluctantly she dug it from her purse and gave it to him. It would have been a lot easier to say good-bye outside the confines of her room. She didn't trust herself alone with him.

He opened the door and they went in. Summer turned on the lamps on either side of the small sofa. She sat down and began pulling the pins from her hair, tossing them onto the table.

He stared at her, following her movements intently. He sank onto the couch cushion next to her and lifted his hands to her hair, brushing hers aside. She froze at his touch. He pulled the last pins from her hair.

Dizzy by the nearness of him, she could barely string together words. "What are you doing?"

"I'm taking your hair down, like I've wanted to all day." He ran his fingers slowly through her hair, gently massaging her scalp.

She closed her eyes with a sigh. "Ummm. That feels good."

He spread her hair out behind her like a fan, fingering the silken tresses, then moving his hands to the base of her skull to massage the tight muscles there.

"You do know how to get on a woman's good side, Ben Carr." She wished she could have this kind of solicitous caring forever. But that was impossible. "I've been thinking, Ben."

"That sounds ominous."

"No, it's not. You've helped me a lot and I appreciate it, but I think you're right that we should end our relationship, such as it is."

"Huh?"

"Put an end to it—like you said."

He shook his head. "That isn't what I mean to put an end to." Ben tilted her head up with a hand beneath her chin. "I'm going to put an end to this heat between us. Maybe it will burn itself out tonight." With that, his lips covered hers. His mouth shaped hers, his teeth nipping her full upper lip, his tongue teasing for entrance. "Open your mouth," he whispered, wetting her lips and sucking gently at them.

Summer moaned. Heat burst through her body. She opened her mouth, granting him entrance and possession. He devoured her offering until that wasn't enough to content him. She knew he wanted more because she wanted more.

"I want you, Summer, in every way." The honesty in his hoarse voice thrilled her as his hands ignited explosions of need everywhere they touched.

Summer slowly relaxed against him. Her breasts felt heavy, almost painful. Instinctively she pressed against his chest, at once easing the painful need and increasing it three-fold.

"And you want me, too."

The smug satisfaction in his voice didn't offend or frighten her. She'd had only a couple of experiences with making love, and that had been with Steven, who had ridiculed her for being a cold fish. Funny, she didn't feel a bit cold. Despite her lack of experience, she knew what her body wanted from this man. She could feel it in her aching breasts, in her throbbing pulse.

His lips traveled along her jaw, leaving fire in their wake. When his mouth slid down her throat to leave little love bites on the juncture of her neck and shoulder, she almost screamed with the fierce pleasure. It seemed so right to want to lie naked in his arms, to make love with him. Taking her courage in hand, she murmured, "I want to make love with you, Ben." And it felt right to tell him so. She'd waited so long for this, for him.

He stilled, his eyes searching her face. "You won't regret it, Summer. I'll make it so special, you'll always remember this night." He stood and pulled her up, lifting her into his arms.

Summer watched his face as he carried her to the huge bed behind them. She knew she'd never forget tonight, because it was the first time she'd ever wanted a man, truly wanted a man. She hoped she could give him enough, because lovemaking was something she hadn't been able to learn from a book.

Ben said nothing. Summer's sweet honesty made him forget his vow not to touch her until she'd abandoned her foolish quest. He thought he'd die if he didn't love her tonight. His burning eyes studied her. How could she even consider going to bed with another man? Marrying another man? The thought made him want to put his fist through the wall. Couldn't she see that she was made for him?

Suddenly Ben wanted to say the words that would make her his. All he had to do was confess his wealth, and she'd be his. Bought and paid for, he jeered mentally. What then?

He stood her beside the bed and undressed her, tossing her clothes into a pile on the floor. His eyes loved her body, but he didn't touch her until both he and she were completely naked.

Her eyes were huge in her face as she studied his body. His manhood seemed to grow even larger and harder as her eyes touched him. Face flaming, she looked quickly away.

For some reason, the fact that she wasn't blase about their nudity made him feel better. He spoke quietly, though he was almost hurting from painful need. "You can look at me if you wish. I like your eyes on me."

"Can I touch you?" Her voice was so soft, he could barely make it out.

"God, yes!"

Summer walked into his arms. Instinctively she pressed against his hard arousal. He groaned aloud and pulled away a little, his mouth seeking hers, spreading tiny kisses down her jawline, over her eyelids, her temples. She swayed against him. Her sweet response destroyed him.

Then his mouth was on hers, slanting and teasing and licking. Summer smiled and opened her mouth to taste his lips in the same teasing manner. His tongue thrust through her lips and boldly stroked the inside of her mouth, scraping her nerve endings and spreading liquid fire everywhere he touched.

Paralyzed by the heat that swept over him, he gasped for air in concert with her. He heard her breath, as shaky as his. He wondered if her legs were as weak as his.

"Kiss me again, Summer," Ben entreated, his mouth taking tiny bites of her mouth, seeking, sucking, stroking, licking. She complied with an ardor that matched his.

When his mouth left hers, she drew in lungfuls of air but then caught her breath as his lips slid down her throat, his teeth nipping the sensitive cord of her neck. She only had enough breath to moan softly, "Yes, Ben, yes!"

Summer didn't see the satisfied smile that played across his face, but she felt it in his lips as they kissed the curve of her cheek. When his mouth returned to sip at hers, she moaned and opened her mouth, met his tongue joyfully, placing wet, wanton kisses along his mouth and jaw. She thrilled at the rough inhalation that indicated he was as undone as she by the feeling between them.

Her breasts ached, her nipples so tight and hard, they burned and throbbed where they brushed against his chest. She rubbed against him, wanting more, begging him to give her what she wanted. Her skin felt as if she'd burst into flame if he touched her again. Yet she knew she'd die if he didn't.

His mouth found hers in a drugging kiss of promise. He lowered her to the bed. Her hammering heart felt the returning beat of his heart. She wanted to remember every moment of tonight, but the galloping desire threatened to consume her. She was desperate to store up the details of this evening so in lonely years to come she could warm herself by the memory and relive it, moment by moment.

"You are so lovely," he said reverently, his hands reaching out to cup the lushness of her ripe body. Summer stared at the contrast of his sun-browned hands against her milk white breasts. Merely looking at him touching her body made her turn to jelly.

Gently he squeezed, then stroked her breasts. Moments later his mouth replaced his questing hands. Summer jerked when his mouth closed over a taut nipple. Through the sensual fog, he pressed her to the bed, his mouth sucking and pulling at first one nipple, then the other. She'd never felt anything so powerful before. His long, lean fingers swept down her legs and up the sleek muscles to the silky blond triangle between her legs. She wanted to weep with the pleasure of it all. His hands couldn't seem to touch her enough. He murmured nonsense love words between his heated kisses.

Summer shivered with the pleasure of his mouth and his hands. She returned kiss for kiss and touch for touch, hoping in some small way, she could make him feel what she was feeling.

He pressed his body against hers. His hard arousal branded her soft, flat stomach.

"Ben, please, please." Summer thought she'd go out of her mind with longing. His hand slid to the soft nest of curls between her legs. Gently he probed, sliding a finger into her hot wetness. His head lifted and he looked into her darkened emerald eyes. "You want me very badly." He found the bud of her desire and spread the slick moisture.

Summer smothered a scream against his shoulder. She lifted her hips, begging, pleading for release. Ben groaned, shattering her with his need. "I can't wait any longer, sweetheart. I have to feel your warmth, your wetness."

"Yes, please," she gasped, nearly unable to think at all. He left her briefly. The sound of tearing paper opened her eyes. She blushed but didn't look away from the sight of his putting on a condom. She looked up to see him watching her watch him.

Without thinking about it, she reached out and touched him, wanting to know what he felt like. With her hands enclosing him, she felt empowered when he groaned and gasped, "Sweetheart, don't."

Summer smiled at him and pulled him to her. His arms bulged with muscles as he held himself from her for a long moment before lowering his body to hers, slowly pushing into her softness.

"Oh, God, sweetheart, you are so tight. So hot," he gasped. Then he slowly pulled out, ignoring her cry of protest. She pounded on his back, and he plunged into her, seating himself to his full length inside her.

Summer gloried in his weight, loved the feel of him deep inside her. Instinctively her hips moved against him, wanting more and wanting it now.

"Not yet!" he cried. With a hoarse shout, he began driving into her as if compelled by a force beyond his control.

Summer felt as if her world tilted on its axis. Something within her tightened and tightened until the tension was unbearable. He plunged harder and faster until a cry tore from her throat and her body convulsed. Ben stiffened and poured himself into her.

Summer thought perhaps she died a little. A feeling almost of sadness filled her. Somehow she knew that her life would never be the same again.

Nine

Ben leaned his forehead against Summer's. His breath mingled with hers as he stroked her and gentled her, calming her and himself. His body trembled with the force of the pleasure he'd found with her. His eyes closed in defeat. He hadn't wanted to become lovers with her until she accepted him as a man, penniless or rich. But he couldn't regret what had happened. He fought against the thought that he loved her.

Mentally he raged at himself. How could he have fallen in love with a woman he'd known for only forty-eight hours? He'd thought he had been in love before, and he'd been wrong. He wanted to beat his fists against the wall, tear his hair, and deny that it had happened.

Yet somehow, he knew he'd finally found the one woman who completed him. He wanted to hold her and protect her and shower her with all the material things she seemed to desire. She excited him beyond reason. With eyes closed, he imagined living with her and making love to her for the rest of his days, until they were both old and gray and ready for a rest home.

Then reality came crashing back as he remembered she wasn't interested in love. She only wanted his money. Except she didn't know he had any, so she wasn't interested in him for any reason—except possibly the sexual gratification she'd just received. She had to have been as overwhelmed as he.

Depressed by his thoughts, he wondered if he could keep

her so aroused that she would forget her damned plan. He moved slightly, slanting his body off hers. When she murmured a protest, he smoothed the damp hair back from her forehead.

He smiled. She'd fallen asleep. He watched her in the dim light, marveling at how thoroughly she'd defeated his control. He tried to remember if he'd ever had sex this good before. He didn't think so—not even with Janine in the early days. It had never been this intense—like the world would come to an end if he didn't make love to her.

The knowledge that she didn't want him pierced his soul. Ruefully he kissed her love-swollen lips and slid from her embrace. Her arms tightened to hold him, but he managed to get up without waking her. He turned out the lamp, double-locked the door, and got back in bed. He turned on his side and pulled her into his arms. Sleep was a long time coming as he thought about the surprising twist his life had taken.

She thought money was power, but she didn't have enough experience with men or with her desires to know that the human sex drive was more powerful than any amount of currency. Sleepily he planned his conquest as meticulously as a general would a military campaign. When his eyes finally closed, he felt confident that he could win her heart because she'd already given him her body. He wanted her, not just for tonight or a week, but forever, he decided. But she had to want him for himself. He couldn't afford to reveal his identity to her even though it rankled him mightily each time she referred to him as Ben Car—. What had started as a joke wasn't amusing anymore.

Summer snuggled next to the source of warmth beneath the covers. She sighed contentedly as she started to drift back to sleep, but a groggy thought intruded. The next moment her eyes flew open. Fearfully she moved her hand along her leg where a hairy, muscled thigh pressed it. She quickly became aware of the hard muscles of another body that lay so close to hers that a piece of paper could not be slid between them.

A groan escaped her lips as the events of the previous night replayed in her mind. What have I done? Eyes closed, her body flamed at the memory of his hands and his mouth and his body. She had to be out of her mind, she decided. How did I end up in bed with Ben when what I intended to do was tell him good-bye?

You idiot! She called herself every name in the book, but that didn't keep the thrill of the evening from possessing her again. She let the memories sweep her away until her body tingled and the only thing she wanted to do was jump atop his body and beg him to make her feel that way again.

No! she thought. I mustn't make that mistake again. He's a loser. What on earth am I thinking about to even consider making love—having sex, her mind brutally interjected—with him again?

She crept out of bed and went to the shower, hoping she could be dressed before he awoke. She couldn't help casting a look of longing at him. The covers were pushed down to just above his hips, revealing his bronzed shoulders and chest, his trim waist with the arrow of dark hair that disappeared below the sheet. She forced herself into the shower.

Deliberately turning the cold water on, she scrubbed herself, vainly trying to eradicate the weakness of her flesh. Just touching herself as she showered brought new awareness to her body. She remembered Ben's hands and mouth trailing fire over the sensitive skin.

Angrily she pushed the shower lever down, turning off the flow of water. She'd gone all her life without giving in to the siren call of the flesh. Why was she obsessed now with her sexuality? Why now, when it was so important she be cool, calm, and collected? Because of Ben. It was his fault! All his fault!

As quietly as possible, she rushed through her morning routine. By ten-thirty she was dressed in beige linen slacks and a black cotton tank top with a matching oversize linen jacket. Her hair hung like a shining curtain about her shoulders. She tied it at the nape of her neck with a black grosgrain ribbon, then put on large oval black onyx earrings and placed a straw boater trimmed with black grosgrain ribbon on her head. Quickly she changed her white handbag for a big straw bag.

Taking the key card to the room, she started to depart but at the last minute decided to leave a note. In the near dark, she tried to hastily compose a diplomatic message to him on the hotel notepad. Something that would keep him from pursuing her. He had what he wanted now, she thought sourly. She scribbled a couple of lines, not alluding to last night's events at all. She ended the note by telling him to visit his family and take care of any other business he had. She'd be in touch with him. With an unhappy sigh, she slipped out of the room.

The quiet click of the closing door woke Ben. He reached his arms out to draw Summer closer to his aroused body but made contact only with the empty bed. Frowning, he opened his eyes and looked around, listening intently. Silence greeted him. What the hell! Where was Summer? He flung the covers back and stalked to the bathroom. His frown turned into a scowl as black as the shiny marble tile.

"Damn it!" he said aloud. Water beaded the ceramic tile shower surround. Her hair dryer and cosmetics were neatly laid out. He touched the blow dryer. Still warm. He'd like to wring her neck for running out on him. If he could get his hands on her, he thought, he'd . . . he'd . . . fling her on the bed and love her until she moaned like she'd done last night.

Ruefully he stared down at his aching hardness. What was he going to do about Summer? How could he keep her entranced and in a fog of sensuality if she kept beating him awake and out the door each day? She wasn't going to make it easy, he realized.

After his shower, he eyed his wrinkled clothes on the floor. They lay next to Summer's discarded pink outfit and lacy lingerie. Seemed as if ever since he'd met Summer, he'd ended up wearing the same clothes day in and day out. But at least I can run up to my room to change this time, he thought.

He decided to call room service and get some coffee sent up. Maybe then he could think straight. He sat on the bed and reached for the phone, knocking over the notepad propped against it. While he waited for room service to answer, he scanned the note Summer had left. His anger returned as he read the sparse lines. So she wanted to pretend last night hadn't happened, did she? Well, tough cookies, lady, he thought.

After growling his request to the room service waiter, he left her room. Just wait until I get that bird dog Blackwood on the phone, he thought, wanting to unleash his anger on someone.

Where had his composure and coolness gone? he wondered as he took the elevator up to the twentieth floor.

Summer dawdled over her coffee and toast, crumbling the bread into her plate rather than eating it. The fresh melon, she welcomed. The pink fruit slid easily down her throat. Seems like she hadn't eaten right since she'd started on this odyssey. It didn't much matter, though, since she was due to have lunch with David Blackwood in another hour.

Oddly, she felt on the verge of tears. She blinked rapidly to dispel the unwanted moisture. I think I've cried more in the last two days than the last two years, she thought, sipping her coffee. All she wanted was to go hide in her room. She called first to see if Ben was still there. As she listened to the phone ring, she refused to admit she felt disappointed at the fact that he'd left. That was what I wanted, she insisted mentally. I want him to stay away.

Summer returned to her room and sat in the wing chair, refusing to sit on the couch, where her seduction had started. She studied the book that had inspired her plan, trying to figure out what she should do next, but the stupid book and its asinine title suddenly disgusted her. She tossed it onto the coffee table next to the small pile of hairpins.

Somehow when she'd sat on the lumpy couch in her little house in Red Rock, she'd thought this plan was worthwhile and possible. And now she was offered her first opportunity to carry out her plan, assuming she and David hit it off today as they had done last night, but she had no interest in it. She felt stupid and shallow for even conceiving the plan.

If she went through with it, she'd have to do with David what she'd done with Ben last night. Summer shuddered. She couldn't imagine giving herself to another man as she had to Ben. It had been right and natural with Ben. Not cheap and mercenary.

Disquieted by the thought, she jumped up and began to pace. Now that she knew what intimacy entailed, she couldn't stop thinking about it. How could she let a stranger touch her and do those things to her? When the phone rang, she knocked it over in her haste to answer it.

"Hello?" Ben, come to me, her heart cried.

"Summer, it's David. I got here a little early, so I thought I'd give you a buzz and see if you wanted to join me now."

"I'll be right down." Resigned to the lunch, Summer gathered her handbag, freshened her lipstick, straightened her hat, then left her room.

"You look great!" David said as he took her arm to escort her into the restaurant. "I love hats on a woman."

"Thank you," Summer murmured. "I've always had an affection for hats. Sometimes I wish I'd lived in the thirties and forties when hats were de rigueur." Summer tried to relax. David really was appealing with his blond good looks, she thought. But not as alluring as Ben, an insidious voice within whispered.

Throughout the meal, that argumentative little voice refused to be silent. It compared everything that David said and did to Ben. Though David was quite nice and she enjoyed his company, she knew she couldn't go to bed with him. She blushed at the thought and hastily looked away.

"What the hell?"

David's exasperated tone made Summer think she had spoken aloud. Horrified, she studied his face, but he was looking past her shoulder.

"Well, well, fancy running into you two." Ben stood next to their table.

Summer wanted to cry. She felt so mixed-up. She had wanted to see Ben, but she knew he showed up just to ruin her lunch with David. Hadn't he already messed things up enough? The warmth in his eyes when she looked up brought a blush to her cheeks. The wretch! *Quit looking at me like that,* she wanted to shout.

Ben pulled out a chair and sat down.

"Do have a seat, old buddy," David said. "Somehow after your call this morning, I figured you'd be joining us."

"Well, thanks, old buddy." Ben's eyes never left Summer's face. "Good morning," he said softly to her.

Summer blushed an even darker shade. "Good morning," she stammered. Her brain went numb. Why had Ben called David? She couldn't think of anything to say to start a conversation. A million questions whirled through her mind.

Silence hung heavy around the table. Summer wondered what David must think, and risked a look at him. To her chagrin, she realized he read the situation accurately. She was mortified.

"Well, old buddy, still just as competitive as you were when you wore short pants," David said. He took a bite of steak and chewed enthusiastically.

Ben waved away the waiter who approached with a menu. "Some things are worth competing for."

Summer's eyes narrowed. What was going on here? Compete! Was that what she was? A prize that David and Ben competed for? A contest! Two dogs fighting over a bone, and she was the bone. Horrified, she wondered if that was why Ben had made love to her last night. Had he been trying to put one over on David?

Angry at the thought, she tossed her napkin on the table and started to rise, but David grasped her hand beneath the table. Rather than make a scene, she stayed. David squeezed her hand and winked at her, confusing her even more.

Summer glared at Ben, her eyes promising retribution to him, not fooled by the innocent look on his face.

"If you'll excuse me a moment, I need to call the office." David rose. "Don't go away, now." He departed with a grin.

Summer resolutely studied the crystal vase of pink carnations on the table and tried not to think of last night.

"Go ahead and say it or you're likely to explode," Ben teased softly.

"I am not some spoils of war to go to the victor of your petty rivalry with David," she sputtered.

"Hey, this isn't petty. He wants you in his bed."

"Don't be crude. He's a perfect gentleman. Unlike you."

"Ha! That perfect gentleman has led more than one girl down the garden path. And let me tell you something in case you're thinking you can get him to propose to you. No woman has ever wrung a proposal from him."

"Of course you'd say that. You don't like him, obviously."

"I never said that. He's one of my best friends."

"Then why are you here? To protect him? You got what you wanted last night. You beat him to the punch, so leave me alone!" *Please deny it, Ben,* she cried, searching his eyes for some clue as to his thoughts.

"Is that what this is all about? You think I made love to you to put one over on David?"

"Well, didn't you?" Summer refused to meet his eyes. The hurt clogged her throat.

"Oh, sweetheart, don't deceive yourself." His hand covered hers. "I made love to you because you are a beautiful, desirable woman. I wanted you. David had nothing to do with it."

Summer considered his words. They melted the ice around her heart at the same time they frightened her to death. What did he want from her? She pulled her hand away. "I wish you wouldn't say things like that." She wanted to run. He made unfamiliar emotions rise inside her, and they scared her to death.

"Well, I'm going to keep on saying them, so you might as well get used to them."

Frightened, Summer saw the months stretch ahead. If she gave in to his seductive words, how long would it be before he tired of her? What if she got pregnant? Would he dump her like her father had dumped her mother? Then what would happen to her? How could she live with her heart stolen from her?

Her heart? No, I'm being foolish, she thought hastily. He can't take something I haven't given him. And I've only given him my body. She couldn't trust the hot passion in his eyes. Even if I give up on my plan. I can't depend on him, she thought. He doesn't love me. Love is just a lie. I've got to cut him out of my life now, while I still have the strength.

"What are you thinking about?" Ben stroked the back of her hand with his thumb.

"About my father," Summer answered honestly.

"I thought you didn't know who he was."

"I don't. When I think of him, he's just a shadow standing next to Mom. Did I tell you why my mother named me Summer?"

Ben shook his head.

"My dad dumped her when she was four months pregnant—just when she began to show. She used to tell me that I was the only thing in the world she had left to love that summer."

"How did you ever survive?" Ben mused, compassion in his voice and eyes.

I don't want your pity, Summer thought. I want your—No! The half-formed thought terrified her. She laughed, the sound ugly. "I guess I was tough. When life got too miserable, I turned to books. I could be anybody I wanted to be in a book. Scarlett O'Hara or Anne of Green Gables or even Tom Sawyer."

"So you became a romantic?"

"I'd hardly classify myself as a romantic."

"Sure you are. You dreamed up this Cinderella story, starring yourself. You plan on winning the hand of Prince Charming. That's romantic. The only difference is that

Cinderella loved Prince Charming. But you just love his money."

"That's not true!" Summer hissed. Agitated, she jerked her hand from his. "I wish you'd quit saying that."

"Sorry. It annoys the hell out of me that you're prepared to throw yourself away on a rich old lech just to have money."

Summer didn't deny his words. How could she tell him she'd changed her mind? That would just give him license to continue using her and to eventually break her heart. "Anyone would think you had more money than brains!"

"What about love, Summer? Does that fit into your plans?"

"Love? What's that? I don't know that emotion you speak of. Was it love that my father felt for my mother when he seduced her, impregnated her, abandoned her? Where was love when my grandmother rejected me? You can take love and shove it."

"I feel sorry for you, Summer." Pain filled his voice. "I'm not the best role model for love, but I know it exists. Right or wrong, I married for love. I used to be bitter about the way my marriage turned out, but not anymore."

"She left you, didn't she, Ben? So what does that prove?"

"You're right, she left me, and it hurt. Loving is part of living. You take your chance, just like everyone else. There aren't any guarantees. Not everyone is lucky. But I know loves exists. I see it each time my mom and dad look at each other. That's the kind of love I want. The kind that lasts for forty years without dying. I just haven't found it yet."

Summer didn't want to hear any more of his seductive lies. "You're the romantic, not me."

"I'm sorry that took so long." David pulled his chair out, apparently unaware of the thick tension between Summer and Ben. He smiled at Summer. "You know, I have a great idea. We're having a small party at the club tonight. The band is supposed to be pretty good. Why don't you go with me, Summer?"

Summer looked first at Ben, who scowled furiously at her. He shook his head slightly. She stuck her chin up. "I'd be happy to go with you."

"I'll pick you up at eight," David replied, then launched into a story about an escapade he and Ben had participated in when they were kids. David went out of his way to charm Summer, telling her other anecdotes about the trouble he and Ben had gotten in through the years. Ben silently stared at her.

Summer laughed politely but wished David would shut up. She enjoyed hearing about Ben too much. Picturing Ben as a boy fed the hunger she needed to kill. When David began asking questions about her background, she tried to answer with open-ended statements that weren't outright lies, but she stumbled over several of her pat answers about her background and her family.

With each near fib, Ben rolled his eyes, and Summer blushed. This was no good. If she could just get through tonight, she would leave Houston and go home to her shabby little bungalow that she suddenly longed to see, she thought. Would lunch never end? she wondered. Summer didn't think she had ever experienced anything quite as nerve-racking before.

"I need to get back, Summer. Would you mind if Ben walked you home, so to speak?" David asked with a grin.

"Oh, there's no need," Summer hurriedly said.

"Say, Ben, why don't you come tonight if you can dig up the right clothes?"

Summer was frightened and so confused. Her traitorous heart couldn't stand another evening around Ben. "Oh, I'm sure he has other plans. He's quite the ladies' man, you know."

"Yeah, I know," David replied. "He's stolen more than one girl from me."

"I'm sure I can find something to wear, old buddy," Ben replied lazily. "I'll be there."

David waved and left.

Summer started to rise. "I have some things to do."

"Sit down," Ben said softly.

Summer sank into the chair.

"It happened. Pretending it didn't won't change things." He pulled her resisting hand from her lap and covered it with both of his.

Rigid, she sat, paralyzed by the emotion that swept through her just at his holding her hand. I'm lost, she thought. Lost.

He lifted her hand and kissed it. "I'll never forget last night. You were magnificent."

Summer couldn't help the swell of feminine pride nor still the words that needed speaking. "Neither will I forget," she whispered. When she looked into his eyes, she read hot desire. Her body responded to the wanton call.

His eyes dropped from her face to focus on her tightened nipples clearly visible through the cotton tank top. A pulse throbbed in her throat.

"I want to love you again," he whispered for her ears only.

"No, Ben, no." Summer tried to pull her hand away.

"Yes, again, and again."

The ferocity of her raging blood frightened her. Don't lose yourself, she exhorted mentally. He's danger. Stay away from him. Run away or he'll destroy you.

Ben held tightly to her hand. "I know you're afraid of the feelings between us, Summer, but don't be. What we feel is good and right."

"No," she almost sobbed. "Ben, I told you not to care

145

about me. You aren't what I want," she lied.

He released her hand. "I forgot. You want a rich man between your lovely thighs."

Miserable, Summer listened to his hateful hurting words.

"How can you even think of another man after last night?"

Summer let the words break over her. "You don't have any room to talk, Ben Carr. It's a safe bet that you've had more sexual liaisons than I have. Are you saying you love only me now?" Summer held her breath, waiting for his words.

"Wouldn't I be a fool to say that when I'm just a dirt-poor redneck you picked up?" Bitterness dripped from his words.

"That's right. I picked you up. I didn't marry you or give you the right to tell me how to live my life. So leave me alone!"

Ten

Summer went back to her room. The hard shell she'd erected around herself lay in ruins. The thought of facing the world without the barrier terrified her. Too tired to think, she crawled between the crisp sheets and cried herself to sleep.

An annoying buzz intruded into her exhaustion. Though she tried to ignore it, the sound grew louder and more irritating. She finally realized the buzzing was the telephone next to the bed. Fumbling in the darkness, she knocked the handset off. Retrieving it, she mumbled groggily, "Hello?"

"I thought you might need a bite to eat before tonight. You didn't eat much at lunch today. It'll be up a little later."

"Thanks, Ben," Summer managed, gripping the receiver until her knuckles turned white.

"Are you sure you want to go to this tonight?"

"Oh, Ben, don't start again."

"I'm not. You just sound pretty tired, that's all. I won't say a word about you and your plan, okay?"

"I'd appreciate that, thank you." Summer replaced the phone and snuggled back into the covers, wishing the world would go away, dreading the coming evening.

She caught herself falling asleep again and forced herself out of bed. A long soak in a tub of tepid water revived her. Her conscience really bothered her about David. Somehow when she'd thought about conniving her way into marrying a rich man, she hadn't thought that the man would be likable

—hadn't thought about his humanity at all. Surely a person as nice as David deserved a wife who loved him.

She sighed as she smoothed misty black hose over her legs. Every time she thought about her idiotic goal, she realized how humiliating it was for all concerned. The black lace bustier dress fitted her as if it had been designed just for her body.

When Summer looked in the mirror, she couldn't help but wonder how Ben would react. She fought the urge to cross her arms over her swelling breasts. The lace bodice revealed more than it concealed, nipping in at the waist and flaring out into a short, flirty skirt that drew the eye to her long legs. Three-inch-high black heels brought her to over six feet tall.

Summer shrugged her shoulders. The purpose of the dress was to attract attention, but now she wasn't interested in that kind of attention. In a few minutes, she had her makeup applied, deciding on a more natural look than she'd originally intended. She let her hair hang loose, brushing it behind her ears so the dangling black jet earrings showed.

After tucking the basic necessities into a beaded black bag the size of her palm, she was ready when Ben knocked at the door.

"Hi," she said. Her eyes rounded. "You look wonderful! He wore a white double-breasted suit that had to be silk. He looked so handsome, it hurt.

Ben's eyes darkened as he took in her appearance. Walking around her, he let out a wolf whistle. "Very sexy. Too sexy."

Anxiously she asked, "Do you think I'll look okay for David's club or is this too much?"

"Don't you have something else you could wear? Like a burlap bag or maybe a dress made of flour sacks?"

"Ben! Don't be silly. Please tell me if I look acceptable."

"My beautiful librarian, you look perfect. I just don't like the idea of every man there wanting you, and they will."

Summer wanted to walk into his arms. Any woman alive would be thrilled at the possessive tone in his voice, even as Summer told herself she was being foolish.

Another knock sounded on the door. "That should be our food," Ben said, opening the door to a waiter who pushed in a cart and made a show of setting it up between the two wing chairs. Ben signed the tab while Summer lifted a silver cover to discover a bowl of sliced strawberries and kiwi. Beads of moisture clung to the chilled surface of the crystal bowl. Another covered dish contained a huge bowl of boiled, peeled shrimp surrounding a small bowl of cocktail sauce. A coffee service and tumblers of ice water completed the light supper.

Summer sat in one of the chairs and poured the coffee. "Next time if I'm paying for it, don't order something as expensive as shrimp. I'm sure they had tuna sandwiches or something cheaper on the menu." The shrimp were delicious, though, she thought, savoring the tang of the cocktail sauce.

"Yes, ma'am." He seemed as determined to be pleasant as Summer was to be waspish.

After a bit, she poured another cup of coffee for each of them and sipped hers as she watched him put away the rest of the shrimp and the fruit. "You certainly have quite an appetite."

"Hey, what can I say, I'm a growing boy."

"Tell me more about this family of yours in Houston that you were so anxious to see."

"Well, there's Tracey, who's married and has a five-year-old son, and Merrick, Faye, and Sissy."

"Goodness! You mean your poor parents had to contend with five of you?"

"Yes, but I was the oldest and kept the others in line."

"I just bet. No wonder you think you're an expert on women—four sisters!"

Ben told of the scrapes they got in as kids, and Summer discovered she liked Ben and his family. Wistfully she thought how lucky he was to grow up with so much laughter and noise in his home, surrounded by two parents and a bunch of sisters. Though he complained mightily about the trouble they caused him, his love for them shone through like a beacon on a dark night.

David interrupted their intimate conversation when he called on the house phone. She told him she'd be right down.

"Don't you have a jacket or something to cover yourself?" His pointed gaze at her breasts had her flushing.

"Don't start," she warned, going to the closet for the matching lace jacket with tight, fitted sleeves. "I'm getting my jacket because air conditioning makes me cold, not to please you."

They walked out the door. When she opened her tiny purse to check to make sure the key card was there, she pulled out several folded bills and proffered them to Ben. "I thought maybe you might need a few bucks tonight—for the parking valet since you're not riding with us."

"Oh, I'm not?"

Summer ignored his question. "I don't want to hurt your feelings or anything, but I know you're short of cash right now, especially if you rented that suit. You can pay me back when you get a job." She didn't want him to think it was charity.

"Oh, right. That running tab of mine that you're keeping. Thanks," he said, handing it back to her, "but I've got it covered this time."

"Oh, all right, if you're sure." Flustered, she put the

money back in her purse. She clutched his jacket sleeve. "Ben, don't say anything to David about—" She broke off, not knowing how to ask him not to tell David about her plan to marry a millionaire. It seemed like such a pathetic joke now. By his expression, she saw immediately that he misunderstood.

"Oh, you don't want David to know that we slept together, is that it?"

"No!" She looked around to see if anyone heard. "Why must you always be so crude?"

"For a librarian, you don't have a very good understanding of words if you think 'crude' is the same as 'honest.' I'm not going to lie about us, if that's what you want."

"There is no *us*." Angrily she stomped toward the elevator, leaving him to trail behind. She stepped into the car when it opened immediately and left him above as she descended to the lobby. David was waiting for her when she stepped out of the elevator.

"Hello, gorgeous!" He leaned over and kissed her cheek.

Summer edged away from him and turned a strained smile on him. "Hello, David. You look pretty gorgeous yourself!" And he did, she kept telling the voice that said he wasn't Ben. His dark silk suit was impeccably tailored, his white shirt flawless, the muted colors of the tie perfect. But he wasn't Ben.

During the drive to his country club, she admired the sumptuous interior of his new BMW. To her dismay, he continued his stories about his and Ben's misspent youth. By the time she stepped from the car at the club, she felt as if she knew every chapter of the amorous adventures of Ben Carr.

She'd given in to her curiosity and asked David if he knew the Carr family particularly well. He'd laughed until tears came into his eyes, as if it were a big joke. Finally he had said no one knew the Carr family that well.

The liveried valet opened the immense carved oak doors for her. It was a good thing she had her hand on David's arm, she decided, otherwise she'd have expired from sheer fright. She'd never seen such an opulent display of wealth before. Oriental carpets covered oak parquet floors in the foyer and the halls. Gigantic Chinese vases, antique or reproduction, she didn't know which, held massive arrangements of fresh flowers.

The men and women milling around fitted the surroundings. She hoped she didn't look as gauche as she felt. David helped her out of her jacket. She folded it over her arm in case she needed it later. She saw more diamonds, pearls, and precious stones than she'd ever seen in any jewelry store. And even though it was the middle of the summer, there were a couple of women there with fur stoles. Surely that was pretentious, she thought, trying to be unobtrusive as she avidly looked around.

"You are, without a doubt, the most beautiful woman here," David said, his eyes on her swelling breasts. He shook his head. "I'm just a day late and a dollar short."

Summer wanted to ask him if he'd even seen the rest of her, but she didn't. After all, this was the image she had planned, she thought punishingly.

They made the rounds of the room. Summer got introduced to so many people that she knew she'd never remember all their names. The only one who stuck out in her mind was a young man named Greg who'd already had too much to drink. She didn't like the way his eyes assessed her.

Across the room, Summer saw Ben talking to an older couple. Her heart began to pound when she saw him, relaxed and laughing. Her pulse quickened at the very sight of him.

She licked her lips, remembering the gentle kisses he'd rained on her mouth.

"Come on, there's someone I want you to meet." David pulled her by the hand. Embarrassed, Summer found herself standing next to Ben and being introduced to Bennett and Irene Carson. Ben took her hand in his. Summer felt the blush that began at her breasts and rose to her hairline.

David smiled at her and patted her shoulder. "You're in good hands now, sugar." He winked at Ben and said to the Carsons, "Nice seeing y'all."

Bennett Carson suddenly cleared his throat with a loud harrumph. "I'd like to know what the devil—"

Ben interrupted him, earning a black look from Bennett Carson. "Your roses are lovely again this year, ma'am." Irene Carson seemed at a total loss for words. Finally she responded, "Yes, they are, aren't they? My *son* always loved the rose beds."

Nervously Summer smiled at the Carsons and tried to chat with them, but their monosyllabic answers defeated her. When they began asking questions more intrusive than cocktail chatter warranted, she felt very uncomfortable as she deftly tried to evade their questions. Not one smile had creased tall, big-boned Bennett Carson's freckled face. His dark-haired, petite wife looked stricken as her brown eyes searched Summer's face.

"If you'll excuse us, the lady promised me the first dance," Ben said with a smile at the Carsons.

Gratefully Summer let him lead her to the dance floor. She came into his arms, swaying to the strains of "My Funny Valentine."

"Hello, librarian."

Summer looked into his eyes and forgot the Carsons and their odd behavior. The desire in Ben's velvety brown eyes unraveled her. She couldn't pull her gaze away.

"You are the most beautiful woman here tonight."

"Thank you," she said, softly, her green gaze locked with his.

"And I want you more than I've ever wanted another woman."

Summer wanted to believe him, needed to believe him. She sighed when she felt his lips brush against her temple. All the tenseness drained from her muscles as she relaxed against him.

When the song ended, they left the dance floor. Ben guided her to a table where David sat. Summer remembered David was supposed to be her date for the evening even if he had handed her off to Ben. Teasingly she asked, "May I have the honor of the next dance, David?"

A woebegone expression flashed across David's face.

"What's wrong?" Summer asked.

David grimaced. "I hate to dance. Cotillion was a traumatic nightmare for me, and I've never got over it."

Ben laughed. "The only kind of dance David can do is the Cotton-eyed Joe, and that's after he's had a few beers."

"But that's okay, sugar," David said. "You just dance your heart out if you want. It won't bother me a bit."

Ben made sure Summer discovered the true meaning of fun as the evening aged. He ordered champagne, and the evening was lost in a fizzy blur. Ben whirled her through a crowd-clearing version of the jitterbug. Summer laughed as he turned her under his arm and she spun out. When the band played the closing notes of "Rock Around the Clock," she collapsed against Ben's chest. They both were breathing as if they had run a marathon. Couples around them applauded as they staggered off the floor.

The band swung into "You Made Me Love You," and Ben

pulled Summer into his arms, whirling her around before settling into a slow, romantic step.

Summer's laughter faded when she looked into his eyes. She felt helpless beneath the onslaught of her emotions. The words to the song echoed in her mind as she wound her arms around Ben's neck. Laying her cheek against his, she pressed against him, breast to chest, stomach to stomach, thigh to thigh.

"Having fun?" he asked in a silky murmur.

She could feel the strong beat of his heart against her breasts. "Oh, yes." Summer smiled, dreamily. "I don't think I've ever had so much fun before."

"Not even last night?"

She missed a step. "Don't bring that up, please."

"Why not? Wasn't that fun?"

"No it was . . . shattering."

He whirled her around and guided her to the edge of the dance floor, where it was darker. "I want you, Summer."

She stumbled over his feet.

"Feel how I want you, Summer." He pressed his aching hardness against her. She shuddered. He rubbed against her belly.

Would it be so bad to give in once more? she wondered, dizzily.

"You can forget about David. He's not for you."

"That's not for you to decide," she said shakily in a last-ditch effort to forestall him.

"Yes, it is. You'd make each other miserable."

"You don't know that. He's very nice. I like him a lot."

"He'll never make you feel . . . shattered. You and I fit together as if we were made for each other. It's never been like that with another woman, Summer. My God! You're not the only one who was shattered." He spoke love words softly into her ear, telling her what he would do later with his mouth and his hands and his body. He seduced her with the words of want and desire.

"Say yes, Summer, say yes."

She pulled back a little so she could look into his eyes. Tears glistened in her green eyes as she solemnly whispered, "Yes." Just once more, she promised herself.

Ben never released her hand until they got in his car. At every red light, he pulled her to him, kissing her, tantalizing her, teasing her, until her nipples were hard pebbles beneath the expensive dress. His hand brushed over her body, stoking the flames that burned through her. "Soon," he whispered against her mouth, "soon." His fingers slid into the bodice of her dress, pinching and rolling her nipples until she moaned aloud.

By the time they stepped off the elevator, they were practically running. As soon as they were inside the room, Ben pressed her against the door with his body, his mouth fitted to hers, his tongue dancing and parrying with hers. His large hands slid down her body and and around, cupping her buttocks and lifting her hips to the waiting hardness barely concealed by his clothes.

His moan filled her mouth. She reached up and unknotted his tie, pulling the ends loose, then slowly slid the buttons through the buttonholes.

Ben unzipped her dress. It fell at her feet, revealing her lovely breasts to his gaze. "My God, but you are beautiful."

Within minutes, he'd ripped off his clothes and stripped her of her panty hose. His breath was hot on her body as he pressed wet, sliding kisses on her neck and down, to capture a creamy pink nipple in his mouth.

"Yes, yes," Summer moaned, thrusting her hips against him.

Unable to make it to the bed, Ben lifted her and braced her against the door. Instinctively Summer wrapped her long legs around him. He saw the faint sheen of perspiration on her body when he entered her. She writhed against him, making him wild as he plunged in and out of her.

Ben didn't think he could hold on a moment longer when Summer suddenly stiffened and cried out. He exploded, pouring into her until he had nothing left.

Exhausted, muscles trembling, he leaned against the door as her legs unlocked and slid down his. He supported her weight for a moment, then found the strength to scoop her into his arms and carry her to bed.

They slept in each other's arms and loved each other awake until exhaustion forced them to slumber. As long as Summer lived, she knew she'd never forget this night.

Eleven

Everything seemed to be bathed in Technicolor hues, Summer thought when she got up the next morning. Surely the sky outside was brighter and a more vivid blue than she'd ever seen before. Her eyes perceived architectural details on the tall buildings that she'd not noticed before.

For the first time since she'd left Red Rock, her mind seemed sharp and clear. The confusion that had plagued her had disappeared. When she thought of Ben, she couldn't keep a secretive smile from lighting up her face, and a dreamy glow made her eyes soft and seductive.

He had left her side just after dawn. He'd told her he had a business appointment but refused to say anything else. She guessed he had a job interview. Suddenly it was very important to their relationship that he get a job, she realized.

Before she had time to get in the shower, the phone rang. A young woman's voice asked for Ben. Summer stiffened. Why had he given out this room number? To the woman she said, "He's not here. May I take a message?"

She felt as if a bucket of icy water had been poured over her when the woman said, "I was supposed to meet him this morning. Never mind. I'll track him down. Thanks anyway."

Hastily Summer asked, "Who is this? Hello? Hello?"

It was no use. She had hung up. Summer felt as if something inside had withered. She sank onto the bed, still holding the phone in her hand. She stared at the phone. Her whole world had crumbled in the space of a few minutes. Gently she replaced the receiver. Her body felt frozen. Her mind was equally numb, and her thought processes had ground to a halt.

Maybe the woman had the wrong room? No, she had asked for Ben. Could there be another Ben with a similar room number? She didn't think it very likely.

Anger began to melt the cold numbness. Jealousy engulfed her. How dare he seduce her and say all those things to her when he didn't mean them. How dare he make her love him! Love him? Oh, no. I can't love him! But Summer knew it was too late. Love had ensnared her heart.

Who was the woman who called? Hurtful, humiliating thoughts pummeled Summer. His girlfriend? Another lover? She thought she would be sick. Janine? No, never. Summer's imagination worked overtime. She'd been right about him. He wasn't interested in commitment. He'd just been using her. She'd been confused for days by her growing attraction to him, and he had played on that. The thought that she'd fallen so easily for him was like bile.

She'd been no match for him. He was a masterful lover with his sneaky words and his slow, caressing hands and his virile body. But he had done more than seduce her body, she cried silently. He had made her love him. Why, she'd actually been thinking about a future with him this morning. What a fool I am, she thought. It's my own fault. I made myself so vulnerable. How could I forget that vulnerability is just weakness?

Angry at herself for letting his fickle actions hurt so much, she rose from the bed. If only he were here. She'd tell him what she thought about him, and in no uncertain terms. She'd show him, she decided. He thought all he had to do was look at her with those bedroom eyes of his and she'd be as complacent as a cow. He had another think coming!

Shame burned in her when she thought of the money she'd given him, the things she'd bought for him, and most of all how easily she'd fallen into bed with him. I must have a screw loose, she thought. As she showered, she continued to castigate herself for yielding to him. I can't stay here for him to return with his lies.

After she'd dried her hair and applied her makeup, she studied the closet, thinking of all the money she'd invested in clothes. What a waste, she thought, jerking a cool mint green cotton slacks set from the closet.

She'd handle her anger and aggression by hitting those stupid little white balls around a golf course. Maybe she'd get lucky and find some rich old geezer out there she could land without feeling repulsed or guilty, she thought defiantly.

"But, Dad, you don't know Summer. She's funny and warm and intelligent," Ben answered the argument in his dad's blue eyes. "She's nothing like Janine."

"Ben, it just worries me. Not about her necessarily, she seems nice enough, but about you. Why are you tricking this young woman into thinking you're somebody you're not? You act like you're ashamed of being a Carson."

"No, Dad, you missed the point." Ben ran his hands through his hair. He looked around the large, country-style kitchen, remembering all the noisy meals the family had eaten there.

"Here, darling, have another pecan waffle." Irene Carson held a platter of warm, fragrant pecan waffles in front of him.

"No, thanks, Mom, I've had enough." Ben pushed his plate away. "Let me try again. You see, my car broke down and I was hitchhiking."

Again his parents exclaimed over such a foolhardy action.

He interrupted by telling about falling and getting muddy, then seeing Summer, then getting picked up by the farm laborers. Ben left out a few details, like sharing her bed at the motel and then becoming lovers with her once they reached Houston. He was pretty sure they could read between the lines. That's probably what bothered them.

He finished with a shrug of his broad shoulders. "So you see, I just wanted to find out what it was like to be a regular person. I needed to know if I could make it on my own without my money and name. Then I transferred that need to my relationship with Summer. I had to know if she could love me if I were just unemployed Ben Carr, not wealthy Bennett Carson."

"Of course, you had the hots for her," Big Ben said bluntly.

His son grinned. "Yeah, you might say that." His grin vanished. "I feel like a heel for deceiving her, but everything moved so fast. The more I was drawn to her, the more important it was to find out if she wanted me—just me."

"And?" His mother asked quietly.

"And what?" Ben sipped his coffee.

"And did you find out?" she asked in exasperation.

He grinned. "Yeah. I did. She wants plain old unemployed Ben Carr. What's more, she loves me, but it's not going to be easy to convince her of that."

"What?" his dad roared.

No way was he going to explain her fortune-hunting plan to them, he decided. "Hey, Mom, Dad, I've got to run. I need to tell Cecil something. I'll let you know when I'm going to bring her over. You'll love her when you get to know her." Ben pushed his chair back.

After he left, Irene and Ben studied each other. "What do you think, honey?" Ben asked his wife.

"I don't know what to think. He's acting like his brain's addled!" Irene exclaimed.

"Well, falling in love does that to a person."

"What if she's like Janine?" Irene looked troubled.

"Then he'll eventually find out for himself. I'm not going to make the same mistake I made last time by shooting my big mouth off about this woman. Nothing I said changed his mind last time. All it did was drive him away."

"Oh, Ben, I hope she truly is different."

"Well, we'll take her at face value. He's older and more experienced, so surely he knows the score. We'll just have to take it a step at a time." Ben opened his arms to his wife. They held each other in the silent kitchen.

Ben tapped on Cecil's apartment door above the garage. When the door flew open, Cecil Johnson stood there with a scowl on his face. The scowl changed to a crooked smile at the sight of Ben. "Git in here, young'un!" He pounded the younger man on the back.

Cecil insisted on pouring Ben a cup of coffee. They sat on the overstuffed beige corduroy sofa and talked about one thing and another before Ben told him about Summer—and her '57 Chevy.

Cecil questioned him intently. "Does it have the Triple-Turbine TurboGlide Transmission? How about the fuel-injected two eighty-three?"

Ben told him he thought it did. "She's having a problem with the solenoid. Do you think you can get one for her?"

"If I can put it on, I can," Cecil bargained.

"Deal," Ben said.

"Tell me, son, does it have the anodized aluminum rear fender panel?"

"No, Cecil, I'm sorry, it doesn't."

"Well, thunderation! That's too bad. What color is it?"

"Restored to the turquoise blue."

"That's a mighty pretty color. Always did like that better than that washed-out yeller." Cecil took a gulp of his coffee. "She's pretty special, huh?" Cecil asked.

Ben knew he was talking about Summer now and not the car. "Yes, she is. You know me, Cecil. I try not to be stupid twice the same way. She's the woman for me."

"Well, bring her around and let me have a look at her."

From the hotel to the rental shop to the golf course took Summer an hour and a half. Finding a set of ladies' golf clubs took more time than she'd thought it would. The third rental shop she'd called had a set of ladies' clubs, along with a collapsible rolling cart to hold them.

Summer parked her car between a shiny Lexus and a Mercedes station wagon and removed the aluminum carrier from the trunk. She settled the clubs in the cart and strolled toward the clubhouse. Huge live oak trees shaded the cedar and stone clubhouse. Yellow day lilies lined the sidewalk, and every blade of grass showed the care of a dedicated grounds keeper.

Despite the pastoral beauty of the scene, Summer felt as strung out as a piano wire being stretched ever and ever tighter. She took a deep breath and tried to relax. If nothing else, she'd end up with an amusing story to tell Annie and Wayne, she thought as she practiced her putts, never managing to maneuver close enough to the cup. She either overshot by many feet or fell short of the hole.

"You're too tense."

Startled, she struck the ball way too hard and it shot off the putting green, hit a tree, and ricocheted off to land in the parking lot.

"Thanks for the advice," she said sourly, turning toward the voice. A young man about her age with a putter over his shoulder got up from the low brick wall where he'd obviously been sitting and watching her.

"Hi, my name's Greg." He gave her a friendly smile.

"I know. I met you last night at the party." She didn't smile, but began to pack her putter away.

"You did?"

Summer nodded.

"Oh, wow. I can tell I made an ass of myself. I'm sorry if I did something to offend you. I wasn't myself last night."

He sounded so sincere and didn't seem a bit slimy in the way he looked at her today. "Who were you?" she asked with a smile.

"Apparently a real jerk." He pulled his sunglasses off to reveal bloodshot eyes.

"Well, we all are sometimes," Summer muttered. "Do you know anything about putting?"

With a laugh, he dropped a golf ball on the carpet of grass and bumped it toward the hole. The yellow ball rolled right into the cup. After he'd done that several times, she called a halt to the exhibition. "I give up. You're depressing me!"

"You want me to show you how to do it?"

"No, maybe some other time," she said.

"Then how about a drink and a bite of lunch?"

"I'd like that very much." She bagged the putter and pulled the cart away. "Would you mind if I put my cart back in my car?"

"No, let me help." He walked into the pro shop with his club and came back empty-handed. Gripping the handle of her cart, he said, "Show me where you're parked."

Summer found out he had played the pro circuit this past year. He practiced at this club because his family had been members here since he'd been in diapers. Old money. The words whispered through her, but she felt no excitement. Instead she found herself listening with interest to stories of getting established on the golfing circuit.

"I'm surprised your family agreed to your bumming around golf courses."

"Well, they weren't really happy about it even though they're both golf nuts. But they figure I'll get it out of my system early and then find something respectable to do."

"Are you any good?"

"Yeah, I am. You'll be reading about me one of these days."

"Then I guess I better get in the habit of reading the sports pages."

"You don't like golf much, do you?" he asked, studying her from beneath sandy lashes.

"No, I cannot tell a lie. Oh, I mean it's okay for you and others who can play, but I just can't get the hang of it."

"You're not a member here either, because I haven't seen you before, and I'd have remembered."

They stopped beneath a huge, spreading oak tree. Summer decided to be honest. "I'm crashing. What if I told you I just came here to meet a rich man?"

Greg guffawed loudly. "That's a good one. What are you really doing here?"

"Honestly, I came to Houston to meet and marry a rich man. Or I thought I did. But everything got crazy." She sighed. "Today I just wanted to to take my frustrations out on inanimate objects."

"Well, I'm not rich yet, at least not until I come into my grandmother's trust, but I've got a few bucks." He grinned.

"You mean you're not shocked?"

"Hey, you're not the first girl who ever had dollar signs in her eyes, but you are the first who was honest enough to admit it. I like that. Summer, I'll be candid with you. I'm not interested in getting married, so you might want to try the putting green again." He gestured over his shoulder.

"Oh, no, I don't think I could take any more today. Perhaps, in the spirit of honesty, I should tell you I've already tossed my plan in the garbage."

"Why did you change your mind?"

Summer sighed, "Well, I met someone."

"Oh, I begin to see. This someone changed your mind?"

She nodded reluctantly.

"Then that leaves platonic friends. You want to have a platonic relationship?" He wagged his eyebrows and winked.

"That sounds like an offer too good to refuse."

They started walking again, cutting across the parking lot to her car. "Wow, a 1957 Chevy Bel Air convertible!" Greg's voice held reverence. "Where did you get this?"

"Actually it belonged to my grandmother." She shook her head. "What is it with you guys and old cars? I don't understand it. You're the second man I've met in the last week who is nuts about this car. My friend said his dad had one. What's your excuse?" she finished with a laugh.

"Hey, don't you know anything about cars? Why, these came out of the plants able to do zero to sixty in under nine seconds. Chevrolet and Ford went head to head in 1957, and Chevrolet was the winner. But they only beat Ford by selling a hundred thirty-six more cars."

"Well, you sure know your auto history."

Sheepishly he grinned. "Actually, I learned all that from a guy that used to live next door. I thought he was so cool. He drove one of these when I was about eight. My dad tried to buy it from him when I turned sixteen, but Mr. Carson wouldn't sell."

"Mr. Carson? That's not the same man I met last night at the party, is it?"

"Yeah. I think he was there." Greg looked at her with humor in his light blue eyes. "Hey, is that why you were at the party last night? Scoping out the rich and famous?"

"Something like that," Summer admitted. "I went to the party with David Blackwood. I guess you know him, too?"

He nodded. "Yeah, if you hang around the money in this town, you pretty well know everyone else in the crowd. In fact, you can't sneeze without someone across town saying gesundheit."

Summer laughed. "I thought it was only like that in small towns like Red Rock, where I'm from."

"Well, the enclave of the rich is like a small town. Is David one of your prospects?"

Summer shook her head. "No, I decided I liked him too much to marry him."

Greg hooted with laughter. "That's a good one. Says a lot about marriage. But it's just as well. He's kind of a confirmed bachelor." He escorted her to the dining room of the clubhouse.

Ben parked at the school where Tracey taught special education. The grounds looked neater than the last time Ben had visited there. The shrubs were all trimmed, and fresh shredded pine bark mulch sent a clean, earthy smell through the air. In the school's office, Ben was told to wait while Tracey was paged in the cafeteria.

"Ben," the long-haired beauty exclaimed, throwing her arms around him.

"Hi, meanness." He jerked a strand of her hair.

She yelped in pretended pain. "I tried to call you at the hotel this morning to tell you I couldn't make breakfast at the old homestead. I even called Summer's room," she said slyly.

"What? Why'd you do that? Of all the . . . ! If I'd known you were going to pull a stunt like that, I'd never have told you about her last night! What did you say? What did she say?"

"Hey, relax. I didn't let your cat out of the bag."

Ben chewed his lower lip. "I hope you haven't caused me problems, Tracey."

"I'm sorry, Ben." Tracey wrinkled her brow. "I didn't tell her my name. Is that good or bad?"

"I don't know, but I guess I'll find out this evening."

She tucked her arm in his. "I'll be glad to call her back and explain who I am."

"No! I mean, no," he said in a calmer voice. "Let me take care of it."

"Come on, there's someone I want you to meet." Tracey tugged him toward the hall.

Ben met the nine kids in Tracey's group. With the principal's permission, he spent the afternoon talking with them and learning from the Down's syndrome kids.

"Aren't they a great bunch of kids?" she asked, her eyes shining with pride as she told him the strides each had made during the summer session.

"Yeah, they really are," he agreed. "Speaking of kids, how's my nephew Chad?"

She rolled her eyes. "Totally spoiled rotten, thanks to Mom and Dad. Despite our protests, they got him a new computer for his birthday. Do you remember when we were kids and they went through that 'learn the value of money' phase by making us work for the big-ticket items we wanted? Well, apparently that doesn't apply to grandchildren."

Ben laughed. "So you and Ryan are taking a page out of their book and making Chad 'earn' his money?"

"We try, but it's difficult. It's harder not to give your kid everything he wants than it is to make him earn it. But he's a good kid. He knows from the work we do with the hunger program and other things of that type that what he has is uncommon. I guess the thing that Ryan and I struggle with most is trying to teach him to judge people by who they are, not what they have."

Tracey kissed him on the cheek when he got ready to leave. "Will I see you and Summer with a big announcement soon?"

"As soon as I can convince her," Ben said, opening the car door. Driving away, he wondered what kind of father he'd make.

Over club sandwiches, Summer learned Greg's last name was Hickel and that he lived in the estate next to the Carson family. She also learned he had just broken up with a girl named Kim whom he'd dated since college. That explained his attempt to drown his sorrows last night, she suspected.

"Why don't you let me take you to dinner tonight?" Greg asked as he put her in her car later in the afternoon.

"Why don't you call Kim and tell her what you told me?"

He hung his head. "Not yet. She's probably still so mad at me that she'd just hang up. Come on, Summer. No strings. Just friends, remember?"

She thought about Ben but decided she didn't want to be at his beck and call after the phone call this morning. "Okay. I'd like to have seafood if that's all right with you?"

"That's great. I'll pick you up at your hotel at seven. Dress casually. I'm going to take you to a wild Cajun kitchen."

With a wave, Summer drove away. After she dropped off the golf clubs at the rental store, she headed back to the hotel. Imagined confrontations with Ben occupied her thoughts.

Her temper had cooled and her emotions had congealed. She knew exactly what she wanted to say to the lecher.

When she reached the lobby, she expected to find some kind of cajoling message, but there was nothing. Where was he? Where had he been all day? She'd wanted to have it out right now, but he hadn't returned and hadn't even left a message for her.

Summer finally decided to do what she'd planned—go to dinner with Greg Hickel. So she showered, standing a long time under the stream of water.

Deciding on a tea-length white linen skirt that buttoned up the front, she paired it with a simple green and white striped T-shirt and her white leather sandals.

Just as she was brushing her hair, the phone rang. Her heart began to hammer. She knew it was Ben. Clenching the hairbrush, she stared at the ringing phone. Should she answer it or ignore it? With every ring, her mind answered the question differently. Yes, answer it. No, ignore it.

Twelve

In the end, Summer couldn't stand the ringing phone. She grabbed it just as the caller hung up. She didn't know whether to be relieved or disappointed. With a glance at her wristwatch, she saw it was still a half hour before Greg should arrive. At loose ends, she paced the room a few minutes, then decided to go sit in the lobby and wait.

With her hand on the brass doorknob, she jumped, startled, when someone knocked on the door. This time, using the peephole, she saw Ben outside her door. Her anger had subsided. Left with the hurt and confusion, she leaned against the door, as uncertain about what to do as she had been when the phone had been ringing.

Ben pounded on the door. "Come on, Summer, I know you're in there. Do you want me to make a scene out here in the hall?"

Summer yanked the door open, his words setting fire to her temper. "I'd appreciate it if you didn't, thank you."

Ben looked at her appraisingly. "Going out?"

"Not that it is any of your business, but yes, I am." She looked him over, wishing he didn't look so appealing in faded jeans and a chambray shirt.

"Are you upset about something?"

"What could I possibly have to be upset about?"

"Well, my sister told me she had called here this morning for me, so I thought—"

"Your sister?" Summer interrupted. "I'm supposed to believe that was your sister?"

"Who else would I give your phone number to?"

"I don't know. You tell me." He sounded sincere. Should she believe him? She tried to maintain her cynical skepticism, but her heart rejoiced at his next words.

"Summer, you can believe me when I say what we have together is too special to risk losing it by seeing another woman." He walked over to look out the window. "This has moved so fast." Turning to face her, he said, "I know we don't know each other very well, but can't you trust the magic between us? For the record, I don't kiss and tell."

Summer shrugged helplessly. "That's just it, Ben, I don't know you at all."

"Oh, sweetheart." He pulled her into his arms, holding her, until the rigidity left her. "I know you've been dumped on a lot in life, but you can trust me. I won't hurt you."

"Oh, Ben." Summer drew a ragged breath. "I thought horrible things. I thought you were just using me," she confessed.

His lips sought hers gently and tenderly. Summer allowed herself to be persuaded. She silenced the distrustful voice inside and luxuriated in the comfort his arms offered her. The meaningless murmurs of solace anesthetized her disquiet.

"Ben, don't ever lie to me. If you want to see someone else, then tell me. But don't ever lie to me."

Ben's hands froze. His breath caught. With a loud exhalation, he said, "I won't, my sweet librarian. I won't."

Their kisses became more and more demanding. He'd thrust his hands through her hair, holding her head still for the assault of his tongue, when someone knocked on the door. With a muttered curse, Ben raised his head. "Who the hell is that?"

"It must be Greg," Summer whispered, her eyes glazed with desire.

Ben's brows snapped together in a furious scowl. "Greg who?" he demanded curtly, his hands sliding to her shoulders.

"Greg Hickel, my date for the evening."

"Greg Hickel! What are you doing going out with him?"

"I met him at the golf course today. He's very nice. We kind of hit it off," she finished lamely.

"Let me see if I get this straight. You were mad as hell at me because you *thought* I had made a date with some woman?"

Summer nodded uneasily.

"Yet you see nothing wrong with you continuing to pursue this insane plan?"

"I just went because I was mad at you!"

"Right. You haven't given up on it yet, have you? I think I'm beginning to understand. You think you'll keep me, poor unemployed stud that I am, on the side, and still marry some rich idiot like that puppy Hickel."

"No! It's not that way at all!" His words hurt her. Did he really have such a low opinion of her?

"Well, you can't have it both ways, Summer." He shoved her away and turned his back. Another knock on the door sounded.

Ben whirled and pierced her with his midnight eyes. "You have to decide now. Me or your fantasy."

Summer paled. What did he mean? The silence stretched between them. Was he offering her a permanent commitment? She looked at Ben, anticipation evident in every fiber of his body. A vision of her mother, wasting away in a hot hovel of a house, rose before her eyes. Summer wiped her hands across her eyes as if to erase the memory. She raised her eyes to his face, searching for the meaning behind his words.

Another knock sounded at the door. Summer stumbled slightly on her way to the door. She opened the door in time to see Greg turn to leave. "Greg, I'm sorry. I was detained."

His easy smile covered his annoyance. "That's okay. Are you ready to corral some crawdads?"

"I'm sorry, Greg, but I must cancel our plans." Summer looked over her shoulder and smiled at Ben. "I've decided to retire from fortune hunting."

"Huh? Come again?" Greg asked, straining to see who stood behind Summer. Greg's eyes widened.

Summer didn't notice the bewilderment on Greg's face. She pulled him into the room. "Greg, I'd like you to meet someone. You and he have a lot in common since you both love old cars."

Ben held his hand out. "Glad to meet you, Hickel."

"Uh, yeah, likewise," Greg mumbled in confusion.

After a few silent moments, Greg mumbled, "Uh, guess I'll go now." Summer turned to walk him to the door and didn't see Ben grab Greg's arm and make frantic signals for Greg to be silent. Nor did she see Greg nod absently.

"Come here," Ben commanded as soon as Greg left.

Summer walked toward him. She hadn't wanted to marry money, she wanted to tell him. All she wanted, without realizing it, was to find someone to belong to—someone to cherish her. Her heart in her eyes, she said, "I choose you, Ben Carr, you poor unemployed stud."

Ben frowned.

Why did he still look upset? she wondered. Had she misunderstood? Hadn't he made a commitment by making her choose?

He walked up to her, looked into her eyes, and said, "You

won't regret this, my darling librarian." With that he kissed her, sealing his commitment in the way she loved best.

Later, lying next to him, she wondered how long she'd have him before he became restless. "I love you, Ben," she whispered to him, secure in the knowledge that he had fallen asleep.

"When are you going to marry me?" he asked, startling her.

She rose up. "I thought you were asleep."

"Don't evade the question, sweetheart."

Marriage. Nonplussed, she thought about being married to him. Living with him, sleeping with him every night. She tingled at the thought, envisioning their life together. They'd work hard through the week then have the weekend to play. In a few years, when they could afford it, maybe they'd have a baby. Tears overflowed her eyes as she thought of a child, part of each of them. "Whenever you like," she said, choking back the tears.

"Hey, sweetheart, why are you crying?"

"Because I never expected this. To fall in love, to have a normal life, a real family."

"Well, you'll certainly have a real family. Maybe more than you bargained for with all my nosy sisters and my parents and all the other assorted nuts in the family tree."

Summer lay next to the man she loved and thought about having relatives, a novel idea. "Do you have aunts and uncles and cousins, too?"

"You bet. Enough to thrill you." He nibbled on her neck.

"Will I get to meet your parents tomorrow? Or am I going to this family reunion of yours that you told me about?"

"Summer, I need to tell you something."

"Yes, you do. I said the words, but you didn't."

"What words?"

"You know, Ben Carr, those three little words."

"My mother always told me actions speak louder than words." He made her forget her plea to hear him speak of his love for her. In fact, she thought he could make her forget her own name as she strained for fulfillment in his arms.

The next morning when she woke, the first thing she thought of was that he had evaded her gentle prodding. He still hadn't said he loved her; at least he hadn't said what he'd taught her on his body. She had him gasping and rigid with need. With a smile, she gave him the relief they both wanted. They shared the shower, and he ordered breakfast while she styled her hair.

Nervously she opted for a sleek, rather severe style with her hair drawn back from her face and twisted tightly into a chignon at the nape of her neck. In dismay, she noticed that dark roots showed already in her hair. She wished she hadn't colored it. What if Ben didn't like the natural color? And what if his parents got the wrong impression of her?

A yellow tropical print skirt paired with a coordinating crocheted top with matching appliqued flowers looked breezy and just right for her meeting, she hoped. Donning white leather flats, she walked from the dressing room.

He stood and seated her. "You look very beautiful this morning." He poured her a cup of coffee from the carafe.

"Thank you for the compliment—and the coffee." She sipped and looked at the rather large breakfast he'd ordered. "Ben, I don't want to rain on our parade. And this is very lovely." Her hand gestured toward the breakfast of honeydew, eggs benedict, fresh orange juice, and coffee. "But if we're going to get married, then we have to start thinking of the future."

"What do you mean?"

"Well, we have to stop ordering room service. And I need

to check out of here and into something more reasonable. Where have you been staying? With your parents?"

"Uh, yeah." He avoided her eyes.

"Well, I guess it wouldn't be right for me to stay there until after we were married."

"Oh, it's all right for us to shack up at the hotel but not under their roof?" A devilish grin crossed his face.

"Don't be—"

"Crude," he finished for her with a grin.

"And don't change the subject," Summer replied. "I'm giving up my fantasy plan, but that doesn't mean I just want to live a hand-to-mouth existence. Between both of us, we should make a good income. And I own a house already if you can find work in Red Rock. . . ." Her voice trailed off. There were no construction jobs in Red Rock except for the occasional need for a handyman.

"Hey, don't look so sad, Summer. We're going to be just fine," Ben promised smugly.

Determinedly she put a smile on her face. "You're right. I still have a few thousand dollars, and I'll be careful with it now. And I don't have to live in Red Rock. I can probably get a job anywhere. I could even sell my house if need be."

"I don't think we need to do that. Let's slow down and take it a step at a time. Before we start planning our careers and how much we're going to spend for electricity and food, shouldn't we get married first?"

She laughed. "I guess so. What kind of wedding do you want?"

"A speedy one!"

"At least we've agreed on that," she said, taking a bite of the hollandaise-drenched eggs. "I'll forgo the forty-foot train and the twenty bridesmaids," she teased.

"Then we'll have to get married by a justice of the peace or at one of the wedding chapels, because if my mom has her way, you'll have forty bridesmaids."

"The only person I really want there is Annie, and her husband Wayne, of course. What about you? Will your sisters come with your mom and dad?"

"Merrick won't be able to get here fast enough, but Tracey and her husband Ryan can, along with Sissy, Faye, and my parents. And I'll ask Blackwood if he promises not to flirt with you."

Summer thought he looked troubled. "Are you worried about what your parents are going to say? I mean, this is sudden. We haven't known each other very long."

Ben was boxed in and there was no way out. He should have told Summer days ago who he was, but it had been so damned hard. Hell! He'd almost forgotten himself that he wasn't Ben Carr.

Then she'd exacted that promise from him to be truthful to her. It got harder and harder to tell her. Frankly, he was worried how she was going to take it. And he couldn't introduce his parents to her since she'd already met them as the Carsons.

He'd wanted to tell her last night but had chickened out. He sighed. He had to tell her. They couldn't get a marriage license until he told her. But he was afraid. Afraid that she'd think he was stringing her along. What was he supposed to do? Simply say, *Oh, by the way, Summer, I'm really as rich as an Arab sheik—I was just conducting a little experiment to see what it was like to be Joe Average*? Somehow he didn't think she'd understand. The longer he kept his secret, the worse he felt. His conscience was eating him alive.

"I'm going to call Annie after breakfast, if that's all right. Then I'll be ready to meet Mom and Pop Carr," she joked.

"Oh, uh, they're busy today," he said lamely.

Her smile slipped a notch, but all she said was, "That's all right. We can study the employment section of the newspaper and draw up a budget. Then we can plan our wedding."

Ben groaned. His stomach churned. He pushed his plate away and watched her eat every bite of her breakfast.

"Thank you. That was wonderful." She kissed him on the cheek. "After we plan our wedding, we can rehearse the honeymoon part again," she whispered in his ear. With a smile, she took a cup of coffee to the couch, where she sat and reached for the phone to call her friend.

Ben had to figure something out and soon, he thought desperately. He rehearsed different scenarios while she talked.

"What do you mean you're getting married?" Annie shrieked.

Summer held the phone away from her ear. She grinned at Ben as he chuckled.

"Do you mean to tell me you actually met a rich man and got him to propose in less than a week?"

"Well," Summer confessed, "I met a wonderful man and he proposed. That part is right, but he's not rich, Annie. In fact, he doesn't even have a job right now." A quick glance in Ben's direction showed a look of pain flash across his face before he stood and waved at her, pantomimed going for a walk.

"What? Summer, hold everything. I'll be there by tonight."

Summer laughed. "Annie, calm down. I don't need you to rescue me from his clutches, but if you'd like to come, I'm getting married Sunday afternoon." She suddenly decided, "At one of the wedding chapels here. Nothing fancy."

Summer ignored Annie's protestations and finally ended the conversation by saying, "If you and Wayne can get away, why don't you come down Friday. That way we'll have a couple of days for you to get to know him."

"Where are you going to live?"

"I don't know. Everything is still pretty much up in the air. We have a lot of decisions to make."

"I knew you'd crack up like this one day, Summer James. You just repressed too long, and the first man you met, you fell for."

Summer laughed. "Come on to Houston, Annie. I miss you and your wacked-out dime-store psychology."

Ben came back fifteen minutes later and took Summer to meet Tracey at her school. He had no doubts left about Summer when he saw her with Tracey's students. There was no cringing when she talked with the kids, just honest, open affection.

"Ben, she's wonderful. You struck oil this time." Tracey looked over to where a little girl sat beside Summer.

Summer looked up and caught Tracey and Ben looking at her. She smiled at them and thought again how familiar Tracey looked to her. She was positive she'd seen her somewhere before.

After lunch at the school, Ben filled the afternoon with a sight-seeing trip to Munger Street to see the Orange Show. "I loved this place as a kid," he explained. "Seeing all those disks of aluminum hanging from all the eaves, twinkling in the sunlight. It was like junk immortalized."

"Kind of a recycler before his time," Summer suggested.

The only cloud on her horizon was that Ben never mentioned going to get their marriage license, and he still hadn't made arrangements for her to meet his parents.

"Let's go back to the hotel for a siesta." Ben leered at her until she laughed.

"Are you sure you're just interested in sleep?"

"Why don't we find out?"

Summer leaned back against the leather seat of the Allante. She'd really miss this opulence when he gave the car back.

He dropped her off at the lobby and went to park the car. She stopped at the desk when the concierge called her name. "A young man has called several times and left messages for you." He handed her several pink slips.

She studied them in the elevator. Why was it so "imperative," she wondered, studying the underlined word, that she call Greg Hickel as soon as she came in? Shrugging, she called as soon as she got to her room.

"Summer, I'm going nuts trying to figure out what to do."

"What do you mean, Greg? Do about what?"

"About you and Ben. I mean I really like him. He was my boyhood idol. This isn't like him. I can't figure it out."

"Greg, what are you rambling about?"

"I wouldn't even have called if I hadn't liked you so much. You remind me of Kim. By the way, we made up. Which is why I thought I should call you, I guess."

Summer rolled her eyes. Greg wasn't making a bit of sense. "Is this about Ben? Do you know Ben?"

"Yeah, I do. Summer, do you know Ben?"

"Greg, this conversation isn't going anywhere. Of course I know him. I introduced you two, remember?"

"That's just it. I already knew him. He indicated to me not to mention it. Summer, his name isn't Carr. It's Carson."

A chill swept over Summer. "No, it isn't. His name is Carr."

"No, it's Carson, Harding Bennett Carson. I should know. His family and mine have lived next to each other since before we both were born."

181

In a strangled whisper Summer asked, "Are you telling me that he's the son of Bennett and Irene Carson, the couple I met who live in River Oaks?"

"Yes! In River Oaks next to my family. I don't know why he's pretending to be somebody he's not, but I don't think it's right. I spoke to his dad earlier, and he said Ben was staying at the Carson suite a few floors above you at the hotel."

He rambled on, but Summer had lost the ability to hear the words, much less understand them. Dazed, she gently placed the phone on the cradle. At first she couldn't make sense of the words Greg had spoken. They bobbed like flotsam on a tide of despair. Gradually the words coalesced into a dark, terrifying thought. Ben had cruelly tricked her. Played with her as if she were some lesser being not due respect.

A painful vise squeezed her heart. It was all her fault. How could she blame him? She'd started it with that stupid plan of hers. She laughed wildly as tears stung her eyes. He'd been having fun with her. Had he enjoyed toying with a money-grubbing conniver like her? That must be what he thought of her.

Like acid poured on a wound, she thought of standing with him next to his parents at the party. They had to have known. And David, and Greg! Ben's sister Tracey. Everyone had known!

Bile boiled from her throat. She ran to the bathroom. Tears streamed down her face as she rinsed her mouth. She felt so tired, so dead. But the memories wouldn't leave her alone. Her lecturing him on the value of a dollar, volunteering to draw up a budget for their future.

Their future! What a cruel joke! Summer understood it all. He'd even warned her about his ex-wife. But she'd put her own interpretation on everything he'd said. He must have decided to teach her a lesson as soon as he'd heard about her plan.

How cruel to seduce her, trick her into loving him. Did he have to make her think they were getting married? She would never marry. She'd always be alone. Summer wept for the dream she'd lost. Even if she ever got over Ben, she'd never be so stupid and naive as to trust a man again.

The hot rage, the tearing grief froze inside her. He'd used her, just like her father had used Rachel. Icy resolve stopped her tears. He wouldn't get away with it, she decided. Maybe he needed to learn a lesson, too, she thought as she washed her face and applied fresh makeup.

He should be up here any minute. She was surprised he hadn't already arrived. Maybe he'd gone up to his room to replenish his supply of birth control, she thought cynically. Surely they'd used up all the ones he'd had last night. At least he couldn't get in without the key card, and she had the only one to her room. She had to figure out what to do before he arrived.

When he knocked, she ignored it. She was no closer to an answer now than she had been an hour ago. What was she to do? Questions plagued her. When had he planned to tell her? On the steps of the courthouse? After one more tumble in bed? Was that why he had brought her back to the hotel?

Relentlessly the questions tortured her until a brittle calmness settled over her. She began to plot her revenge. She must let Annie know not to come. Summer thought of a million details to keep from thinking about Ben and the way he kissed her and held her when he was so deep inside her that she thought he had pierced her soul.

Thirteen

When Summer jerked the door open and saw Ben, for a moment she wanted to crumple at his feet and beg him to tell her it wasn't true. His beloved face caused an ache deep inside. How could she never look on his face again without dying a little, day by day? But the moment passed. Her next impulse was to slap that handsome face until his ears rang. She curled her fingers into fists. How could he have done this to her? What kind of heartless, demented person was he?

"What took you so long to open the door?" He kissed her cheek as he walked past, pulling his shirttail out.

So he thought he could waltz in here and snap his fingers and she'd hop into bed with him! He'd been too spoiled by women falling at his feet, obviously.

"Oh, I was trying to decide what to wear tonight," she said breezily, walking past him to her closet.

"How about your birthday suit?" He walked up behind her, his hands stroking familiarly over her rounded buttocks.

She slid away as if to peer into the closet. "Ben, not now. We're going out!"

"We are?" He frowned.

"Aren't we going to the courthouse for our marriage license? Then I thought afterwards, we could go celebrate."

"Oh, uh, well, the license division will be closed by the time we could get over there. Let's do it first thing in the morning. We have a lot to talk about tonight." He hung his head. "There are some things I want to tell you."

Yeah, she thought, I just bet there are. Things like *You're a fool, Summer James!* Aloud she said, "Well, I guess waiting one more day won't be a problem. But come on, let's go celebrate anyway," she said with forced gaiety she didn't feel.

"Sure, if that's what you want," he said, quickly pulling her into his arms.

She stood as still as a statue, praying not to feel a thing when he kissed her, denying her body's quickening. He shaped her lips with his own, drawing the unwilling response from her. In a panic, she pushed him away and untangled herself.

"Oh, I'm such a mess. I feel so sticky. This Houston humidity is really something." She laughed nervously. "Why don't you go change into something dashing, and I'll meet you downstairs in an hour?" She pushed him toward the door.

He looked hurt. "Sure, if that's what you want." With a puzzled look, he turned and left. She double-locked the door behind him and leaned weakly against it.

With sheer grit, she pulled herself together. Automatically she went through the ritual of grooming herself. When she looked into the mirror, she saw a white-faced stranger looking back. She applied more blusher, stroking the coral powder lightly over her clammy skin. The woman in the mirror looked like one of those black-and-white pictures from *Vogue.* All angles and hollows. That's what Summer felt like, brittle and hollow. As if her heart and soul and brain had been removed. A walking, talking zombie, ladies and gentlemen!

The tight, crinkle-knit black dress emphasized her body and left little to the imagination. She pulled the stretchy fabric lower on her arms so that her shoulders and a greater expanse of creamy skin were revealed. The built-in bra cups pushed her breasts up until they seemed ready to pop out of the bodice.

Summer nodded in approval. She looked as dangerous as she felt. With shaking hands, she tugged on her hair, fluffing and pulling it out, spraying it with liquid styling gel until it was a wild, scrunched halo around her overly made-up face.

When she walked into the lobby, Ben wasn't the only man who stared. Summer swaggered up to him, deliberately swaying her hips more than necessary. The heels she wore, the highest she owned, put her nearly at eye level with him. She was determined to seduce him tonight, have him salivating after her, wanting her as much as he'd made her want him. Then she'd be the one to drop him like a soiled tissue.

He took her to an elegant French restaurant on Westheimer and impressed her by ordering in French. She didn't comment on his command of the language. He'd just tell another outlandish lie. When she thought of all the lies, the dumb coincidences that she'd never questioned, she cringed at her stupidity.

A harpist played music that sounded like water sliding over smooth stones. The quiet strings should have soothed Summer, but her mind and body were in such turmoil that she doubted anything would have calmed her.

She slipped her black silk pump off and ran her toes up the calf of Ben's legs. When he jumped as if struck by an electric wire, she smiled, satisfied at his response. The week hadn't been a total loss, she thought. She'd more than made up for her lack of experience in the sexual arena, thanks to Ben. Next she squeezed his knee and lightly traced the crease of his trousers.

He gripped her hand. "What are you doing?" His eyes burned in a face suffused with heat.

"I don't know. I must not be doing it right if you have to

ask," she whispered, licking her lips slowly. Her eyes met his boldly, then dropped down to slide over his body.

He actually squirmed. Before he could speak, the wine steward brought their wine. Summer watched Ben go through the ritual, and after the steward left, Ben lifted his glass and said, "To the most maddening woman I've ever met."

Summer inclined her head and drank deeply; the icy Chardonnay slid easily down her throat. "Um, that's very good. I'll have another, please."

Ben filled her glass, frowning when she lifted it and drank half of it. "Don't you think you should slow down? It's been a long time since lunch."

"Well, that depends. Am I paying for this wine?"

Ben looked as if she'd slapped him. "I guess so," he said tightly.

She drained her glass. "Then I'll have another." Summer wished the wine would remove some of the coldness, but she didn't feel any effect from the alcohol at all. But she'd keep drinking, because it obviously upset him. And anything that upset Mr. Harding Bennett Carson pleased her mightily.

He didn't say anything when she reached out for the bottle and refilled her own glass. This time she didn't drink, though. She decided to explore the art of conversation.

"Tell me, darling, more about your ex-wife. Janine."

"I've already told you everything important about her."

"Where does she live now?"

"In Los Angeles. She hooked up with a video producer."

"Do you still carry a torch for her?"

"How can you ask that after us?" He looked more puzzled than angry, she decided.

"Well, sometimes I still think about Steven." She sighed.

"Who the hell is Steven?" His voice drew the attention of several other diners.

"Ben, really, must you be so loud?" She sipped her wine, planning what to say. "He was my first love." Summer spun a tale of lusty young love, embroidering the episode considerably. By the time his face looked like he was ready to explode, she changed the subject. "You know where I'd love to live after we're married?"

"No," he asked cautiously, "where?"

"In Los Angeles, just like your ex-wife. What an exciting city! Why, think of all the things to do and people to see." She added as an afterthought, "Oh, and there must be a lot of jobs for laborers in a place that big. Or you could always sign up for welfare?" She batted her eyes at him.

"I'm not a laborer," he ground out between clenched teeth, "and I wouldn't live in L.A. even if they guaranteed it wouldn't fall off into the ocean someday." He tossed back his wine and poured another.

"What the hell is wrong with you tonight?" His hand gestured toward her. "The way you look. Then you tell me you want to move to L.A. And you tell me about some bozo you were in love with who was every woman's dream. Do you still love that idiot? I thought by the way you responded to me . . ." His voice trailed off.

He looked as confused and as hurt as she felt. No, she amended. He couldn't possibly hurt as bad as she did.

Their dinner was served, and Summer decided to let him stew in his bewilderment. She didn't want to push him too far—yet.

Picking at the bundle of whole green beans tied with a carrot strip, she systematically cut them into half-inch pieces. She managed a few bites of the squash puree but thought she'd choke if she tackled the broiled lobster.

Halfway through their meal, she resumed her campaign. "You look very handsome tonight, Ben." She laid her knife and fork down. Her right hand disappeared from the table and landed lightly on his leg, trailing up his thigh, sliding toward the warmth at the juncture of his legs.

Despite his earlier anger with her, his eyes flared. Men were so predictable, she thought scornfully.

With her left hand, she picked up her wineglass and sipped. She hadn't managed to eat enough of the expensive meal to absorb the alcohol. Even though the wine had begun to make her feel light-headed, she kept sipping it to moisten her dry mouth.

This time, instead of scolding her for her actions, he laid his hand atop hers and pressed her hand to his groin. Her breath quickened when she felt the iron-hardness of his desire. He groaned softly. Branded by his touch, she jerked her hand away.

"I know I implied I didn't like the way you're dressed," he whispered, "but I didn't mean it." He reached up and captured her hand, pulling her tight fist into his warm palm. "You look like every man's fantasy. I just don't like other men looking at what I claim as mine." His eyes caressed her breasts.

"So you see this dress as a problem?"

"Yes," he said, grinning, "but the problem is easily removed. Why don't we go back to the hotel, and we'll eliminate the problem."

Summer felt the tables turn.

He leaned closer to her. "Do you have on panty hose?"

She shook her head; her senses reeled, visualizing how it would be with his mouth on her body, kissing her inch by inch as the clothes were slowly removed. "I have on a black lace garter belt with matching panties."

"Oh, hell," he croaked. He raised his hand to call their waiter over.

Summer ran the tip of her tongue around her lips again. His eyes followed her pink tongue. "If we don't get out of here soon, you'll be ravished right here on the tabletop."

Summer's heart pounded. This wasn't a game anymore. She wanted to curse at the desire that flooded her body. The blood pounded through her veins, and she didn't think she could wait until he made love to her. "I think the tabletop might be okay," she whispered huskily.

"You're playing with fire, librarian."

"Am I?" She lowered her eyes, staring at his groin.

"Check, please!"

On the way back to the hotel, he steadfastly refused to look at her or touch her. Even though he didn't touch her, he could still smell her, that elusive musky scent that drove him wild. He remembered smelling it between her breasts when he kissed her there and at her waist and knee and ankle.

Stop, he commanded himself, pressing the accelerator harder. He thought back to earlier in the evening when she'd acted so strangely. Had that been her or the wine talking? And if the wine had released that torrent of nonsense, had it been uninhibited truth or mere girlish prattling?

He didn't know the answers to those questions, and that bothered him. Maybe she wasn't the woman he thought? He refused to consider that. He couldn't be fooled twice in a row.

He wished he'd told her the truth already, then he could stop this pretense of being penniless. He wanted to shower her with gifts, anything her heart desired. He hated her thinking he was sponging off her.

When they reached the hotel, he let the valet have the car. They squeezed into the revolving door together, Summer giggling. He smelled the wine on her breath. When they entered the lobby, arm in arm, he couldn't help notice the way every man's eyes groped her.

He didn't like it, but he'd have to get used to it. He couldn't very well make her wear burlap sacks. And he knew the dress she wore and her hairstyle were all very *in* now. With a sigh, he resigned himself to being a silently possessive husband.

Behind the locked door of her room, he decided he could live with that. He kept a tight rein on his emotions as he slowly peeled the dress from her. His body, hot and tight, threatened to explode. Summer's eyes were so dark, they looked almost black. He noticed the slight shaking of her breasts with each pulsating beat of her heart. He kissed the throbbing pulse in her throat.

When he brought her to fulfillment, she wept, huge tears sliding from between tightly closed eyes, sobs shaking her slender shoulders.

"Sweetheart! What's wrong?" He stroked her hair from her face and wiped her tears gently with his fingers. He didn't understand what was happening. Something was bothering her, but she wouldn't confide in him.

"Nothing is wrong. It was just so . . . so completely devastating."

He grinned. Her words appealed to his male ego. "For me, too," he admitted, kissing her closed eyes.

If only he didn't have the secret of his identity hanging over him. Wryly he wondered if perhaps he should just change his name to Ben Carr. It sure would avoid the problem. He'd rather die in her arms than hurt her, he realized. He was afraid she wasn't going to take it very well, because he'd been over it in his mind, wondering how he would have felt. He'd come to the conclusion that he'd have felt like someone was playing a dirty trick on him. But he wasn't tricking her. He intended to marry her, so that would make it all right, he rationalized again.

Summer pushed at Ben. He obligingly rolled away. She got up from the bed and went to shower. She needed to wash his scent from her body. Resentfully she stared at his sleeping form.

She'd failed tonight. Instead of teasing and tormenting him, then telling him off and leaving, she'd become caught in her own trap. The shower cleared the fuzziness from her head. She slipped into a nightgown for the first time since she'd started sleeping with Ben.

She dashed from the bathroom to pick up the phone when it rang. With surprise, she noted that it was only eleven o'clock.

"This is Annie. I'm downstairs. You didn't tell me your room number this morning, and these officious idiots here won't give it to me."

"Oh, Annie, I'm so glad you're here. Come on up." Summer gave her the room number, put her robe on, and ran to the door, opening it a crack so she could catch Annie before she knocked.

She embraced her friend, pulling her into the room. "Oh, Annie!" she cried, fighting tears.

"Summer, I came to talk some sense into you." Annie stopped, staring at Ben sprawled in the bed. "Wow! He really is gorgeous." Then her eyes swung to Summer's attire. "Oh!"

Summer blushed furiously.

Just then Ben stirred. The two women stilled, but he roused further, finally opening his eyes and looking at them. "You must be Summer's friend Annie." He grinned and pulled the sheet up to where he was more modestly covered.

"Yes, I'm Annie Redmond. How do you do?"

"Very well, thank you." He smiled as Annie blushed to the roots of her hair.

"Yes, well," Annie looked around helplessly.

"If you ladies will turn your backs, I'll go shower. You can have a nice chat while I dress."

Warily they eyed the bathroom door. The sound of the shower was their signal to start talking. They sat together while Summer told Annie the whole story, leaving out nothing.

"I can't believe it. This sounds like something in a soap opera. I told you not to do this!"

"Oh, Annie, I don't need an *I told you so.* I need to get out of here as soon as possible."

"But you love him, don't you? How can you just walk away?"

"Because he doesn't love me." Summer wrung her hands. "Oh, he was really hurt by his ex-wife. He told me once that she just married him for what he had. Now I know that means millions of dollars."

"But why propose to you and, and . . ." Annie waved her hand toward the bed.

"I don't know. I've been over and over it in my mind. I think he got fixated on teaching me a lesson. Maybe it all started as some kind of joke. Kind of a punitive example for other fortune hunters. I don't care why he did it. All I know is, I'm going to make him pay for what he's done to me." *For making me love him,* she cried, her heart breaking.

"Take it easy. None of this makes any sense, Summer. I think you need a cooling-off period. You sound as crazy as he is. And if what you say is true, he's not just crazy, he's depraved!"

Ben stepped out of the shower to grab Summer's shampoo

from the vanity. The women's voices carried. He heard Summer say, "Annie, he's got millions. He's a regular golden boy when it comes to business, I understand. He's going to pay in a big way."

The blood drained from Ben's face. He gripped the vanity to keep from falling.

"What happens when he finds out you knew all along?" Annie asked.

"It won't matter, Annie. I'll have the last laugh on Harding Bennett Carson."

Ben hung his head.

"He'll pay," Summer repeated.

Ben thought the room actually swayed. Blood roared in his ears. Was this what it felt like to die? he wondered. This hurt so much worse than Janine's betrayal. Summer's words damned his plans for a life with her and broke his heart.

Summer knew who he was. Had known all along probably. She had executed her plan perfectly. She'd come to Houston to find some rich moron to marry but had lucked out by finding one along the way. When had she learned his true identity? He searched his mind trying to discover a moment when he could have told by her expression that she knew.

He leaned both hands against the vanity, gripping the cold marble edge to keep from falling to his knees and howling his outrage at the world. How had he fallen for another lying, deceiving woman? Was he congenitally stupid? Oh, she was good with her innocent act, her sanctimonious parsimony. Everything about her was an act, a lie.

The words burned in his mind like acid. So she planned on making him pay? Savagely he thought, we'll see who pays. He switched the shower water to cold and stepped under its spray. The water couldn't match the chill in his heart as he coldly plotted his revenge against the woman who'd betrayed him.

Making a lot of noise, Ben exited the bathroom, taking satisfaction in the startled faces of the two women.

"I know you two have a lot to catch up on so, I think I'll mosey on back to my dad's humble abode," he said sarcastically.

"Nice meeting you, Annie," he said blandly, looking over the small woman. Another schemer, he decided. Had they hatched this together?

"Yes, Ben, same here." Annie looked rather green when she attempted to smile.

He turned to Summer. His smile didn't reach his eyes, but she didn't notice since she was staring at Annie's sickly face. "Walk me to the door?"

Summer hurried to do his bidding. At the door when he smiled at her, she smiled back tremulously.

He held his arms wide. She hesitated, then walked into them. His arms wrapped around her, tightening until she complained, "Ben, you're hurting me."

"Sorry," he said, releasing her. He wished he could crush the deceit out and distill her into the essence of the woman he thought she was.

"Love me?" His voice was raspy and uneven. He glanced at Annie, who promptly looked away.

Summer hesitated a moment, her eyes cast down, then said, "Yes."

"Show me how much you love me," he demanded, pulling her into his arms and fitting his mouth to hers.

Her arms hung lifelessly by her side, but he wouldn't allow her to be uninvolved. His big hands cupped her buttocks, pressing her into the cradle of his burgeoning hardness. His mouth ground into hers until her whimper halted him.

Damn her! Damn him! Ben thought. He'd wanted to punish her but had ended by tormenting himself. "Where's Annie staying tonight?"

"She and Wayne are booked into a Holiday Inn. He's there waiting for her. She just wanted to come over to talk to me."

Yeah, he thought sourly, lucky for him he'd heard the conversation.

"I'll see you early in the morning. Let's have a late breakfast around ten, then go to the courthouse for our license. Just think, in a few days you'll be Mrs. Ben *Carr*." He studied her impassively as he said t*he name. He thought he detected a flicker of emotion in her deep green eyes.*

"Yes," she replied, "Mrs. Carr."

He heard the door lock behind him. When he got to the elevator, he stabbed the button for the top floor. Tomorrow Summer James would get the payoff she deserved, he vowed, eyes narrowed in thought.

Fourteen

After Summer called Annie, she stowed away her luggage in the trunk of her car. She felt like a criminal, sneaking the cases out of her room one by one.

I'm a gutless coward, she thought, but she couldn't chance being around him anymore. She'd decided during the night that she couldn't pull off the arrogant farewell scene she'd planned. Her heart wasn't in it. She just wanted to leave quietly. To tuck my tail and run back to my side of the tracks, she thought disparagingly.

She didn't even want him to find out she was checking out. When she'd gone to settle her bill, she'd found out he had paid the entire tab already. Evidently he planned on lowering the boom on her today. Her cheeks burned when she thought about him having a suite at this hotel. Everyone who worked here knew all about their fling, she was sure. They probably reported her every movement to him. The whole city was having a good laugh at her expense. Well, Ben Carson was going to have to laugh alone, she'd decided early this morning.

With the big cases stowed away in the trunk of her car, she walked back to the room for her purse and her makeup bag. Then she'd leave this cursed town. She wished she'd never heard of Houston or Ben Carson or that damned book. Last night she'd shredded the book into the bathroom wastebasket, taking physical delight in tearing out

197

the pages and crumpling them.

With a last look around at the beautiful room, she turned to leave. When she opened the door, she stepped back in shock. Ben towered there, looking as immovable as granite.

"You're really in a hurry to get that license, aren't you?" he taunted.

Summer stepped back. She didn't know what to say.

"Aren't you dressed a little casually for such a momentous event?" He gestured toward her denim skirt and cotton blouse and canvas espadrilles.

Her silence seemed to displease him. He stepped into the room and locked the door.

"Love me?" he asked, his voice as rough as it had been last night when he'd asked.

Tears filled Summer's eyes. She'd never see him again, she realized. Yes, she loved him, she wanted to cry out; at least she loved the man she had known as Ben Carr. With a shaking hand, she reached out and cupped the curve of his cheek. She felt his jaw clench. "Yes," she whispered, meaning it and knowing that it sentenced her to a life of unhappiness. "I do love you." *And will never ever forget you,* she added silently.

"Show me how much you love me," he demanded, as he had last night. But this time, he made no move to touch her.

Summer stepped close to him, so close she swore she could hear the thunder of his heartbeat. She closed her eyes and leaned toward him. She'd never see him again after this day. Her hands slid up his chest, encircled his neck. Pressing her lips to his, she nipped the chiseled line, pleading for entrance.

He didn't respond. Puzzled, she tried harder to pleasure him with her mouth, the way he had taught her. All the pent-up hurt and love inside bloomed to an unbelievable ache. Suddenly she wanted to shower him with all the love she had. The love that was his alone. If only she could impress herself upon his heart and mind, the way he had upon hers. Futilely she wanted him to remember her. Would he recall her face a year from now?

Then he moved jerkily. His arms enfolded her tightly, but she didn't protest. She kissed him until his tongue plundered her mouth demandingly.

"Touch me," he demanded harshly.

Feverishly she compiled, her hands stroking his shoulders and chest; sliding the buttons from their position, she kissed her way down to his waist. When her tongue circled his flat male nipples, he groaned, and she delighted in it. In a frenzy to make love with him one more time, she spread her hands over his belly and his groin, caressing the hard bulge.

"Summer!" he cried, yanking at his belt, opening his trousers.

Summer didn't understand his anguish, but she recognized that he was as powerless in the grip of desire as she was.

He took her to the bed, flipping her skirt up, pushing her pink panties down, and entered her.

She cried out at the exquisite sensation. Then her hands stroked his back, urging him and pleading with him.

Frantically they sought release, riding the crest of a punishing desire. He couldn't wait as he always had before to make certain her pleasure peaked before taking his. He poured himself into her, crying out, drowning her own moan of repletion.

Summer lay there, her body tired, her heart aching. How could she feel like they were one when she knew it was a lie? His breath still came in quick, short pants when Ben pulled himself from her. He walked to the bathroom. She heard the water running. Looking down at herself, shame overwhelmed her. Her skirt lay bunched at her waist, and her blouse gaped open. Her panties tangled around her ankles. She still had her shoes on. The harsh morning light made her nakedness seem obscene.

Summer smothered a sob. She felt ashamed. Used. She couldn't meet his eyes when he walked into the bedroom. He didn't say anything. The quiet buzz of his zipper closing made her eyes fly open. He hadn't even removed his clothes.

The man who stood there wasn't the man she loved. This man must be Bennett Carson, she thought with a flash of fear. He looked every inch the arrogant millionaire.

"Do you still love me, Summer?"

She winced at the harsh question. Softly, resigned to what she couldn't change, she said, "Yes, I still love you." Oh, God, she wished it weren't true.

"You liar! You just love the millions I have in the bank."

He knew. Stunned, she shook her head. "No."

"You know who I am, don't you?"

Summer jumped when he repeated the question in a cold, merciless voice.

"Yes, I know." Tiredly her brain tried to analyze the situation. Something was wrong. He was enraged. He was acting as if he had been wronged. But she was the injured party. He'd played her for a sucker. Perhaps more so than she'd imagined, she realized.

"You do know I'm rich, don't you?"

The moment froze in time. Summer knew she'd always remember the hate in his dark eyes.

"Yes, I know," she whispered.

"Yeah. I guess you do. You probably have an eight-by-ten color glossy of me in your file on the richest men in Texas."

"No." Summer shook her head in denial.

He snorted in disbelief. While she watched, he pulled his

wallet from his back pocket and opened it. "I figure even the highest-priced call girl doesn't earn more than a few hundred a night. Here's a week's worth. I've even tipped you out by paying for this room." He tossed the money across her naked belly.

"You're sick," she whispered, brushing the money from her body as if it burned her white flesh.

"No, Summer," he said, his voice cold and hard, "I just don't take kindly to betrayal." He turned to leave. "Oh, by the way, unless you've got a strong desire for personal humiliation, I'd advise you not to try to get any more money out of me. I've got a lawyer who'll tie you in knots and take every penny you've got. I think you know him—David Blackwood?"

He looked her over. She didn't have the energy to cover herself. She stared at the velvet draperies. Her voice was so quiet, he barely heard her "Get out of here."

"Sure thing, honey. You've got till noon to get your things and head back to Hicksville."

Summer heard the door close quietly. She lay there for a long time, unaware of the passing minutes, unable to think. Eventually she was able to pull herself together enough to leave the bed. Carefully she gathered the crisp hundred-dollar bills from where they had fallen and found an envelope in the desk to stuff them in. With shaking fingers, she wrote his name on the front.

Oddly enough, she didn't feel the need to cry. Perhaps all the love she'd had for Ben had simply been killed, stabbed to death by his hateful words. She found the strength to walk to his suite and slide the envelope under the door.

When she got in her car, it wouldn't start. All she heard when she turned the key was the whirring and clicking. That's when the tears started. She leaned her head on the steering wheel and sobbed her heart out.

An hour later, face red, eyes swollen, and nose stuffy, she got the hammer out of the trunk and tapped under the hood on the solenoid. The car started the next time she tried.

Crying and cursing, she headed out of the garage. At a red light, she hunted for tissues in her purse but didn't find any. Tears continued to stream down her face. Anyone who saw her would surely think she was crazy. And she was, because she still loved Ben. Crazy in love with a crazy man. She laughed wildly. Crazy with heartache.

She headed north toward home, leaving Houston and its oil industry and its heartless rich people behind. She never wanted to see the place again.

Driving until she had to stop for gasoline, she retraced the route she'd followed the week before. How could my life change so much in such a short period of time? she wondered. From the heights of ecstasy to the depths of despair. From uncertainty to love to humiliation. She'd made the trip in record time.

After midnight, she pulled into the gravel driveway of her small home. The full moonlight shone through the branches of the old cedars when she wearily unlocked the house, then lugged her bags into the bedroom.

The hot, musty air trapped in the small building since she'd left made her gag. She went around opening windows, letting the comfortable night air in. Slipping off her wrinkled clothes, she wadded them into a ball and dropped them into the trash. She never wanted to see them again. Never wanted to remember the way she'd looked when Ben had finished with her.

She slipped on a loose white cotton dress and lay down on the bed. Though exhausted, she couldn't sleep. Too many memories haunted her. She paced each room until she couldn't stand being cooped up indoors anymore. Finally she collapsed in the old porch swing. Her eyes felt like two burning embers. She pressed the heels of her hands against her eyes.

Summer wanted to stop thinking about Ben. She hated the fact that she missed him. If only she could be in his arms right now, not for passion, but for comfort. She desperately needed someone to hold her. Just before dawn, she fell asleep.

"What the hell are you doing, son?" Big Ben Carson roared, his bushy eyebrows drawn together in a scowl.

"I'm getting drunk." Ben grinned lopsidedly at his father.

"Well, do you have to do it with my best brandy?" his father asked, pulling the decanter from Ben's limp hands. "Hell! A bottle of Thunderbird would serve the same purpose."

Ben laughed and tipped back the water glass. He might as well get it over with and tell his dad. "Hey, Dad, you were right again. Turns out Summer was just after my money. Just like Janine."

"Ben, I never said anything about this Summer of yours. What in hell are you talking about?"

"I just eshcaped . . . escaped, that is, by the shin of my teeth, the *skin* of my teeth, another monumental matrimonial mistake," Ben enunciated carefully.

Big Ben rubbed his eyes. "Son, do you want to tell me what's going on?"

"Nope." Ben drank deeply, emptying the Waterford tumbler. "Where's that decanter?"

"Don't you think you've had enough?"

"Nope. There isn't enough in the whole damn state to be enough." Ben stood, swaying. "I'll see you later, Dad. Didn't mean to wake up the house."

"If you didn't mean to wake me up, you shouldn't have sounded like a bull elephant in a china shop."

Ben swayed and bumped against his father when he tried to walk past the older gentleman.

"Here, son, let me help you."

"Why, thanks, Dad. That's mighty nice of you."

Big Ben helped him up the stairs to his old room, motioning Irene, who waited in the upstairs hall, to open the door for him. He commiserated with his son and pulled the story from Ben, piece by drunken piece.

When they reached Ben's room, his dad gave him a little shove toward the bed. Ben collapsed onto it. His reddened eyes closed. "I thought you were different, Summer," he mumbled before passing out. Loud snores echoed in the quiet room.

Irene winced at the noise. "Is he going to be all right?" she asked in a whisper.

Her husband nodded. "Oh, yeah, he'll be fine, but he's going to have a hell of a hangover."

"No, darling, this thing with Summer. Do you think he'll get over it?"

"Sure, in time. He got over Janine, didn't he?" He pulled his wife out of the room. "Let's let him sleep it off."

"I don't understand, dear. He seemed on top of the world yesterday. How could that . . . that hussy do this to him?"

"I don't know, sweetie pie." Big Ben looked back at his son. "Maybe he'll tell us." He and Irene walked back to their room.

Moisture misted Irene's eyes. "I would have gone to his little wedding and kept my mouth shut no matter what I thought about that girl. If she was what he wanted, then I would have done my best to love her, too."

Big Ben enfolded her in his arms. "I know, Irene. I know. I wouldn't have risked losing him a second time either."

Fifteen

Summer passed the hot days of August trying to come to grips with what had happened in Houston. Oddly enough, she didn't blame Ben for the mess she'd made of her life. She realized that the seeds of her own destruction had been planted years before. The harvest had just been more dramatic than most.

Though Summer had denied Annie's charge that what she really wanted was love, she knew now that her friend was right. Summer had wanted to belong to someone—even if she had to sell herself to accomplish that. Money might feed the body, but love fed the soul. Each night seemed to last a century, and Summer's soul hungered for Ben's arms to hold her.

Summer stretched, relieving the strain on her back. She straightened a chair, then stepped back to admire the combination of her grandmother's old oak pedestal table, which she had refinished, and the six oak chairs she'd found at a flea market.

When the kitchen phone rang, she lifted the receiver, sighing as she listened to her best friend.

"Annie, I'm perfectly fine," Summer insisted. "I'm not going to spend another Friday and Saturday night at your house, playing cards with you and Wayne."

"Honestly, Summer, we enjoy your company. Besides, what is the point of moping around all by yourself in that empty house?"

"My house has always been empty, and I've survived just fine."

"But that was before," Annie replied.

Summer looked at the plaster dust that covered everything. "I've got so much cleaning up to do around here that I won't have time to mope. Then when I finish here, I'm going to organize my new garage. The guys finished installing the door opener today."

Grudgingly Annie conceded. "Okay, but next weekend you are coming to dinner Friday night, and I won't take no for an answer. In fact, wear something kind of nice."

Summer sighed in exasperation. "Annie, if you have any more thoughts of matchmaking, do us both a favor and forget it. The last Friday night dinner was a disaster. For goodness' sake! I couldn't stand that guy, or his big cigars! I can't believe you really did that!"

"I just think you need to meet other men."

"Not now, Annie. The time isn't right." Ben's face flashed before her eyes.

"Will the time ever be right? Summer, you deserve to be happy. You're a warm, wonderful woman."

"Eventually I may be ready to think about a relationship. But I'm still learning about myself. I wouldn't be any good for anyone else right now. You know, in a way, I owe Ben a favor."

"What!"

"He held a mirror to my face, and I didn't like what I saw. What I wanted to do was cheap and insulting. I've spent so much time thinking about this. Annie, for some reason, he really thought I had targeted him and that everything that had happened between us was part of an elaborate plot to snare him."

"Then if you still love him, why haven't you tried to call him and explain?"

Summer shivered, remembering the hate in his eyes. "He'd never believe me. He'd just think I was still trying to catch myself a rich husband."

"I'm so sorry it turned out this way, Summer."

"It's okay, Annie. I'm okay." They changed the subject and talked about Summer's remodeling projects and about school starting the following week.

After Summer hung up the phone, she turned on the vacuum. A smile lit her face as she worked. Looking around her home, she marveled at the changes a month had brought.

The week after she'd returned home, she had hired a contractor to remodel her house. Though it had exhausted her savings account and her energy, she didn't regret having spent the money. It was a far wiser use of her hard-earned dollars than the narcissistic endeavor she'd made in packaging herself as a gold digger.

Now the house was a cozy, comfortable bungalow. Next year she planned to remodel the hall bathroom and, if she had enough money, build a deck out back.

The long, sculptured nails Annie had laughed at were history, made obsolete by hard work. Despite the contractor's protests, Summer had hammered along with the work crew and had stripped varnish and layer upon layer of paint from the woodwork.

Fresh pine green shutters gleamed darkly against the new white paint on the exterior of the house. New storm doors replaced the rusted screen doors that had squawked like wounded geese.

Spider lilies bloomed alongside fading summer flowers in the beds that Summer had recovered from the wild tangle of yard, and hanging baskets of scarlet petunias hung along the breezeway that connected the new two-car garage to the back of the house.

Summer had made other changes in her life also. For the first time since she'd moved to Red Rock, she made an attempt to become part of the community. She joined the church where her grandmother had been a member.

She didn't feel ashamed either or feel that the other members were talking about Erma James's illegitimate granddaughter when she walked through the door. Everyone had welcomed her. Though she realized there would be a certain amount of gossip, it didn't bother her. She'd laid that ghost to rest along with many others.

But Ben continued to haunt her. Though she worked like a demon during the day, sleep eluded her. During the long, sleepless nights, thoughts of what might have been possessed her, and memories of love kept vigil with her as she restlessly prowled the house, often ending up dozing in the porch swing.

Bennett Carson entered the lobby of the Claremont and saw Toshiro Ishikawa immediately. They greeted each other warmly and exchanged pleasantries about the weather.

"Excuse me, Mr. Carson." The concierge held out an envelope.

"Yes, Albert, what is it?"

"This was found on the floor of your suite. I would have called you about it, but I kept expecting your son to come back to the hotel."

"Oh, uh, he's been staying with his mother and me for a visit." Ben eyed the hotel linen stationery. "I'll take that to him, thank you."

Albert nodded and handed him the envelope. For a moment Big Ben studied it, then with a shrug, he placed it in his inside coat pocket. He'd give it to Ben tonight when he got home.

"Now, Toshi, let me treat you to a Texas-size steak while we talk about this little idea you've had." Big Ben clapped Ishikawa on the shoulder, and they left the hotel.

After Ishikawa had been dropped back at the Claremont, Bennett Carson drove home. The little gold Allante was gone.

"Where's Ben?" he asked, kissing his wife on the cheek.

"He's gone back to Dallas," Irene said sadly. "I asked him to stay longer, but he just grinned like he used to when he wanted to get his way and said he was going to run down to the Bahamas for a couple of weeks to get in some snorkeling before he headed back to work."

"Irene, he's a grown man. We can't keep him here forever."

"I know. I'm glad he's over her and getting on with his life. It's just that it was nice having him home again."

"Well, he'll be back."

Later, when he hung up his suit coat, he found the envelope. Feeling of it, he wondered why it was so bulky. He tossed it on the wooden clothes valet shelf. He'd try to remember to ask Irene to mail it to Ben, he thought sleepily.

Summer refused Annie's dinner invitation by saying she had a hair appointment in Dallas. Though Annie sputtered, Summer remained obstinate. She had no intention of being a surprise dinner partner for Wayne's old college buddy who just happened to be visiting.

"You are a magician, Monsieur Claude," Summer declared, turning her head to stare at the shining strands of honey blond hair. Her transformation back to the old Summer was complete.

Well, not exactly the old Summer, she thought, conscious of how her clothes hung on her. Fifteen pounds had dropped from her frame, leaving her too thin, Annie claimed. And she still wore contact lenses, only changing to daily-wear lenses instead of the extended-wear contacts she'd worn in Houston because she'd developed an eye abrasion from sleeping in the long-wear lenses.

"Thank you, Monsieur Claude."

He bowed over her hand and said imperiously, "Do not ever color your beautiful hair again, young lady."

Summer promised she wouldn't and started to leave.

"Make an appointment with Cathy," he ordered.

Summer waved and did as he asked. Why not? she thought. I'm worth the price of a good haircut, and driving to Dallas hadn't been as traumatic as I thought.

At first she had been terrified that she might see Ben. Then she'd chided herself for being silly since the odds against seeing one specific person out of a couple million people were tremendous.

I have to get on with life. And I'll live it more fully and with more enjoyment than I have in the past, she vowed, driving home. Surely the day would come when she didn't think about Ben all the time. Wondering where he was, what he was doing, who he was with.

Summer enjoyed the wind blowing through her hair as she drove home. Thankfully, she hadn't had any more trouble with her convertible. At first she'd been inclined to sell the Chevy because of the memories associated with it, but defiantly she'd decided to keep it. It had kind of grown on her. Her mechanic was on the lookout for a starter solenoid that would fit so she wouldn't have to worry about getting stranded somewhere. It was just a matter of time before it went on the permanent blink. Then no matter how much tapping she did with the hammer, it wouldn't start.

The dizziness didn't hit Summer until she was making a

pot of coffee to go with the chicken salad sandwich she'd prepared for a late supper. Summer clutched her stomach, positive that she was going to lose the enchiladas she'd had at lunch. Cold sweat popped out on her forehead. She couldn't discern whether it was the aroma of the coffee or the onions in the chicken salad. What appetite she'd had fled as quickly as she dashed to the bathroom.

Later, she dragged herself to the kitchen and fixed a glass of iced tea. She lay on her new couch, propped against the Indian print pillows, and tried to ignore the roiling nausea that troubled her.

Summer drifted off to sleep but awoke with her body throbbing with painful desire. She'd dreamed of Ben's lips on hers, his large hands gliding passionately over her trembling body. She wanted him so fiercely, she ached. Knowing that she'd never know the heaven again that she'd found in his arms, she wanted to cry. But she'd shed so many tears. It seemed as if she shouldn't have any left.

With a sigh, she rose from the couch, tentatively waiting to see if the dizziness and nausea returned. Hmmm, she thought, must have been something in the enchiladas. The sickness didn't trouble her again over the weekend.

When school opened on schedule Monday morning, Summer realized how much she'd missed seeing the energetic elementary students. They were so sweet and funny and enthusiastic. Though Summer's days overflowed with activities, she couldn't find enough to fill the empty hours between sunset and sunrise. Disturbingly, the episodes of dizziness and nausea continued, taking more weight from her.

When Ben returned from his vacation, he put into action the plans he'd made. Determined to move back to Houston, he started arranging his business affairs to facilitate that move. First, he thought with a sigh, he had to get through the mountain of paperwork and correspondence his secretary had set aside for him.

"What's this, Linda?" Ben asked, holding a wad of hundred-dollar bills paper-clipped together.

"Oh, they must have got separated from the envelope." Linda sorted through the in-box. "Here it is. Your mom sent this to the office while you were in the Bahamas. When I opened the envelope, another envelope from the Claremont was inside. I opened it, and all that money was in there."

Ben took the envelope from her.

"Are you okay, Mr. Carson?"

"Yeah, I'm fine. That's all for tonight, Linda."

She hesitated, then shrugged her shoulders and went to her desk to gather her things.

Ben stared at the envelope in one hand and the money he held in his other hand.

"She didn't take it," he said in a whisper. He leaned against his high-back leather chair and closed his eyes tiredly, remembering Summer the way he'd last seen her, her beautiful green eyes filled with pain and loathing. He hated himself for what he'd done to her. No one deserved to be treated that way. He should have just told her to run along and find another sucker, but the pain at her betrayal had exploded in rage. Ben shook his head, remembering how out of control he'd been. He'd frightened himself.

He brushed a finger across his name that she'd written on the envelope, then carefully placed the money back in it and locked it in his desk drawer.

Summer, he thought, I'm sorry. I'm sorry I hurt you, but most of all I'm sorry you didn't love me. Would she ever stop haunting him? he wondered.

★ ★ ★ ★ ★

One day, at lunch in the school cafeteria, Annie noticed Summer push her plate away again. "Okay, I haven't said anything before, but I can't keep still any longer. You haven't eaten right since you came back from Houston. You're a walking scarecrow. Summer, you've got to stop this."

"But, Annie, this has nothing to do with Ben."

"The hell it doesn't," Annie whispered. "You make a doctor's appointment today or I'll make it for you. You've let yourself get run-down, and you're probably anemic by now. That's why you're so dizzy all the time."

After much nagging, Summer agreed and made an appointment for the following Friday, notifying her principal, who also told her she should have gone before now.

"Mrs. Gates, you know me. I'm usually as healthy as a horse."

"I know, my dear," the silver-haired lady replied, "but you haven't looked like yourself since school started. I've been meaning to speak to you about it."

"I'm fine, really. This is a lot of fuss over nothing."

On the day of her appointment, Summer drove to the doctor's office. As she filled out the questionnaire, her heart began to hammer when she came to the blank that asked for the date of her last period.

Frantically she thought back to the hot days of July. The last time had been before she'd gone to Houston. How could she have ignored—she counted on her fingers—two missed periods, almost three?

She felt faint. No! Fate couldn't play such a dirty trick on her! Thinking back, she realized there'd been two times when Ben hadn't taken precautions. The first had been after the party at David Blackwood's club. They'd been too lost in their passion to think about such things.

The other had been the morning she'd left. Her face

burned at the memory. In his haste, he hadn't thought of contraception, only of having her one last time. And she'd thought only of having him fill her, one last time. And he had. She paled; perhaps he'd given her more than he knew.

"I think I know what might be wrong," she began hesitantly, red staining her cheeks, as the doctor examined her. Summer discussed the possibility of pregnancy with Dr. Morris.

"Well, judging by your exam, I think you're probably right, but we'll do a test to make sure."

After Summer was dressed and seated in front of the doctor's desk, Angela Morris asked, "So you think the dates you gave me are accurate?"

"Yes, you see, it was the only times I didn't . . . that is, we didn't . . ."

"Use protection?" the doctor finished with a smile.

Summer nodded. Still trying to come to grips with the fact that she could be pregnant, she responded automatically to the questions until Dr. Morris asked, "If you are indeed pregnant, are you going to go through with the pregnancy?"

Summer stared into kind gray eyes, shocked at the question even though she knew she had a choice. She thought of what it had been like growing up without a father. The rejection of her grandmother, the ridicule of other children, illegitimate. What an ugly word. But surely times had changed.

"I have to ask," the doctor stated gently, "especially since you're not married."

Summer looked ahead through the years, understanding how difficult it would be and was frightened at the thought she might bear a child and then unforeseen events might leave the child an orphan as she had been. Could she take the responsibility of bringing a child into the world when life was so uncertain?

But how could she not bear this child? A part of Ben was

growing within her. She'd have a child, maybe with his eyes, a part of him she could hold forever.

"I'll go through with the pregnancy."

"Good." The doctor smiled. "I'm always personally delighted when that is the decision."

An hour later when Summer left the doctor's office, she still hadn't fully accepted the fact that she was pregnant. She was going to have a baby. A baby to love. A child who would love her and fill the emptiness in her heart.

Every so often a smile flitted across her face and she'd find herself glancing at her flat stomach. It was impossible to believe there was a new life within her. A spark that had been created by their loving. Was that how her mother had felt when she found herself pregnant? Had she still loved Summer's father even after he'd rejected her and their baby?

On the way home, Summer wondered what her pregnancy would mean to her future with the school district. She'd not heard of any unmarried pregnant woman employed by the district. She prayed that she would still have a job after she told Mrs. Gates.

When she arrived home, she wanted to tell someone—had to tell someone or she'd burst. The one person she wanted most to tell was Ben, but she couldn't. Perhaps one day she'd tell her child about Ben, but that was a decision far in the future.

Her mood shifted to despair when she thought of the months ahead of her and realized she wanted Ben to share them with her. She wanted him to watch her belly enlarge. She wanted him there when she felt the baby kick the first time. When she was wheeled into the delivery room. But I'll be alone, so I might as well accept it now, she thought, frightened at the enormity of the step she was taking.

Summer decided everything would work out in its own

time. She wasn't going to worry. Instead, she'd enjoy being pregnant since it might never happen again. She couldn't quite picture herself ever getting married, though Annie assured her she was being melodramatic over the situation. "I'll make a wonderful mother," she promised aloud.

She couldn't call Ben, but she could share the news with Annie tonight, she decided, with a quick glance at the clock.

"You're what?" Annie shrieked.

"You heard me. I'm pregnant." Summer hastened to add, "And I'm quite happy about it also."

Dead silence greeted Summer's words.

When Annie finally spoke, Summer wished she'd kept the news to herself awhile longer. Sometimes her friend acted as if she were Summer's mother.

"Summer James, haven't you heard of condoms?" Annie sputtered.

"Of course I have." Summer blushed and was glad Annie couldn't see as she tried for a casual tone. "Unfortunately we got carried away a couple of times."

"And now you have to pay the price while that . . . that playboy . . . gets off scot-free."

"Annie, I told you I'm very happy about this. I can support myself and the baby quite nicely and have no need of anything from Ben." Except his love, she thought. "I don't intend to tell him."

"You could get child support from him!"

"I don't want it." If I can't have him, I certainly don't want his money. Pain stabbed her at the thought. "Won't you be happy for me, too?"

"Well, if you put it that way," Annie grumbled with ill grace. "Of course, I'm happy if you're happy."

After a few minutes, Annie asked, "After everything that's happened, you still love him, don't you?"

"Yes, I guess I'll always love him."

"Are you going to tell him?"

Summer sighed. "He'd just think it was a plot to get his money. Annie, he'd already been burned by his first wife before he met me." Summer said firmly, "He need never know."

Summer and Annie talked for a short while longer. Annie reassured Summer that the school board couldn't fire her in this day and age but that she was going to be the subject of quite a few conversations.

"There's not such a stigma attached to unwed mothers now, Annie. Times have changed."

"Not in Red Rock, they haven't."

Reluctantly Summer agreed with her and privately thought Annie might be wrong about the school board having to keep her on. After she said good-bye to Annie, Summer sat down with pen and paper and began to do a budget forecast. Though she'd come to appreciate her position as librarian here, it didn't pay much. Money would be tight for a while with the expenses of her pregnancy and delivery, but she should be able to manage.

Just in case the school board decided to fire her, she thought she should be prepared, and planned to type up her resume before the week was out. If she could get a position as librarian for a private company, a law firm in Fort Worth, for instance, she'd make a lot more money. Of course, she'd have to commute, and the longer workday meant more time away from the baby. But if she had to, she'd do it.

If she kept her job here, she could do some free-lance research work for some of the professors at the universities in the Dallas and Forth Worth areas. She'd done a little of that last year.

With a thousand thoughts tumbling around in her head, she began to get a headache.

★ ★ ★ ★ ★

Annie stared at the phone, her face a mask of indecision. "The heck with it," she said aloud. Taking a deep breath, she picked up the receiver and called the number long distance information had given her. Disgusted when an answering machine took the call, she left a message, wishing she could have talked to the rotten playboy himself. She'd like to give him a piece of her mind since he obviously didn't have enough brains to know love when he had it. She slammed the receiver down.

"What's the matter, hon?" Annie's husband, Wayne, asked.

"It took me all last night and all day today to get my courage up to call Ben Carson. I finally do it, and all I get is the stupid answering machine."

"You shouldn't interfere," Wayne warned with a frown.

"Well, somebody has to help Summer. She thinks the school board will turn a blind eye to her pregnancy. But they won't. You know how this town is."

Wayne massaged the tense muscles in his wife's shoulder. He kissed the side of her neck. "Well, come to bed, Miss Busybody, and you can keep my body busy."

Annie cuffed him lightly on the arm. "Men. You're all alike. All you think about is sex."

"And aren't you delighted about it?" Annie giggled and let him lead her to bed.

Ben stared at the envelope he'd taken from his locked desk drawer, tracing his name with his finger. This was all he had left of Summer, the handwriting on an envelope. He tossed it to the desktop and rose, walking to the bar to pour himself another Scotch.

Catching sight of himself in the mirror, he barely recognized the gaunt face that looked back at him. The ravages of the last couple of months were clearly evident in his face and body. He looked as mean as he felt. Dark circles surrounded his sunken eyes. His face felt as if it would crack were he to smile. Though God knew he hadn't smiled since Summer had left.

Summer! Pain twisted his features. At first he'd refused to think about her. He'd cursed her and got drunk so he wouldn't be aware when she slithered into his mind. But she followed him to the Bahamas, then to Dallas. She whispered from the shadows of the room until he thought he would go insane.

As each endless day passed, he found himself welcoming her into his mind, because that was the only thing left of her —his memories. Sometimes when he was walking down the street, he'd glimpse a white blond head of hair and his heart would hammer. He'd get closer only to discover that it wasn't Summer.

His body clenched with desire when he lay in bed at night, trying to sleep. He'd thought about releasing that kind of tension with another woman but had spurned the thought. He didn't want another woman. He wanted Summer.

Startled, he thought again. I want Summer. His heart hammered. He wanted her even if she only wanted him because of his money. And if that's what it took to get her, then so be it, he decided. He'd have enough love for both of them. By God, he vowed, I can love her enough to make up for her not loving me. As long as we're together, there's a chance she'll learn to love me. He slammed his drink down.

Galvanized into action, he ran from the office. "Cancel all my appointments, Linda, I'll be out of town awhile."

"But what about—"

Ben ignored her. All he could think about was getting

219

home and packing. He needed to find a map to figure out where Red Rock was. There was no use in calling. After the way he'd treated her the last time, he figured she'd slam the phone down as soon as she heard his voice. Of course, she might meet him at the door with a shotgun when he got there, he thought. But somehow between now and the time I arrive on her doorstep, I'll figure out a way to earn her forgiveness. He prayed he hadn't hurt her so much that she hated him now.

The phone rang as he grabbed his keys. He ignored it. The answering machine could get it. He raced out the door.

For the first time since the day she'd left, he felt alive again. By tomorrow, he'd be with Summer. She could have his damned money, as long as she'd take him with it.

Sixteen

Ben ordered a huge breakfast at the diner by the railroad tracks near downtown Red Rock. He looked around with a smile. Red Rock's downtown consisted of about four blocks and looked for all the world like a Norman Rockwell painting.

He hadn't had much appetite for weeks but suddenly felt ravenous when the waitress placed a platter of hash brown potatoes, scrambled eggs, and thick patty sausages in front of him.

He was finally here. Actually, he'd arrived in the wee hours of the morning but hadn't a clue as to how to find Summer's home. He'd thought he'd wait until morning and call Annie Redmond and get directions from her—if she'd talk to him. Since the small town had no motel, he'd ended up sleeping in his car parked in front of the post office.

When he finished breakfast, he found the Redmonds listed in the phone book, but there was no answer when he called. Ben walked back to his seat at the counter. The waitress topped off his coffee cup. He smiled and sipped the steaming brew.

"Excuse me, ma'am," he asked the white-haired waitress, "would you happen to know a young woman who is the librarian at the elementary school here?"

"You mean Erma James's granddaughter?"

Ben nodded.

"You a friend of hers, you say?"

"Yes, ma'am."

"Where do you know her from?"

"I met her in Houston this summer."

"Ohhhh." She drew the sound out. "You wouldn't happen to be that young man that broke her heart, would you?"

Ben flushed. No, he thought silently, she broke my heart.

The woman looked him up and down, then a smile slowly unfolded across her creased face. "You come up here to fetch her, didn't you?"

Ben grinned foolishly. "Yes, ma'am. I'm Ben Carson." He reached over the counter to shake her hand.

"I'm Clorice Clancy."

"Tell me, Mrs. Clancy, do you know how to get to her house?"

"Well, Ben, you go back out of town like you're headed to Fort Worth and turn left past the feed store. You drive out that old farm road about three miles till you come to a fork in the road by the old abandoned Pentecostal church, where you turn right. Go about a half mile and her property is on the right. You can't miss it. The turnoff has a new sign that says 'Summer's Fortune.' "

Ben choked on his coffee. "Summer's Fortune?"

"That's right." Clorice cackled, the jowls in her face bouncing merrily. "When she got back from Houston this summer, she redid that whole house. She joked with everybody about putting a fortune into her granny's old house. Annie Redmond—you know Annie, her best friend." The woman rattled on without giving him a chance to answer. "She had that sign made as a joke—kind of a housewarming present, I guess."

Ben let Clorice fill his coffee cup again and listened to her for another thirty minutes. He wondered if Clorice knew everyone's business as thoroughly as she knew Summer's.

"If you ask me, it weren't right what Erma did to that little girl. Lettin' her be raised in foster homes and that orphanage." Clorice snorted. "Old Erma was a sour one for sure. The only reason she left her place to Summer was because she knew she was dying and wanted to try to get into heaven."

Ben thought of how lonely Summer's life must have been. He vowed to give her enough love and kindness to make up for all the hurt she'd known. If she'd give him a chance.

As time had passed, he'd become convinced that what he'd seen in her eyes that last morning wasn't disappointment at losing a fortune. It was hurt. If he hadn't been in such a rage, he'd have noted it then. Maybe she had planned to catch him, but she wasn't as coldhearted as he'd imagined her to be.

No woman could have responded as freely as she had if she'd only been interested in money. It was amazing that she'd been able to love as freely and unselfishly as she had, given her past. He hung on to the hope that if she'd cared about him once, he could make her care again.

When he thought he'd have a caffeine overdose if he drank any more coffee, he said good-bye, leaving a generous tip.

"You come back now, Ben Carson." Clorice pocketed the tip and headed toward the telephone. Ben heard her say, "Hello, Donna Sue? You'll never guess who just left the diner!"

Ben followed Clorice's directions, still chuckling. He grinned when he passed the yellow sign that read in black letters, SUMMER'S FORTUNE. The gravel pelted the underside of the Allante as he pulled into her driveway.

He wiped his suddenly clammy hands on his trousers. How would Summer react when she saw him? He studied her house as he drove up, approving of the green-shuttered bungalow, bordered by shrubbery and shaded by towering trees.

Apprehensively he let the shiny brass knocker fall against the door.

Summer opened the door and froze, rooted to the spot. Shock glazed her eyes.

Ben stood there, his eyes devouring her. He touched the dark honey strands of hair. "I knew your hair must be beautiful." His dark eyes glittered as they devoured her face, her beautiful green eyes. "I'm going to give you emeralds," he murmured.

All the blood drained from her face, leaving it as white as the enamel on the door. Had she conjured him from her dreams? She swayed, leaning weakly against the doorjamb.

"Summer!" Ben jerked the storm door open and grabbed her.

"I'm all right. I'm all right," Summer said as Ben led her into the house and forced her to sit on the couch. "It was such a shock seeing you standing there when I've thought so many times about—" She pressed her lips together to stop the words.

Her head fell back to rest on the cushion. She stared at the ceiling. Why was he here? Why now? His nearness had her heart hammering. Remembered pain flooded her senses. She inhaled, remembering his own special scent, wanting to bury her face in the curve of his neck.

Ben rubbed her hands. His worried look faded when her face took on a healthier pink cast. He touched the pulse that throbbed in her throat.

Summer jerked as if scalded. "What are you doing here?" Even to her ears, her voice sounded breathless.

"I couldn't stay away." He edged closer.

Summer edged away from him. "What do you mean?"

"Ever since you left, I've been a zombie—moving through the days, hardly sleeping at night. I can't eat. I can't sleep. I can't get you out of my mind."

Nonplussed, Summer didn't know what to do or say. In her wildest longings, she'd never imagined that she'd see him again.

"I came to ask you, beg you if necessary, to have mercy on me." He grinned the lopsided grin she'd found so charming the first time she saw him.

I can't fall for his charm this time, she thought, wondering why he was really here. He couldn't know about the baby. She hardened her heart against the charm he wielded so carelessly.

"Mercy? You want me to have mercy on you? That's a laugh. How much mercy did you have on me?" Humiliation at their last encounter flooded her. "You are totally demented if you think I'm going to have anything to do with you. Now, get out of my house!" Dramatically she pointed toward the door.

"No," he said, crossing his arms over his chest.

"What do you mean, 'No'? I want you to leave."

"And I want you."

She was stunned at his words. "Don't say that," she whispered shakily. "Don't ever say that to me again."

He got up and walked to her. "Summer, I need you. I need your forgiveness. But most of all I need you. Please say you'll marry me or live with me. Whatever you want. Your terms. You can have every plug nickel I've got. Hell, I'll sign over half of everything I own if that's what it will take. I don't care why you marry me, whether it's for me or my money."

Tears filled her eyes. "You must have quite an opinion of me, Ben Carson." She drew herself up, spine straight, and looked him in the eye. "You can't buy me." Pain closed her eyes for a moment. "Maybe at one time I thought money was what I wanted, but I've learned it wasn't. I don't want your money." She turned away and said quietly, "Please, just leave me."

"But I can't." His whisper lingered in the air. She felt his hand on her shoulder. He turned her around. She was so weak where he was concerned. She'd been so lonely without him. But his sudden appearance didn't make sense.

He pulled her into his arms. She didn't resist, but she didn't encourage him either. He pressed her against him, and her heart took off like a rocket.

"Tell me you don't want me to hold you. Tell me your blood isn't hot and pounding through your veins the way mine is. You could tell me all that and more, and I'd know you were lying." He cupped her breasts, brushing her hardened nipples with his thumbs. "Your body remembers me. It was good between us, Summer. It can be that way again."

"No," Summer moaned, fighting the sensual spell he wove so effortlessly about her. She pushed at his chest, putting some distance between them. "Why do you want me now, after all these weeks? Why now?"

An ugly suspicion began to form in her mind. Maybe he did know about the baby. Was this his noble gesture? "And don't tell me that you suddenly realized you loved me." A bitter laugh accompanied her last statement.

"Why would it be so hard to believe I love you?"

Summer didn't have the energy to argue with him. If he'd come because of the baby, she didn't want him. And that had to be the only reason he was here.

"I've forgotten you, Ben, so just leave. I don't need you or your money," Summer repeated.

Ben ran his fingers through his ebony hair. He sighed.

"What's the matter, Mr. Carson? Did you think I'd just fall into your arms like nothing ever happened?"

"I was hoping, but I can understand the depth of your

hurt, because that was how I felt when I overheard you and Annie talking about my millions and making me pay."

"Oh." Summer remembered the conversation. "You must not have heard the entire conversation." He hadn't trusted her love enough to confront her with what he'd heard. If he had been that cruel to her over part of an overheard conversation, then he could do the same thing to her again through another misunderstanding. "Well, you know they say eavesdroppers never hear any good of themselves."

"What do you mean I didn't hear the whole conversation?"

"You figure it out, Sherlock!"

Outside, a car horn sounded. "Oh, dear. I forgot." She looked at Ben. "I was getting ready for church. I was supposed to ride with Miss Nettie."

"Car not running?"

Summer nodded. She opened the door and called, "I'm not quite ready, Miss Nettie. Can you wait a few minutes?"

Ben called from over Summer's shoulder, "It's all right, Miss Nettie. I'll take Summer to church."

"Oh, no, you won't. I'm sure you need to get back for a cocktail party or a polo match or whatever you rich people do to pass the time."

"No, I've sold my business in Dallas, and the condo is up for sale. I have nothing but time and money. And I'm prepared to share that with you."

Summer shivered. She didn't know what kind of game he was playing or what the rules were, but suddenly she felt like little Red Riding Hood, and he distinctly reminded her of the big, bad wolf. She thought of the way they had spent their time together.

"I can still make you blush, I see." His eyes swept over her body. "Does it still rise from your beautiful breasts like a pink tide?" His rough whisper reminded her of the times he'd loved her, speaking soft, seductive words to her.

"What's going on here, Summer?" A little old lady with impossibly red hair opened the door and peeked in. Her face crinkled into a million lines when she looked at Ben. "And who are you, dear?"

Ben introduced himself and once again found himself given the third degree by one of Red Rock's senior citizens. To Summer's consternation, he embroidered on the story of their meeting in Houston, describing how deeply in love they fell.

Miss Nettie giggled like a schoolgirl. "I simply must get to church before services start," she declared.

Summer was awash with indignation. She followed Ben and Miss Nettie out, waving good-bye to the old lady as she climbed into an ancient white De Soto.

"You don't know what you've done," Summer moaned, watching Miss Nettie speed out the driveway and hurry toward church.

With an innocent grin, Ben asked. "What do you mean?"

"She's got to get to church early so she can tell everyone there about you and our grand love affair! Why did you tell her all that garbage? I don't know what you're up to, but I'll have none of it!"

"It wasn't garbage. All of it was true."

She snorted. "Sure."

"So I changed a few details."

"I'll say. Like you forgot to mention I picked you up at a Dairy Queen. And what we fell into was lust, not love, or more precisely, we fell into a bed at a cheap motel."

"Summer, Summer, you have no romance in your soul. You poor baby. You've led such a deprived life," he teased. When he tried to take her into his arms again, she stood stiff and unresponsive. He sighed. "Get your purse and let's go. We don't want to be late for church."

"You can't go into church with me," she gasped, horrified.

"And why not?"

"Why, because, because everyone will know about us."

"Surely you don't think we are the first two people to have sex before marriage?"

"No, of course not."

"Church is a place for people striving to live better lives, right?"

She nodded.

"Then let's go. Besides, I'm going to make an honest woman out of you."

"I am already an honest woman, thank you very much." She stalked from the room, pulling on a cranberry jacket that coordinated with her floral dress.

Ben grinned as he escorted her to his car.

Startled, Summer stared at the gold Allante they'd driven all over Houston. It was a good reminder of her stupidity, she thought.

He seated her, then buckled his seat belt and backed out the driveway.

She couldn't maintain her silence. "Did you buy this the first day I arrived in Houston?"

"No," he answered quietly. "A friend of mine does own a dealership, and he did loan it to me."

"Because he thought you might buy it?"

"Probably, but also because I didn't have any wheels and he's a friend."

"Do you own it now or is it still on loan?"

"I bought it. You seemed to like it, and I thought you might want it. Kind of a wedding present?"

"Wedding present! There's not going to be any wedding. I

don't trust you, Ben Carr—Carson. So just go back to Houston or Dallas or wherever you hang your hat now." The rest of the drive to the church was made in silence. Ben let her stew in her thoughts.

The church she directed him to was a simple frame building erected at the turn of the century. Beautiful stained-glass windows adorned the sides of the building, and a ginger-bread-trimmed cupola topped by a cross drew the eye up.

As they walked from the parking lot on the side to the front doors of the church, Summer felt every eye on her and Ben. She groaned. Without a doubt, by nightfall everyone in Red Rock would know about Ben Carson.

"Ben, you came!"

Summer and Ben turned toward Annie and Wayne Redmond, bearing down on them.

Puzzled, Ben asked, "What do you mean?"

Annie looked surprised. "Oh, I meant to say you're here! What a surprise!" she finished lamely. Hurriedly she introduced her husband. The two men shook hands.

Summer's eyes narrowed. She'd known it. Annie had meddled where she shouldn't have. She must have called Ben as soon as Summer had notified her about the baby. He came to Red Rock to do the honorable thing, not because he loved her.

She pulled her arm from his grasp and turned on him. "I think I understand why you're here now. You can take your noble gesture and . . . and stick it—"

"Summer," Annie gasped, jerking her head to where the pastor stood chatting with Miss Nettie.

Summer compressed her lips until they hurt.

"I don't understand what's going on here." Ben shook his head. "Do you always talk in riddles and nonsensical sentences?"

Summer ignored him and started into the church. Ben hurried after her, sliding into the pew next to her.

Summer didn't know what to do. She didn't want him sitting next to her. Oh, Lord, but she was troubled. When the organ began to play, she closed her eyes and prayed for guidance and strength. His presence brought all the hurt to the surface again. His thigh brushing hers ignited the desire to be in his arms again. She prayed harder.

"Hello again, Mr. Carson," Miss Nettie whispered as she seated herself behind them.

Summer tried to ignore the whispers between Miss Nettie and her group of "girls" who controlled the gossip mill in the town. The church service was the longest hour of her life. She thought it would never end.

As she stood in line to shake Reverend Cleveland's hand, she listened to the many voices who bid Ben welcome to their church. His cheerful voice grated on her nerves until she thought she'd scream. She was holding up fine until she heard him introduce himself to the minister as her fiancé. That was the straw that broke the camel's back!

"Now, darling, don't be shy about telling our good news," Ben admonished, putting his arm around her.

Short of making a scene, Summer could do nothing. Once inside Ben's car and headed home, though, she told him what she thought of his high-handed actions.

"This isn't the way to my house."

"I know. I thought we'd get a bite to eat. I had breakfast at this really great diner on Main Street."

"Oh, no!" Summer groaned, putting her head in her hands. "You didn't talk to Clorice Clancy, did you?"

"A real sweet old lady with white hair?"

"I'm lost. There's no hope for me now." She thought of what the grapevine would have to work with now that Ben had appeared. As soon as she showed in her pregnancy, there'd be no doubt in anyone's mind who the father was. She groaned aloud.

"I don't know why you're acting the way you are. It's not like I'm offering you an indecent proposition. I want to marry you. I thought by the way you acted in Houston that you would kind of like the idea, too. After all, that is what we'd planned on doing." He drove a few miles in silence.

"Ben, turn around. Let's go to my house. I'll fix lunch. I can't face Clorice today. Not after Miss Nettie, the minister, and everyone else."

Ben obliged her, and soon they were back at her house. While Summer fixed sandwiches and heated soup from a can, Ben explored her house. It was small, but he liked it. He eyed the huge bed and grinned. "Maybe later," he said aloud.

Over lunch he chatted, steering clear of any references to Houston and what had happened there. He drew Summer out, and her natural enthusiasm for her job made her forget their unusual circumstances.

"You really like children, don't you?"

She smiled. "Yes, I do. I never thought about it much until lately, but I guess I've always enjoyed being around kids." She played with her soup.

"Have you ever thought about having any of your own?" he asked gently.

Startled, she met his eyes. So he wanted to talk about it now. Why didn't he just bring the subject out in the open instead of beating around the bush? "Yes, I've thought about it a lot. I want children." She danced around the issue. "I guess I've always wanted someone to love and to love me. Compensating for a loveless childhood, Annie would say, but that's not it entirely. My mother was great. She gave me as much love as it's possible to give a child. She was my whole world. Now I can give that kind of love to a child, my child."

"I love you, Summer."

"No, you don't." Summer's eyes shifted from his. She didn't know what to do when he said things like that. Especially since she knew he was just trying to be noble.

"Why do you look so sad when I say that?"

"Ben, you don't love me. I know it, so don't say it anymore, please."

"I'm curious. Just how do you know I don't?" He leaned back in his chair, his eyes somber as they studied her.

"I don't want to talk about it anymore. Excuse me while I change clothes." She stopped at the doorway and said, "It was nice of you to come and I'll always be grateful you made the offer, but it's not necessary."

"Is that supposed to be your way of telling me to get the hell out of Dodge?"

She flushed. "I'm sure you won't want to linger now that you've been exonerated. I have some paperwork to do. When I'm finished, I don't want to find you here." She refused to listen to the traitorous part of her that said to take him up on his offer.

"Exonerated?" Ben cleaned up the kitchen while she was locked in her bedroom. He went about the task efficiently, his mind obviously on another problem. Suddenly he pounded one fist into the palm of his other hand. He shook his head in bewilderment. Going to the phone, he called Annie Redmond's number again.

When she answered, he said, "Annie, this is Ben Carson. There's something going on that I don't understand. But I'm going to get to the bottom of it. I have a suspicion that you can help me out." Ben made arrangements to pick her up at school for lunch the next day.

When Summer came out of the bedroom, she found Ben

on the couch fast asleep, gently snoring. Two football teams battled on the television, their actions a silent pantomime in the quiet room. She couldn't dredge up any anger that he'd disobeyed her edict to leave. If she was honest, she'd have to admit she craved the sight of him. While he was asleep, she could look her fill at him.

Summer wished she could curl up next to him and rest. She remembered how safe she felt in his arms. Her hands gently stroked her flat stomach. She hoped her baby looked like him.

She pulled the colorful afghan from the back of the couch and spread it over him. Frowning, she noticed the dark circles under his eyes. He looked as if he'd lost weight, too.

Curling into the armchair opposite the couch, she tucked her housecoat beneath her feet and picked up the latest Dean Koontz thriller in hopes of losing herself in its pages. The afternoon passed slowly, the mantel clock ticking quietly, the television buzzing in the background. Summer's head lolled on the cushion. Her eyes closed and she drifted to sleep also.

When Ben awoke, he saw Summer curled in a ball in the roomy chair. She was going to have a crick in her neck from her head being in such an awkward position against the cushions. He stretched and kicked the afghan off, smiling as he fingered the bright fringe.

He stood and softly left the living room. A short while later he returned, grabbed the afghan, and hoisted Summer into his arms. His body trembled as he clutched her to him. He brushed a kiss against her forehead as he carried her to the bedroom.

She never stirred until he lay down next to her and spread the afghan over them. She murmured sleepily when he pulled her against him. She didn't feel his rigidity. He moaned as she rubbed against his groin. He pulled her into his arms and willed himself to sleep.

Monday morning, Summer didn't look at Ben as she scurried around getting ready for work. The alarm clock hadn't been set the night before and she'd overslept. Her need for sleep seemed to have doubled since finding out she was pregnant, she thought as she turned the key in the old rusty Toyota. Lucky for her it started, since she'd made no arrangements for a ride to school.

The day passed faster than Summer would have liked. She didn't know whether Ben would be at her house when she returned or if he'd given up and left for Houston.

Summer stopped in the act of shelving a Nancy Drew mystery. All day her attention had been distracted by the memory of last evening. She had awakened in Ben's arms. She closed her eyes and savored the memory of his body next to hers, fitting like a glove to the curve of her spine, warm and strong.

Why did he have to come now, stirring up everything just when she'd accepted that he would never be a part of her life? She couldn't let him marry her out of pity or to give her baby a name.

But she couldn't be around him all the time without succumbing to him, she feared. And if he kept proposing and saying he loved her, she might take the easy way out and marry him so he would be hers for keeps.

No, she had to do the right thing for the baby. The trouble was, she didn't know what was right for the baby. If Ben cared enough to marry her so his baby would have his name, then perhaps that was the right thing. She cocked her head to the side. Even if he didn't love her, he was apparently willing to do the honorable thing. Perhaps she could strike a deal with him. He could marry her so she could keep her job. In return, she wouldn't make any financial claims against him for the baby, and she'd agree to a quick divorce whenever he wanted.

No, she was doing it again. She was rationalizing the situation. It wouldn't be fair to Ben. She needed to talk to someone, but Annie was the only one she could trust. And Annie had left at lunchtime and hadn't returned.

An hour before the final bell, Summer had a raging headache but no answers to her problems. Giggling children walked down the hall, leading Ben to Summer's desk.

"Here she is, mister," they giggled.

Surprised, Summer looked up. Her hesitant smile faded at his expression. He was furious, she realized, fear striking her. He looked the way he'd looked that morning at the hotel.

"When were you going to tell me?" The ice in his voice chilled her.

"Tell you what?"

"That you're pregnant—with my baby. My baby." He stabbed at his chest to punctuate the last two words.

"But you knew already."

"How could I have known? I'm not clairvoyant."

"But Annie called you. She must have."

"Well, if she did, she spoke to my answering machine. You can ask her. I was on my way to see you when she called."

"Wait a minute. I'm terribly confused. Isn't that why you came here and asked me to marry you?"

"No. I didn't find out you were pregnant until this afternoon when I took your good friend Annie to lunch."

"Then why did you propose to me?"

He stared at her, and gradually some of the stiffness left his features. "Is it so impossible to believe that I might actually love you?"

Summer shook her head in denial. "You can't."

"Why can't I?"

"Because I lied to you. You said . . ." Her voice trailed off. She couldn't repeat the hurtful words.

Ben reached for her. "Summer, I'm sorry. I never meant

those things. I thought you had known all along who I was. I thought you were just out after a rich man, as you had told me."

"Don't you still think that? Aren't you here just out of some outdated sense of nobility? To give your baby a name?"

"No, I could acknowledge and support our baby without marrying you. Sweetheart, I realized during the last few weeks that I'd been an idiot. You couldn't have given yourself so unselfishly to me if you hadn't loved me. It took a while for me to put the pieces together, but I know you weren't faking the love you gave me."

Summer wanted with all her heart to believe him.

"Then I discovered a blinding truth. Even if you were only after my money, I still wanted you. To live with you. To wake up in the same bed with you every day. To marry you if you'd have me."

"Oh, Ben," Summer cried brokenly. "I thought I'd lost you. I don't care about the money. I just want you. I'll sign a prenuptial agreement; in fact, I insist on it. I'll just live with you if you prefer. We don't have to get married."

"Not get married? Forget it, darling! I want some kind of permanent commitment from you." He tilted her head up. "If you'll give me fifty or sixty years, I'll do my best to see you never regret it. I'll give you anything you want, whatever your heart desires."

Tears blinded Summer. "A very wise woman once told me that everyone should get their heart's desire once in a while," she said, her voice breaking. "Ben, if you'll just hold me and love me, that's all my heart will ever desire." She walked into his waiting arms.

Oblivious to the giggling children who had stopped to watch them, Summer and Ben kissed, their mouths gentle and tender as they pledged their love.

Epilogue

"What name do you give this child?" the minister asked.

Summer and Ben looked at each other, then at the black-haired baby she held in her arms. The ivory heirloom christening dress spilled over her arms.

Summer's heart overflowed with love for the tiny, green-eyed child. Tears that sparkled brighter than the diamonds on her fingers ran down her cheeks. Overcome by emotion, she couldn't speak for a moment.

"Rachel Renee." Tremulously she spoke in unison with Ben's strong voice. Rachel for you, Mom, she thought silently. And Renee, Latin for reborn, which is what happened to me when I fell in love with Ben.

She handed the baby to the minister, who smiled and proceeded with the age-old ritual. Rachel giggled and cooed when she was handed back into her father's waiting hands. Summer and Ben clasped hands as the minister prayed.

As soon as he said amen, Irene and Big Ben Carson clustered around, hugging Summer and vying for their new granddaughter's attention.

Tracey wanted to hold the baby next. Her son Chad told his dad, Ryan, that he didn't know what the big deal was; the baby wasn't even old enough to play Nintendo.

Ben's sisters Merrick, Faye, and Sissy good-naturedly squabbled with one another over whose turn it was after Tracey. A few aunts, uncles, and a dozen or so cousins added to the noise and confusion.

Summer remembered the mad crush at the River Oaks home when they'd all arrived en masse last night. Of course, it hadn't been nearly as bad as at their wedding. She still shook when she remembered the three hundred people who attended her *small* wedding. Summer smiled, rejoicing in her new family.

Ben retrieved his daughter from her eager aunts. Summer kissed her daughter's cheek, laughing when Rachel's tiny fingers grabbed at her face and captured an earlobe.

Ben gently unwrapped the tiny fingers from around the antique ruby earring Summer wore. Rachel immediately curled her small fingers around his index finger. When he looked up at his wife from Rachel's sweet face, Summer saw all the love in the world shining from his eyes.